There are two sides
 to every story...

WEST

A From The Wreckage Novel

- *Michele G. Miller*

West
Copyright © 2016 Michele G Miller
Published by Enchanted Ink Press

ISBN-13: 978-1530283675
ISBN-10: 1530283671

All rights reserved. No part of this book may be reproduced or transmitted in any form or by any means, electronic or mechanical, including photocopying, recording, or by any information storage and retrieval systems without permission in writing from the author. Copyright infringement is against the law. This is a work of fiction. Names, characters, places and incidents are the product of the author's imagination or are used fictitiously, any resemblance to any actual persons, living or dead, events, or locales is purely coincidental and not intended by the author. The author acknowledges the trademarked status and trademark owners of various products referenced in this work of fiction, which have been used without permission. The publication/use of these trademarks is not authorized, associated with, or sponsored by the trademark owner.
All right reserved.

West is edited by Samantha Eaton-Roberts
Cover design by Designs by Starla
Cover photography by Regina Wamba of www.maeidesign.com
Cover Models: Calen Dehen and Bryden Giving

Other Titles by Author

From The Wreckage Series - Coming of Age Drama
From The Wreckage
Out of Ruins
All That Remains
West

The Wrecked Series - Coming of Age Drama (From The Wreckage spin-offs)
Into the Fire - Dani's story

The Prophecy of Tyalbrook Trilogy - YA Fantasy Romance
Never Let You Fall
Never Let You Go
Never Without You - Coming soon

Individual titles
Last Call - New Adult Romance

Visit my website for updates
https://michelegmillerbooks.squarespace.com/

"There are far better things ahead than any we leave behind."

~ C.S. Lewis

To the ones clinging to the pain. Let it go.
Use your past to fuel your big, bright, beautiful future.

One

"Still can't miss a game?" Jeff jumps onto the bench of the picnic table at The Ice Shack and takes a seat next to me. I've been sitting here watching students from Hillsdale High show up in droves for the past twenty minutes. The Shack is always the place to hang after Friday night games; with tonight being the first game of the new school year, it's especially packed.

His shoulder knocks into mine. "Why do you keep showing up if it bothers you?"

"Who said it bothers me?"

"Seriously?" Jeff's right brow cocks up as one corner of his mouth turns down.

"Whatever," I mutter. He knows me well. I kick at his foot with the toe of my boot, changing the subject as we watch the crowd. "You played a good game tonight. A little weak to the right, but you keep it up and A&M won't regret recruiting you." He plays defensive back for our high school and he's exceptional. It's why he's been heavily recruited by every school in the state—and then some.

He shakes off my comment. "It's a long season, West." He sighs, "Wow, this is it. Senior year."

"Senior year," I repeat, sending a knowing smile his way. "Hard to believe we've almost made it."

Jeff scoffs. "Hell, it's hard to believe we've survived this long. Hey, why don't you come hang out with the living for a change tonight?" He nods his blond head toward the crowd of jocks and other students from Hillsdale congregating around the parking lot. I shrug, ignoring his intentional dig at my choice of friends, and am spared the need to refuse by the uptick in crowd noise that grabs Jeff's attention.

A smile forms on his face and he rubs his hands together before hopping down from the table. He walks backwards, motioning over his shoulder to the car sitting in the middle of the parking lot, the headlights flickering on and off. "Gotta run. My girl's here."

"You and Katie? Again, man?" I groan, although I know it's pointless to argue. "Will you ever learn?" I call after him as I survey the scene behind his back. The car belongs to Tanya Rivera—Katie's best friend—and she's unable to move thanks to two guys who are re-enacting their own version of Magic Mike in the beam of her headlights. Cheers at their antics ring out.

"Come over," Jeff offers again, and I shake my head at him and the showboaters. "Don't pretend those little skirts have no effect on you, Rutledge. I know where, and who, your eyes focus on," Jeff shouts with laughter as he jogs backward to join the others. I flip him off before turning my back to the crowd.

Instead of joining them I remain seated on the table to the left of The Shack, gazing at the shadowy field before me. The late August air is humid and a trail of sweat trickles down the small of my back as a light breeze picks up. It's the last weekend of summer break. Come Monday, I'm a senior; I'm not sure if I'm relieved or not. I have no concrete plans for my life after high school.

Not anymore.

I'll still go to A&M—because it's what Rutledge boys do—but I won't be doing what I'd always planned. Instead I'll spend my Saturdays cheering on one of my best friends, Jeff, and my brother Austin as they chase their dreams on the football field without me. The notion leaves a bitter taste in my mouth. A hollow sensation sinks into my chest, but I push it aside as my ears pick up the cheers and name calling around me.

The loud blare of a horn puts a smile on my face as Tanya's curses carry from the parking lot to my hiding spot. Funny enough, I don't feel as though I'm missing out on much. I enjoy it here in my dark corner away from the people I've known for most of my life. Flipping a flask around between my fingers, I contemplate what Jeff said when he first showed up. Going to football games, the ones I should be playing in, doesn't bother me. Not usually. It's been four years since I took an official snap, threw a pass under the Friday night lights, and hoisted a teammate into the air after an amazing connection. Four years since I gave it up. Yet I show up to every game my old teammates play and I watch. I find myself studying their moves and deciphering the playbook mentally. I curse their stupid mistakes as though they affect me, and I begrudgingly cheer their wins.

Begrudgingly.

My breath catches at the word. Perhaps I care more than I'd like to admit, but it's too late now.

"Poor Tanya, that can't be comfortable."

The unmistakable voice of Jules Blacklin—head cheerleader, town sweetheart, and the Quarterback's girlfriend—interrupts my complicated thoughts. Startled, I shift and look over my shoulder. Jules has taken a seat at my picnic table with her back to me. Her tiny cheerleading uniform hugs her figure; the pleated skirt riding low on her hips offers me a tantalizing glance at the smooth skin of her lower back. I bite back an admiring smile and a dozen dirty thoughts. "You always talk to yourself, cheerleader?"

Red hair flies around as Jules' head snaps my way. This girl is gorgeous, as one would expect a cliché golden girl in high school to be. She looks at me, her blue eyes wide with surprise; she obviously didn't see me sitting here in the dark. I suppress my grin as I study the little wrinkles in her forehead and the pink tint to her face. Even in the dark her skin reminds me of a damn peach. I recall a time, years ago, when I touched those smooth cheeks and gazed into those crystal blues. The thought stirs something within. *Damn it.* While I sit here and lose my ever-loving mind at the sight of her, she merely blinks as though she's trying to recognize me. I attempt to not let her indifference bruise my ego.

"Excuse me?"

"You're excused, Buffy," I drawl. I grin at my clever joke as I tip my head to the side and allow my eyes to rove over her backside again. We go way back—elementary school, pee wee football, middle school team events—she's part of a past life. I've spoken to Jules a handful of times in the past four years. Less since she started dating Stuart Daniels during our sophomore year. I've watched her though; she's hard to ignore.

Jules studies me, her head tilting side to side before one russet brow arches and a self-satisfied look washes over her face. "Does that make you Spike? Sitting here brooding in the dark with your flask?"

I don't suppress my approval of her witty comeback. *Touché.* I lift the flask in question, saluting her with a mock toast. Jules' eyes narrow on my mouth and a million thoughts whirl through my mind. Why the hell is she sitting here? I assumed she'd walk away the moment I spoke, and I certainly didn't expect her to fire teasing comments back at me. But now, not only has she remained sitting, but she's watching me. No, not watching me, she's watching my mouth as though she wants to taste the liquid dripping from my bottom lip. My stomach clenches at the thought and I swallow hard. Making the decision to enjoy this rare encounter, I face her fully and lean my forearms on my knees. As though the weight of my stare is too much, Jules stands with a shake of her head.

"I think I could live with you calling me Spike," I say, hoping for another round of verbal boxing with her. A breeze rolls by, lifting her red and white pleated skirt. A guy's gotta love those little skirts.

"Really?" Her hand presses her pleats down. "You do know Buffy and Spike hated each other?" she asks. There's surprise in her tone. She sounds hurt somehow, and I can't fathom why she'd feel disappointment. I brush the ridiculous notion aside.

The lights inside The Shack flicker once, but I pay little attention. I'm too engaged in verbal sword play with a beautiful girl. Jules pointed out Buffy and Spike's disdain for one another, but I'm reminded of the enemies-to-lovers story arc between the characters. Silently thanking my ex Carley for forcing her addiction to the show upon me when we were dating, I lower my voice and correct Jules' statement with a grin.

"At first."

Her eyes narrow. "At first?"

"Jules," interrupts Katie as she jogs our way. "Can you believe this? Every freaking weekend they do this crap. Can't we just get Tanya and go? I'm so tired of all the pissing contests."

Straightening, I pay Jeff's on-again, off-again girl no heed as my eyes lock on Jules' eyes. I will her to grasp the meaning behind my comment. Katie barely glances my way as she grabs Jules' hand, ready to pull her back to her friends, but Jules doesn't budge. I sense the moment she catches it, the double meaning of my words.

Her blue eyes widen and she stammers, "Oh, at first."

Her face lights up and I'm transfixed. Without warning, my memories fly back to the seventh grade and a kiss with the girl I wanted to impress so badly that I manufactured our being picked for the age old game of Seven Minutes in Heaven. This is the girl Jeff was referring to only moments ago as he laughed at me. The one my eyes always go to, the one who might have been mine once upon a time, if not for cancer.

If not for Stuart Daniels.

If not for my being a quitter.

Jules Blacklin.

My memories mean nothing as the lights flicker on and off once more and beside me Katie whines as she tugs on Jules' arm. "Come on."

Irritated at my thoughts, I salute the girls with a chuckle. "See ya around, Buff," I say as I slide down from the picnic table, forcing myself to leave.

Or I would have left if not for the shouting.

Katie's angry interruption makes sense now as I look to where she came from. A fight has broken out in the parking lot and I shake my head, mumbling beneath my breath, "Stupid pricks."

I'm not able to identify the participants rolling around on the ground before their shouts are drowned out by a sound infinitely more terrifying.

My pulse quickens as the piercing scream of the early warning storm sirens go off, making me and everyone around jump at the signal. The Ice Shack goes silent and I hold my breath as I look past the crowd and down the highway toward the normally cheerful town of Tyler, Texas. It currently resembles a disco, the lights flashing on and off, and I know—we all know—something isn't right.

Two

This is a test of the emergency broadcast system . . . The robotic voice plays through my mind as the scene around me morphs from frozen disbelief to pandemonium. A dust-filled gust whips my face, causing my eyes to water as a transformer blows in the distance, throwing the parking lot into darkness.

"Come on! Let's go," Katie yells at Jules, who looks from me to the town and back. My eyes shift from her back to the waves of people attempting to flee the area in their cars. They're creating a traffic jam worthy of a Dallas highway in less than one minute. There's no way we're getting out of the parking lot by vehicle.

Safety.

The word supersedes all other sounds, hurling into my brain, and I listen. We must find shelter. Something underground. *If this had been a real test . . .* the robotic voice persists as all the years of weather drills and warnings return to me.

A hole, a basement—we need a basement!

Wasting no time, I latch on to Jules' arm before she can leave my sight with Katie. She turns to me, confusion etched across her face, and I raise my voice over the mayhem, "No! We need to find a safe shelter. You can't outrun a tornado." I tug at Jules in an attempt to force her to follow me. Her eyes are filled with fear as she shouts for Katie over her shoulder. In the distance, a rumbling vibration breaks through the thick Texas air. *Shit!* I'm done standing around. "Come on," I order, pulling Jules' arm again. This time she follows, dragging Katie with her.

Katie's frantic shouts reach me as we jump over the low-lying hedges separating The Shack's property from the fields next door.

"Tanya! Jeff!"

Their names float past me on the wind and I shake my head, pushing them out of my mind. There's no time. We need to run.

I'm focused on Grier house coming into view in front of us. The chipping white paint of the vacant farmhouse glows in the shadowed moonlight. A beacon, as hell breaks loose all around us.

Behind us there are explosions—transformers—and trees groaning. Shouts of terror mix with the persistent blaring of horns and something large falls on the highway back by The Ice Shake. The sound of metal scrapes the asphalt and sparks shoot into the air. *Debris.* My mind goes to the inevitable. If there's debris reaching us, then there's a tornado behind us somewhere.

I don't take the time to look back. I squeeze Jules' hand in mine and I run. I run until my body is yanked backward, then I pause when, out of the corner of my eye, I catch her stumbling. Tightening my grip, I jerk hard on Jules' arm. I give her the slightest moment to regain her footing, and we're off running again.

Safety. Shelter. Run.

Those are my three objectives.

It's nearly impossible to hear over the howl of the wind, but Jules' voice reaches me. I turn, intending to yell at her to keep running, and see Katie is no longer with us. Jules is frantic, her head swinging back and forth as she searches for Katie. Shutting off my emotions, I force myself to ignore Jules' fear.

Safety. Shelter. Run.

Three objectives. Two goals. *Save yourself, save Jules.*

I can't stop and search for Katie, a girl I've known all my life. My best friend's girl. Stopping puts me at risk. It puts Jules at risk. Not happening. I keep running, continuing to move forward as Jules wrenches back. Her fight forces me to hesitate and I peer over my shoulder, scanning the black field looking for the blonde bob I know belongs to Katie.

The racing silhouettes of my peers greet me instead. It's surreal. We're all running for our lives. A moment ago each person here had their own objective, their own goal for the night. Now we all have the same purpose—survival.

The outline of a body comes into view directly to my free side. It's Big Ruben, a Hillsdale football player and one of my former teammates. He drags Katie in his wake and I release a sigh of relief. Ruben shouts, but his words are lost on the wind. He waves us forward and I assume he's merely trying to reassure us he'll take care of Katie, but Jules isn't having it. Her grip on my hand loosens as she stretches for her friend, and I snap.

"Don't you dare let go, Buffy! We need to run!" I warn, hauling her into my side and wrapping my arm around her waist for a more secure grip.

"I can't leave Katie!" she argues as tiny wisps of her hair whip at my face in the increasing onset of wind."

"We're not leaving her. She's with Ruben. Now come on!" My eyes flick to Ruben and Katie once more, confirming they're with us. The shadow of Katie's hand extends forward, looking for a connection with Jules. *Damn it.*

I slow up.

It's only a step or two. One step could mean the difference between life or death for us, but I can reach Katie. I can't not try. I can't leave her behind. I focus on her fingers and not my fear of what's chasing us as I stretch back. I slow and I extend and my hand seizes Katie's wrist, my fingers tightening their hold. I speed up again and I don't look back.

My heart races and my stomach protests, the fear and stress within making me sick as we reach the house and hustle to the front porch.

"This way!" I say.

We make our way up the front steps, joining the small group of people who are already there. Why are they all outside? I look around. Fists and bodies beat at the boarded up windows and door of the house. *Shit.* I join in, kicking at the plywood-covered door with my motorcycle boots in an attempt to break in.

"What are we doing?" Jules asks over my shoulder, her voice unsure.

Maybe this plan wasn't the best. My mind races through our options, but I come up blank. There are shadows of other people running straight by us, by this house, as they seek their own safety. They're fools. There's nothing more in this field. This house is it.

Jules shuffles around beside me, her tremors of terror flowing through our connected hands. I stop, worried she'll freak out and bolt down the stairs with the others who are giving up on the house. Facing her, I touch her arm in an attempt to help her maintain focus.

"There's a basement here." I search her face in the dark, making sure she heard me. "Stay by my side! Don't leave!" I shout louder. She nods and I release her hand.

"How do you know there's a basement?" asks Katie, who's now hugging Jules with both arms.

All the parties I've been to in this house over the last three years come to mind, but they aren't important. "I just do," I answer as I punch Ruben in the arm and throw myself back at the door. "Ruben, help me!"

Pain surges through my shoulder as I hurl my body against the boarded-up house again and again. Ruben and I take turns kicking, punching, and slamming into the plywood. Another shot of pain hits me and I curse, thinking of how handy my old football pads would be at this moment.

"We're gonna die."

The three words are a whisper in my ear when Jules says them, and they cause my stomach to drop. Gritting my teeth, I slam my shoulder into the boarded-up door again, harder this time. I refuse to let her prediction become a reality.

Then renewed hope comes from an unfamiliar voice. "Help me! I've got it loose!"

Following the shout, Ruben and I push through the others to where someone has managed to force a corner of the large piece of plywood covering a broken window back enough for us to get our fingers beneath the frame. Glancing over the heads of the guys around me, I search for and spot Jules' red hair, ensuring her proximity, before I focus on the board. We work together, a dozen pairs of hands finding their grip around the edges of the board and attempting to pull and break the wood or wrench the nails free from the window casing.

"Watch the nails!" the guy next to me shouts as we form a human crowbar. We pry and pull until we hear the blessed sound of nails squealing and loosening, creating a hole large enough for a small body to crawl through. *Jules,* I think, and as though Ruben has read my mind, his deep voice calls out.

"Katie! Jules! Get in there. Any other girls?"

The howling of the tornado picks up and the energy within the crowd heightens as panic grows.

"Hurry up!" a voice demands as Jules steers a girl up to the window. There are three of them. Three girls standing there. Jules, Katie, and one I don't know. Where is everyone else?

"There's a basement somewhere. You need to find it and go downstairs," Jules tells the new girl. I catch the younger girl's eyes and chime in.

"It's in the back, in the kitchen. There's a door; you won't miss it." She nods as she climbs through the window. I turn to Jules, "Your turn." I want her in the house and downstairs. I can think of nothing else at this moment.

"No," she argues and shoves a crying Katie my way. "Katie, you go!"

Katie seems paralyzed and I want to pitch her through the hole myself as Jules takes control, yelling at her. Another shout mixes with hers.

"Jules!" Jeff's voice reaches me as he wends his way through the small crowd. Our eyes meet and I feel the same fearful relief I see in his face. Relief at knowing my oldest and closest friend is here, and fear because we're not through this yet.

My reaction is nothing compared to Katie's. Her body is already halfway inside the house when she hears his voice. "Jeff! Jeff!" she screams, attempting to climb out of the house before Jeff pushes into her line of sight.

"I'm here, K. Get in there. Go to the basement," he orders.

Katie's terror is too much for Jules and her face crumbles before me.

"Let me go in and I'll punch at the boards from the other side. We can't all fit through this hole," a guy offers, and others join in. Bodies jostle for position.

"Hey!" Jules shouts as she slams into my side and my hands slip from the wood as the crowd surges forward. Ruben's hands slip as well and the board crashes against the window casing, the hole we'd created no longer there. Trapped inside the house, Katie screams and pounds against the plywood.

What little order we've maintained is lost as in the distance mass chaos explodes in the echo of thousands of branches cracking and splintering apart. From my vantage point I can't see what causes the noise, but the way Jules clutches my shirt with her mouth hanging open speaks for itself.

"Oh. My—" My ears register her small voice release the two words before the others' shouts of panic overtake hers.

"It's here!"

"Open the windows!"

Fists, bodies, and feet batter the windows and door again. Next to me, Ruben props his back against the house, lifts his arms above his head, and works to push the plywood away from the window once more. I position myself on the opposite side, pulling as I shout for Jules to go in. Taking the cue, Jeff wrenches Jules away from my side and forces her to duck under Ruben's arms and through the broken window, whispering something into her ear.

Before she climbs through, our eyes meet and hold. The look in her gaze will remain with me for as long as I live—there's a promise there, a moment the two of us will forever share. Then she disappears into the dark house and a heavy weight lands on my chest.

Once the girls are inside, a short line forms behind us. One by one, people I know, and some I don't, climb through the window in their haste for safety. "Next," they shout as their feet hit the floor inside.

When three guys have made their way in, they pound on the board from the inside. As I stand there holding the plywood, I catch the flash of a dim light in the house. Someone yells Jules' name, and Stuart's too, then she starts arguing. I pull the board harder. Nails pop and the board loosens more. *What is she doing?* Sweat drips into my eyes and my biceps burn from the task of holding the plywood. I want to scream, to power through this the way The Rock would and break this shit right off the wall so I can get to her. The adrenaline courses through my body and with a final growl as Ruben and I look at each other and the guys inside the house count to three, we all push and pull with every ounce of strength we possess.

Time stands still until, at last, the plywood cracks and breaks in half, falling free from the house.

"Go, hurry!" yell multiple voices at once as we toss the broken board over our heads. The crowd on the porch is gone, dwindled down from fear of waiting, and I say a silent prayer that they find safety elsewhere. The last three guys enter the house before I watch as Jeff climbs in, followed by Ruben. Mentally I tick off the body count. *Twelve.* Twelve people remained with us and went into the house.

Looking around, I verify I'm the last person and pause. It feels as though it's been an hour since the sirens went off, since we started running, since Jules disappeared from my sight. It's been mere minutes, a few thousand seconds of sheer terror unlike anything I've felt in my life. I dare one last glance back at The Ice Shack and now I see what the others already saw. Nothing. The Shack is gone and in its place is a dark, swirling mass of debris and cloud heading my way. I quickly realize that I have seconds to find safety.

I throw myself through the window in time to hear a panicked Jules question Ruben, "Where's West?"

"Hey, Buffy. Miss me?" I tease as my boots hit the floor.

Her reaction floors me. She hurtles herself into my chest, her arms expelling the air from my lungs as they tighten around my waist. My mind doesn't choose what happens next, my body simply reacts on instinct, and my arms go around her as I press a kiss to her silky hair.

"Basement," I whisper, practically carrying her in the direction of the door I know will lead us down.

"Is everyone in? Everyone who was out there?" Jules asks, and I'm again struck by her concern. In the past few years I've allowed myself to think of Jules as some shallow cheerleader. Thinking of her superstar boyfriend as a bad influence on her and assuming she's turned into a Grade A Bitch made ignoring her easier. Her asking about the safety of others, her waiting for me before finding shelter herself, those things don't fit with the Jules I created. Of course I know she's not a bitch. She's never snubbed me or done anything to gain the reputation I've given her in my head. I'm the Grade A Ass. The guy who finds it easier to pretend everyone else isn't worth my time because it makes it painless to walk away. I'm the fraud.

"The porch was empty," I assure her as we descend into the concrete-walled basement.

My eyes scan the area, looking for the best place to hide. *Against the wall*, I remind myself as I tug Jules into the back of the basement. Katie, Jeff, and Ruben are in the right back corner and I'm tempted to head their way, but change my mind and lead Jules left instead. That corner is empty. More room equals two walls to sandwich between and more safety.

I move to pull her to the ground as our world changes forever.

Everything magnifies, every groan and creak, each snap and crack. The tornado is on top of us, and as my ears go deaf to the cacophony of sounds, I throw Jules forward into the corner and land on top of her.

"I don't want to die!" she screams, taking my hand in hers as I cover her body. The faces of my dad and brothers flash through my mind. *No!* I push them away.

"We're not gonna die tonight, Buffy." I press my face into the side of her head, my lips kissing her hair as I shout. "I'll be damned if I finally get the nerve to speak to you again, only to die in this place."

An ear-splitting crash above us drowns out any other thoughts I might have. The house over our heads lifts and falls, and then shatters to pieces all around our bodies.

Three

My hand clings to Jules' as debris rains down on us. "Cover your mouth, Jules. Don't breathe in all this dust," I shout over the noise, pulling the neck of my tee up to use as a face mask.

I focus on her whimpers as pain slices through my back, as dust burns my eyes, and as the sound of the storm fills my ears. I focus on her warm palm in mine, on the way her body trembles beneath me, and on the smell of her hair pressed to my cheek. Anything to keep my mind from focusing on what's happening above us.

Then it's gone.

Passing over us with the same speed as it arrived.

And a new dilemma hits me as fast as the storm did. We're trapped under a house. I don't have to open my eyes to know that what used to be above us is now on top of us. I heard it all come down; the scream and tear of nails lifting and boards snapping has my ears ringing. I lift my head as the sounds of the storm fade away, replaced with shouts of fear, and bump it on something a few inches above me. Gathering my bearings, I take stock of my position. My back is pressed against the wall of the basement and Jules is partially below and in front of me. She's laying on my right arm which is wrapped around her. Our interlaced fingers are pressed against her chest. The racing of her heart tells me she's alright. Terrified, but alright.

"Everyone okay?" someone shouts. Weak moans and curses reply.

The girl I don't know cries, her sobs filled with terror as she worries about being buried alive. Her words set the others off. Calls for help ring out as the sound of movement picks up.

Next to me, Jules' head swivels from side to side. I lower my cheek to the top of her hair in an offer of comfort as she groans. The voices pick up around me.

"We can't panic." My voice is hoarse and I cough, attempting to strengthen it in order to yell for my friends. "We can't panic! Stop and listen!" Jules flinches at my shout. "Sorry. Are you okay?" Her head nods against me and her fingers tighten around mine.

"Yo!" Ruben's baritone voice rises above the rest and echoes off the walls. "Chill out, everyone."

The voices fade, leaving muffled sobs and the shifting of debris in their wake. *Who's hurt and who's okay?* An internal voice prods me to take inventory of my friends. The urge to cross my fingers overcomes me as I call out for Jeff. Uncertain of what I'm about to hear, I hold my breath as I listen for his voice.

"I'm good, man, and so is Katie."

Thank you, Lord.

Jules sighs, her body relaxing as the others proceed to do a roll call. Jeff shouts for Mark, and Mark accounts for those in his corner by calling out more names. As Mark calls a couple of guys names out, Jules fidgets beneath me. Her movements are small, but with our bodies pressed together I'm aware of everything she does. She intakes a sharp breath, stiffening.

"Jules? What's wrong? Are you hurt somewhere?"

"There's something on my leg." Her left leg wriggles as she shifts around again. Her breathing picks up pace. "West? Are you up against the basement wall?"

"Yeah, I'm leaning against it. Why?"

"We're trapped. There's stuff everywhere in front of me—sheetrock, plywood—oh no. The whole damn house fell on us, didn't it? How are we going to get out?" Her voice rises in octaves with each word. I draw in a breath of air, knowing that I do not have the luxury of panicking.

"Jules! Jules, what's wrong?" Katie calls as Jules' panic escalates and reaches them. She sucks in a breath beneath me.

"Katie! I'm all right, I'm not hurt," Jules replies. "How about you? You okay?"

"Yeah, I'm fine. I fainted. Where are you?"

"I'm with West and we're in the back corner. We're trapped under a bunch of debris."

I'm impressed with her composure as she talks to her friend. Her voice is unexpectedly strong and sure. Regardless of her fear, she's making sure her friends believe she's calm. Her concern for Katie's feelings serves as another reminder of how perfect this girl is. What an idiot I was to think otherwise.

"Hey, West, man—can you guys see our cell phone lights?" It's Jeff who asks and I lift my head in search of a light, any light in our dark surroundings.

"I can't see anything but black" My stomach sinks. "Can you?" I ask Jules.

Her head lifts from the crook of my arm and shoulder before she drops back down with a heavy sigh. "Nothing."

Cursing under my breath, I relay our situation. "Jeff, we're pretty deep in the rubble here. We can't see a thing."

"Yeah, it looks like all the debris stacked up in the corner where you two are. We're pretty good over here."

"Good, then go get us help!" Jules orders, and I choke back a laugh at her demand.

"Jules, hun, you know I would love to, but the stairs are gone. We can't get out." Jeff's reply is teasing, but I pick up the nerves in his tone.

"Hey," I touch Jules' face as her breathing speeds up again. "Hey, don't freak out on me, Buffy. We're gonna be fine. Our parents will be looking for us, and the cops will know to check the Shack," I soothe as she begins hyperventilating. Her heart races against my hand that she's still clinging to.

"What if they're all dead?" she moans, her voice broken. "What happened to everyone else, West? There's only a handful of us down here. Where did they all go?"

My mind envisions a giant vortex sucking up everything and everyone I know and love. The last image I saw before I climbed through the window was a vivid one. The Shack was reduced to matchsticks and the tornado was heading straight for me. I blink the idea of a destroyed town from my head. I can't let myself think that way. I won't let myself worry about anything but what's in front of me right now. *I'll focus on Jules and me and getting out of this twister-made coffin,* I promise myself.

Rubbing her bare arm as her muffled cries surround us, I focus on the way her body shakes. She's fading fast. "Jules?" I slide my hand down her side, rubbing her thigh in an attempt to soothe her. "You need to calm down. Slow breaths, or you're going to go into shock."

"I c-c-a-a-n't."

Her broken speech concerns me and I change tactics.

"Dang, girl. I thought you were Buffy? You're ruining the fantasy here," I tease with a bite to my tone.

"I'm . . . n-o-o-o-t-t-t. Wa-a-a-nt home," she mumbles, and my heart breaks.

"I know, Jules. Me too," I whisper. "We're going to go home, I promise. You need to calm down for me. Close your eyes and try to breathe. Can you do that?"

She doesn't answer, but I continue to rub her leg and hip as I whisper about going home. I'm not sure if I'm saying it for her benefit or mine anymore, but either way it works. The rapid rising and falling of her breath has steadied and her body quits its spasms.

"That's it, keep doing whatever you're doing," I tell her as I shift off of her and attempt to slip further between her body and the wall at my back. The sharp stab in my back returns as I press it against whatever is behind me, and I bite the inside of my cheek to stop from cursing.

"Don't move," she cries as I shift. I stop. She said there was something against her leg, I must have disturbed it.

"I'm sorry. Sorry, is this . . . let me see if I can get whatever it is pressing against you off," I offer, working into a position to feel around us.

Her hips jerk back into mine. "No, no, no. It hurts and might collapse. Don't, please."

"Jules, I'm going to see if I can lift it with my boot enough for you to pull free. I won't move anything. We'll go real slow," I promise.

"I'm pretty sure I might pass out if you touch it, West. Please leave it."

Ignoring her, I poke around the area using the toe of my boot, searching for whatever landed on her. When I find a board, I tap at it, testing its strength and weight load.

"Damn it, you're taking this Spike thing too far."

Her ire brings a smile to my face as I kick the board a second time. "Ha, you know you like it, Buffy." She huffs and tightens her grip on my hand, turning my fingers numb. "Okay. Look, all I have to do is kick it and it's going to slide off easy, like Jenga."

"Jenga?" she growls. "This isn't a game, West. The whole thing could come crashing down on us."

"It's hurting you, I'm getting it off. Look, like I said, it's Jenga."

"Oh my word, what does Jenga have to do with this?" she shouts. I pinch her hip in frustration.

"If you'd shut up I'd tell you, geez," I snap. "If the entire pile of rubble was resting on that board, I wouldn't be able to move it. Just like the game—how you move the easy pieces because you know it won't affect the pile—got it?"

"But what if you're wrong?" Jules asks, and her worry tempers my reply.

"If I thought for a second I could hurt you, do you think I would try this?" My chest tightens as I say the words. I'd never hurt this girl.

Where in the hell did this concern for Jules Blacklin come from? I wonder, not for the first time tonight. Sure, I've harbored a crush—or perhaps it's something more akin to lust nowadays—for her for years. I have no intention of acting on it. Ever. She is the girl who got away. The girl who I assumed wouldn't ever be mine because the boy she might have wanted, the one she'd kissed at a party four years ago, died when his mother did a few weeks later.

"Ummm, I don't know. You're the crazy rebel, remember?" she flings back. I make a mental note to give her hell about her sugar and spice attitude the moment we're out of here.

"Wow. That hurts, Buffy. I know we're supposed to be enemies, but really?"

"If this doesn't work and that pile comes crashing down, I'm so hitting you with a stake to the heart," she threatens on a pitiful moan.

"You already did, cheerleader," I acknowledge. Jules inhales sharply, then chokes and coughs.

"Fine, try it," she manages on a rasp.

"On three I'll push it and you try to pull your leg out at the same time. Ready?"

"Mmmhmmm," she nods against me.

Lifting my hand to protect both our heads, I shift as close to her body as possible and count to three. I kick at the board over and over, feeling it give a little each time. Dust shifts around us. I close my eyes and kick again. My hips press against Jules' backside as my foot reaches forward and my mind contemplates all of the things I would prefer to be doing with Jules and her body right now in this position. The thoughts torment me as I kick the board again, a low grunt of frustration ripping from my throat. This time when my toe connects, the board flies out and the pile above us shifts. I can't see Jules, but I feel her body bend forward. She tucks her thighs into her chest, folding into a ball, as things move around us, and I follow, bracing for the worst.

"West! What's happening?" Jeff shouts, his voice full of concern.

It worked. Nothing collapses down on us. So far, anyway.

"It's all good, we're just making a little room under here."

Jules sniffs. "Making a little room? You mean you're trying to kill me?" Sarcasm has replaced her earlier worry and I smile though she can't see it.

"Why not? The way I see it we already beat death once tonight."

"West?"

"Yup?"

"You're not funny."

"You're not stuck anymore and you've calmed down, right?" I point out. "Don't knock the methods if they work."

Her reply is an exasperated puff of air.

Stretching my legs, I close my eyes and listen to the muted voices of our friends as they shift and discuss their options for getting help. Somewhere in the distance the sirens of a rescue vehicle ring out and I pray they're heading our way. I return my hand back to Jules' hip for lack of no place else to put it. She leaps at the touch, but she doesn't protest.

After a few minutes, Jules chuckles and I wonder what she finds humorous, so I listen to the chaos on the other side of our pile. I focus in on the conversations. There's an amusing argument going on between Katie and Jeff, or it would be if we weren't trapped in tornado debris. Katie argues with the guys about making some sort of human ladder to lift her out of the basement and Jeff seems angry.

"And then what, K? Who knows what's out there, and I can't let you go alone," he argues.

"We need to get help."

"Hey, Jeff you're strong enough, if we lifted you up after she climbs out, you could pull yourself out. We've got this. We'll get you both out, and you can get us help." That calm voice of reason belongs to Mark Jones, another member of the football team, Mark has always been a leader. The smart, studious guy who I could never quite figure out because he doesn't fit the stereotypical jock M.O.

There's a moment of silence before Jeff agrees with the plan.

"What are you guys doing out there?" Jules shouts, startling me.

"We're going to get Katie and Jeff out of here so they can get help, Jules. We don't know how long it will take anyone to find us. Who knows what the town looks like, you know?" Mark replies. He must be taking the role of leader out there. The others are quiet now, all complaining has ceased, and the unknown girl's crying has stopped.

"Whose idea was it?" Jules asks and I swear I detect humor in her tone.

Katie laughs as though she's telling a private joke. "It was all me, Ju-ju-be."

"Ju-ju-be?" I repeat with quiet laughter. "I like that almost as much as Buffy."

"Way to go, K. Be careful!" Jules replies before she shifts her body. It's pitch black in our tomb, but by the twist of her back I can tell she's looking over her shoulder at me. "And only Katie and Tanya are allowed to call me that, Spike," she points out, and I wish I could see her blue eyes flashing at me when she speaks.

I do my best to be serious. "Duly noted."

"Did I ask you if you were all right yet?"

"Yeah, you did. I think I'm okay." I curl my shoulders in, stretching my back, and experience the burning pain again. "I'm sure something took a chunk out of my back, but I can manage."

"What?!"

"I'm fine. It hurts and I can tell I'm bleeding, but it's not bad. I've had plenty of injuries, Buffy."

"We're trapped in tornado wreckage. Think you could stop making fun now?" Her voice wavers, the way a weak radio signal does.

"Jules?"

"I don't feel so good. I feel dizzy."

"Dizzy? Did you hit your head? Jules, are you sure you're not injured? Are you bleeding anywhere?"

"I don't think so. I don't know . . . my temple hurts, though. West, are we going to get out of here?"

"Yes, most definitely," I promise without hesitation as I search her head for cuts or bumps. Coming from a family of football players, I'm immediately concerned about a head injury. "I don't feel any blood."

"That's a good thing, since you're an evil vampire and all."

"Then you better stay awake, Jules. You wouldn't want me to take advantage of you, after all," I snap as her voice fades out again.

I shake her arm when she doesn't poke back at me. *Shit.* "Jules? Jules? C'mon now, wake up."

"Buffy . . ." she whispers.

I nod. "Yes, Buffy—that's right. Stay with me then, Buffy, okay?"

No answer.

"Buff?" Fear races in. "C'mon, Jules, you can't do this to me. Jules!"

"West?" Jeff shouts, his voice is clearer, as though he's standing closer to us than before.

"You need to get help, Jeff. Jules is out cold." I'm not sure I recognize my own voice. I've never been this scared.

Katie shouts, her tone full of worry, but I don't hear her over the blood pounding in my ears and Jeff's reply. "We're going, man. Hang in there, 'kay?" I trust him to find help.

My hand rubs Jules' hip and thigh again as I listen to the sounds of people working together to hoist Katie and Jeff from the basement. I sigh with relief once they're out. Now, there's nothing to do but wait.

Four

My fingers travel the length of Jules' side. Her bare skin is warm, a good sign. My brain works to recall what I've seen on medical shows and in science classes about the signs of shock. Cold would be bad.

"Weston—"

"Yeah, Momma?" She rarely calls me Weston, unless I'm in trouble, so I realize she's looking for my father, but I hurry to her side anyway. I hate how weak her voice is. She's so tiny now on the large chaise, all withered down to skin and bones. The chemo that's supposed to make her better is killing her treatment by treatment.

"Oh . . . hi, baby. Where's Dad?" Her body shivers violently under the pile of blankets tucked around her. It's late July in Texas and she's freezing.

"You're cold," I say, more to myself than her, as I walk to the ever present pile of blankets stacked in the game room. "Dad will be back soon, he took Austin to practice." Returning to her side, I spread another blanket over her legs.

"Lay with me?" she asks. Her shadowed eyes crinkle around the edges, the only sign of a smile she can give most days, and I crawl next to her, my thirteen-year-old body taking up twice the space hers does. "What are we watching?"

My eyes glance to the television on the wall. I've been staring at it, not watching, with the sound muted. "Oh, the usual," I say as her head touches my shoulder.

"More sports," she whispers, her eyes drifting closed again. "You should have gone to the fields with your daddy, West. Don't stop playing . . . you love it best . . . "

She trails off, her shallow, even breaths letting me know she's asleep once more, and I sigh. "No, Momma. I love you best."

Jules moans, a harsh cough rattling her chest as she shifts in my arms. The feeling so eerily similar to the moments shared with my mother that I have to remind myself where I am. Blinking away the memories of the past, I move my free hand to Jules' face and touch her cheek. She no longer has her top over her mouth, it's no wonder her breathing is so labored. Worried about what we might be inhaling under the debris of a one hundred-year-old house, I tug at her uniform in an attempt to cover her mouth and nose. She groans.

"Jules?" I touch her shoulder, hoping she's coming too.

"Hmmm?"

It's about time. "You passed out. You okay? Are you in pain?"

"Passed . . . out?" she wheezes with another cough. "How . . . you?"

As she struggles to form words, the warning lights go off in my brain. *Dizziness, losing consciousness, slurred speech*—her behavior is consistent with the symptoms of a concussion.

Jules' body jerks side to side and I know a moment of panic—thinking she is having convulsions—until the movement changes to the shakes and wiggles of someone who's merely restless. I press my fingers into her hip in warning. "Don't move. You might hurt yourself or knock something."

"Have . . . to . . ." she insists, pulling her hand free from mine for the first time since we entered the house. She groans, twisting her body about. Realizing what she's doing, I reposition my arm to shield her head as I tug at her waist in an attempt to help her roll in place. Her knee bumps my leg and I chuckle as she grunts her way into a new position.

"Wow, Buffy—good thing you're so tiny."

"No fair," she whispers with labored breaths as her face meets my chest. "The air seems . . . cleaner over here."

That reminds me. "Here," I say as I search for her hand in our new position and guide it down toward my waist. She pulls back, a small gasp escaping her lips as though I have nefarious plans for her. I wish the move I was making was one of pleasure. I suppress a dirty grin at the direction of her thoughts and clasp her hand again, steering it up under my shirt. "Hold it to your face and breathe through it."

The cotton lifts from my body as her arm snakes up, her forearm grazing and resting against my stomach as she stretches the fabric to her face to use as a mask. I chew the inside of my cheek, distracting myself at the way her touch affects me. The torture is worth it when her breathing becomes deeper and more pronounced.

We're cuddling face-to-face now instead of spooning as we were before. My left arm acts as pillow to Jules' head still, but my hand is empty now that she's rolled away from it. I touch the back of her head and allow my fingers to brush through her hair.

"We're gonna be okay," I tell her with confidence.

"How long do you think we've been down here?"

"Not long. They'll look for us, we'll be okay," I repeat. *We'll be okay*, I won't stop thinking it.

Time ticks by and my right hand becomes restless. It brushes Jules' shoulder, her waist, then her hip before I can't stand it and I weave up and under the arm she has in my shirt. My fingers skim her forearm as they seek out their target. Her fingers are spread wide as they hold my shirt to her face and I cover them with a sigh, happy to once again be holding hands with her. *I'm a weak man*. If she calls me out on it, I'll use an excuse. Tell her I wanted to give her a break from holding the shirt, or pretend I'm worried she'll pass out again and I want to be sure she can breathe safely. I form several replies to cover why I had to hold her hand, but she doesn't question me at all.

I get the impression she wants my hand in hers as much as I do. Somehow I know it.

"I feel sick," Jules moans. I cringe on her behalf. I had a concussion once, it's comparable to hell. I felt both drunk and sick at the same time as my brain beat against my skull in an attempt to escape my head. I certainly don't envy her right now.

"That's normal if you have a concussion. Just breathe deeply and try to stay awake," I remind her as she shakes her head. "Keep talking to me, Jules."

"Fine, tell me something I don't know," she mutters.

Your boyfriend can be a real prick.

You're the sweetest girl I've ever known.

"I was at the game tonight," I say out of the blue.

"Our game?" As though there were a million other games I might have been at tonight.

"Yeah, Buff. Your game. I never miss one."

"You—really? Why haven't I—didn't know?" she flounders and I decipher her words the best I can. She's wondering why she hasn't seen me? Years of games and she's never noticed me there. I don't take it personally. I go out of my way to not be seen by those who might question my appearance. I've been working on perfecting my I-could-care-less attitude since the eighth grade. Plus, it's not as though I attend the games to stalk her, or anyone for that matter. I go because I can't help it. I've tried to skip out, and when I do, I'm always miserable. My heart wants to be there, with my best friend and old teammates, doing what it loves. *Damn, the truth hurts sometimes.*

I admit the truth out loud to someone for the first time in years. "I miss playing."

"Why—"

"We've been here for an hour," shouts Mark, interrupting Jules, saving me from opening a can of worms best left on the shelf. "West, Jules, you two still good?"

"Yeah, I do want to speak with management about the conditions of our room when we get out though," I reply sarcastically. "What do you think, Buff, want to order some room service?"

No answer.

"Jules?"

Her hand goes limp under mine. She's out again.

Five

Waiting sucks. Outside our pocket of safety, I attempt to follow the muted conversations being tossed about by my classmates. I've learned that their cell phones don't work, the other girl who sought refuge with us is named Lola, and Ruben is hungry. Occasionally Mark comes closer to our pile and shifts things around, looking for an opening to help us.

Jules jolts in my arms. She's restless, so I press her head into my chest to keep her from jumping the way she did the last time she came to.

"Where—can't breathe—what—"

"Hey, Jules. It's West. You're okay, I've got you," I soothe as her panicked questions evolve into painful sobs.

"I want to go home," she cries, stretching her arm around my waist and pulling herself closer to my body. Her hot tears sear my skin as I tuck her head under my chin.

"Me too. Soon okay?"

"I can't—I can't stay here."

"Yes, you can. Close your eyes and take deep breaths." I obey my own instructions, hoping she'll follow. Instead, she continues to cry, her raw emotion brings tears to my eyes for the first time in years. I'd whispered those exact words to my mother once upon a time. They're the same ones she'd whispered to me as a child after I'd have nightmares.

"Close your eyes and take deep breaths, my sweet boy," she would say, smoothing my sweaty hair from my head and kissing my cheek. *"Let them go."*

Let them go. I haven't allowed myself to think of those days—her last days—in years. Let them go, I'd told her . . .

"Who will cook you boys dinner when I'm gone?" she asks brokenly one night while we rest together on her chaise, the television the only light in the room. *"Who will wash your uniforms and make sure your homework gets done?"*

"Mom, stop. You're not going anywhere. You're going to get better." I repeat the words my father has drilled into us boys. We don't believe them anymore, but we speak them. For her. Or maybe they're for us.

"I wanted to see you grow up, West. I'm sorry."

My voice breaks with hers as I wrap her in as tight a hug as I dare. *"Momma, you will see me. You'll be with me forever and ever."*

Her cries lessen as mine grow. Her frail voice tells me what I already know. *"I'm so tired, baby. I'm sorry. I'm so tired, but I'm scared. I want to see you and your brothers live. I don't want to miss it, but I'm going to."*

"I don't want you to be afraid for me. For any of us, Mom. We'll be okay knowing you're better. Let them go. Close your eyes, take deep breaths, and let them go. Remember that?" I ask with a watery smile as I recall her words of wisdom. *"Let the monsters in your head go, and rest."*

"I love you, my MVP," she says as she surrenders to sleep.

I close my eyes at the poignant memories, willing them to go away as, once again, Jules stirs in my arms. It's been two hours. Mark called the time a moment ago. Two hours, and while we hear sirens in the distance, no one has come to this area yet.

"I'm scared."

I've trapped her top leg between mine and I give it a squeeze with my knees. "Why?"

"Why?" she asks incredulously, her voice stronger this time. "Well, hmm—we're stuck under the rubble of a house, a tornado has hit our town, and we have no idea what's going on out there. Listen to all of those sirens. It sounds like a war zone."

"O, ye of little faith. This is nothing. I've got you."

"You've got me?"

"Yeah, Buff. I've got you. I'm here and I'll keep you safe. No worries, okay?"

She's primed for a freak out; I can feel the tension in her body. Her arm, pressed between our chests, pushes against me, and she wiggles her legs as though she's going to change something. It's as though she thinks some magical portal is going to open up and swallow us through the floor to safety.

"Hey," I warn, frustrated with her movements and worried she'll kick something loose. "Calm down. Breathe."

"I want out of here. I can't breathe, my head hurts, and I want my mom and dad. What if they're hurt?" Her shoulders shake. "What's taking them so long to get help?"

Her fear tamps down my frustration.

"Jules. Baby, you can't freak out on me now, please. I need you to stay calm." Removing my hand from her hair, I find her face and cup her cheek in my palm. "Look at me."

"I can't—I can't see anything," she gasps.

Her fear is tangible. And understandable. I feel claustrophobic myself, the heat is oppressive, the air stale and dirty. Every inch of my body aches. My muscles are constantly tense as they wait for the ceiling to drop on us. But, freaking out won't get us out of here. So I focus on Jules' hand, the vision of her red hair blowing in the wind, and her perfect legs and body doing cheers under the Friday night lights. The visuals work for me. They calm the storm inside my chest every time I want to break free of this prison we're in. Maybe the same tactic will work on her?

"Pretend, then. Listen to my voice and picture my face in your head. Picture the Ice Shack from before all of this happened." Moisture hits my hand as she takes a deep breath, and I envision her face. Tears dripping from her blue eyes, fear creasing her forehead. My thumb caresses her cheek and she stills. "That's good. I can feel you calming down already. I told you we're not gonna die tonight. Trust me. Will you do that?"

"How do you know?" she sniffles, "What if—"

My thumb shifts over her lips, stopping her from getting worked up again. "Because I've got stuff I want to do in this life, and I'll be damned if this is the end."

Her teeth graze my thumb as it rubs across her lip. The touch sends a jolt of unexpected desire through me and I lower my voice. "Plus, while I've always dreamed of dying in a beautiful woman's arms, this wasn't exactly the way I planned it."

"Oh wow, was that a pick up line?" Her mouth parts under my thumb and I remove my hand as though I've been burned. The reaction my body has to her simple smile floors me. If this house isn't the death of me, she will be

"No, gorgeous, that was the truth. I'd show you what I envisioned, but I don't think we have enough room in this little cave of ours," I tease boldly.

"It's a shame our accommodations are so shabby then. Should I offer you a rain check?" she asks with a touch of humor. I jump at the offer.

"Hell yeah you should. I'm taking you up on that, too. No backing out now," I say meaningfully, and she snorts, pressing her face into my chest. I'm on cloud nine for the simple fact that I made her laugh and calm down.

○○○○○○○○

"I feel as though I'd have to fight off a lot of girls if you tried," Jules says after a while.

I've been weaving in and out of sleep, the oppressive heat rendering my eyelids heavy as we lay in the dark.

"Sorry?" I ask as I roll my head around in an attempt to wake up.

"Are you dating anyone?"

"No." *But you are,* I think with a frown. She's got Stuart, and she'll go back to him the moment we're free from this pit. I can't forget that, I remind myself even as my fingers rub the base of her skull and tangle in the knots of her hair. Letting her go isn't going to be easy.

Subject change. "Tell me about you and Stuart."

She refuses, and I pester her. "Come on. Don't pass up this golden opportunity to gush about the amazing Stuart Daniels."

Her head rests on my bicep, and though our surroundings are pitch black, I can tell she's looking at me. Her head shifts, cocking up as she speaks with exasperation. "You don't sound like you want to hear about him."

"Ha." She flinches at the abnormally loud sound. "Of course I do. Tell me." In reality, she's correct; I don't want to talk about him, but I'm curious now.

"Tell you what?"

"About your boyfriend."

She sighs. "There's nothing to tell."

Nothing to tell? Her answer fuels something irrational within me, a wave of jealousy so strong it would knock me off my feet if I were standing rushes in. If I were her boyfriend, there would be a whole lot to tell.

There's a cracking sound amongst the boards around us before a sharp snap fills the air.

"Oh no," Jules moans.

Things shift. My hand covers Jules' head as we brace ourselves for the worst. The dust and dirt of dry wall rain upon us as. Something bounces off my chin, scratching me. Outside the hole, our friends shout our names. Then things settle as quickly as they shifted.

"We're good," I call out to Mark and the others once our muscles relax again. I feel both of our frantic heartbeats against my hand that's still attached to hers and resting between our bodies. *Don't let her return to panic mode,* my inner voice prompts me. Inhaling deeply, I return to our conversation as though the threat of imminent death did not interrupt our conversation.

"Do you love him?"

"What?"

"Do you love Stuart? You've been together forever."

"Yeah, I love him." Her heart rate picks up. "No," she shakes her head.

"No?" I repeat. *Did I hear that correctly?*

"Yeah."

"Jules, I'm used to chicks confusing the hell out of me, but you're winning by a landslide right now," I groan, trapping her head under my chin again as more debris shifts around us. I close my eyes, wondering how much longer we have. Something must have landed right on top of us that is keeping all of the remnants of an entire house from crushing us. What if it breaks? Each time I hear a creak or dirt falls on us, I picture our safety bubble popping. I don't want to think about it. I'm tired of being scared down here. Apparently Jules is too because this time—after things quiet—she returns to our conversation and explains her answer.

"I mean that if I'm honest then, yeah, I love him, but I'm not in love with him anymore."

Maintain calm. "Since when?"

"I don't know. It's been a while, I think."

"Then why are you still with him?"

"I don't know. He loves me. He's good to me, and like you said, we've been together forever."

"That's stupid." *Did I say that out loud?*

"Excuse me?" She jerks back, the top of her skull cracking painfully into my chin.

"Damn, girl, stay in one spot."

"Can I punch you when we get out of here?" she fires back, shifting around beneath me again.

"If we get out of here, Buffy, you can do whatever you want to me."

She stops. "If?"

Shit. I take another deep breath, mentally kicking myself for making such a comment. I cover the slip-up with a laugh. "I meant when. Don't get your panties in a bunch."

"Wow, you're a charmer," she mumbles.

Our conversation has taken a drastically wrong turn somewhere, but I lower my voice, happy to irritate this beautifully infuriating girl if it keeps her mind off of worst case scenarios. "Oh, I'm sorry, cheerleader. Did you want me to be charming?" I drawl in my best seductive voice.

There's no humor in her reply. "No."

Six

"If I'm going to die, just let me die already." Jules' words fall from her lips as though they're being forced from her mouth. "I'm scared. It hurts," she whines. Her voice is so raw I barely recognize it. The debris causes my own throat to burn each time I swallow what little moisture I can produce.

"I wanted to skip school and see a Broadway show," she continues.

"Jules?" I brush her temple with my thumb as she mumbles incoherently.

"And we have homecoming, and prom, and I want to see Jase grow up—"

"Jules, sweetie, what are you talking about?"

"My list."

"Your list?" I ask, confused at the way her mind leaps from subject to subject.

"Don't you have one?"

"One what? What kind of list are you talking about?"

"A bucket list. The girls and I, we made one years ago," she explains. "I want to see Paris and kiss under the Eiffel Tower."

"I want to travel too," I tell her, thinking of the plans our family made for when Mom recovered. "And scuba dive, and jump from a plane someday." I chuckle, recalling all of the crazy things I've always planned on doing.

"Why?" she asks.

"I don't know." That's not the truth, but the why doesn't matter. "How about you? What's another item on your list?"

"Kick a field goal," she says with a giggle. "That's stupid, isn't it?"

"Nah, I like that one. It's different." I love her passion for football. "I want to gamble large sums of money in Vegas," I tell her, opening up to the idea of a bucket list.

"Why?" she asks again.

"Do I need a reason?"

"You do. Wanting something isn't good enough, you need to have a reason for it. Not just because."

"A reason, huh? Well, I want to live. I want to do everything I can to celebrate being alive. That's my reason."

"If we get out of here, I'm not going to care what people think of me anymore. I'm tired of trying to be the perfect girl. Staying with—" she cuts herself off.

Her forehead rubs against my chest as she clears her throat and shifts on her side. Staying with? What was she about to say?

"I want to fall in love." My stomach flips because it's Jules' face I see when I think of being in love and I can't believe I shared that aloud.

"I want to have sex before I die," she mumbles. I bite my cheek, surprised at the revelation. "I don't want to die in a heap of rubble, West. I have so many things I want to do."

My eyes close as fear enters her voice once again. "Jules, listen to me. You will do all those things. I'll make sure of it. We will get out of here and—"

"Would you take me to Paris?" Her voice fades in and out, as though she's losing consciousness again.

"I would if you'd let me," I promise, kissing her forehead. "I'd kiss you under the Eiffel tower too. Hell, I'd kiss you right now if I could."

"I'd let you," she says, "cause I—I want to live too."

"If you'd let me, I'd fall in love with you, cheerleader," I admit to myself and to the dark. Jules is out again.

Each time Jules blacks out I'm stuck with nothing but my own reflections. My thoughts have never been pretty, but now, when I'm faced with the idea of being buried alive, they're impossible to handle. Talking about living, and about the things I want to do in life, only reaffirms all of the things I've given up. I think about my brothers, the two people I've always looked up to the most, and how they handled our mother's death. They moved on, they played on. Why didn't I? I picture my mom in her chair, laying with me day after day during her last month, and I hear her words, *"Live, West. Do all of the things you want to do, sweetheart, because you never know."*

"I see lights! West, Jules, there are lights coming our way." Ruben declares, his voice filled with elation. The basement goes from silence to cheers at the glorious news and I smile into Jules' hair. For the first time this evening the shrill echo of sirens is steady and close; moving toward us instead of away. My muscles relax with relief as I hug Jules tighter. She's fallen into another fitful sleep against my body and I whisper promises of our pending rescue into the dark as I listen to the outside world and wait for help.

Then, from beneath our pile, I make out masculine voices in the distance. Their calls are answered by shouts of "Help us!" and "Down here!", and my heart races as a dog's excited barking fills the air.

"You kids okay?" a new voice shouts. *Dad?*

Mark replies with calm, using my father's name, confirming it is indeed him. I'm not hallucinating.

"Dad!" I shout, but my hoarse voice doesn't carry. I cover Jules' ear and try again. "Dad!"

My only reply is the clanking of metal ladders and more voices moving closer. *They're here!*

"Where are they?" my dad asks. He's nearby now; he sounds as though he's in the basement with us. Mark's reply is muffled over the rest of the sounds. A moment later, my father's voice is closer than ever.

"West! Can you hear me?" Tears spring to my eyes.

"Dad! I can hear you, can you hear me?" I shout painfully.

"I hear you, son. Hold on, okay? There's a crew setting up. We're going to dig you out."

I don't reply. I can't. My throat has closed up, whether from the dust and lack of moisture or from the relief I feel, I'm not sure. All I know is we've been found and my dad will do whatever it takes to get us out alive.

I lay there, mentally counting as I wait. I sing songs. I envision movies and moments of my life. I remain patient as time drags by with little to show for it. The stress in their voices makes it clear this rescue mission isn't a simple one. Men shout, my dad argues, and lights shine on us from up above. The sight of light, although dim and only through a few cracks, gives me hope. I have hope they'll find spots to work on soon. Spots where they can carefully remove the wreckage on top of us until we are dug out of this nightmare. Dad says it's a good thing I can see light. It means the debris pile isn't thick in those spots. The men go to work, meticulously shifting the wreckage around us.

I've adjusted my position once more, throwing a leg over Jules and pulling her as close as humanly possible. She's repositioned as well, settling her face into the crook of my neck. The warmth of her breath against my skin gives me chills. Her hands and arms remain between us, one under my shirt intertwined with mine, and the other is up near her chin. Those fingers tickle the base of my neck on and off as they press against me.

I don't know how it happened, but everything within me craves this girl. The relief I feel at being rescued is at odds with the indescribable pain I'm beginning to feel at losing her once we're free.

Around us, dirt and debris is stirred up as the rescue crew digs through it.

"Jules?" I say as she rouses, her hips pressing against my thighs as she works herself closer to my body.

"Hmmm?"

"Jules, it's okay. We're okay. You just woke up, but we are going to be okay."

There's a shout as a pile shifts without warning. Boards tumble and a weight presses across our legs as something slides above us. Jules and I both gasp, her hand tightening in mine. My other hand digs into her silky hair, keeping her head close to me.

"West!" my dad shouts in a tone of terror I've never heard.

"Gooood!" I manage to answer.

"Almost there, son. You okay? How's Jules?"

I couldn't answer those questions if I tried. It doesn't matter how she is. It doesn't matter how I am. Who knows how we will ever be after this.

"Just get us out of here. Hurry!" I tell him before once again reassuring Jules, and myself, of our future.

"I promise you, we are going to live, babe. We are living."

Seven

The first blast of fresh air I've breathed in hours hits my face and I squint, turning my head away from the spotlight shining on Jules and I.

"He's here," a voice calls out above me. "Good to see you, West."

I take great gulps of the fresh air as I shield my eyes and look up at the shadowed face. Another large piece disappears near our heads and my father comes into view. His gloved hand reaches over the ledge of debris still trapping us in and touches my hair. His face is full of relief. "You okay?"

"Yeah, ready to get out of here though." His eyes move to Jules who is snuggled close to me. "She's been out of it for a while now, Dad. We need to get her checked out."

"Almost there," he assures me as his face moves out of view.

The rescue team pulls a few more pieces of wreckage away from us, then we're free. Our hours in this coffin come to an end as they pry an unconscious Jules from my arms. There's a whirlwind of activity now. They place Jules on a backboard, a precaution, Dad assures me as I watch them lift her from the basement.

Our friends—Mark, Ruben, and the others—have already left the site, taken to whatever shelter authorities have set up. I climb out of the basement on my own, swearing I'm fine and not in immediate need of medical care.

I emerge to a sight I will never be able to erase. Grier field is dotted with torn trees, cars, and other objects. Red and blue lights flash everywhere. Teams of people scour the field for survivors, flashlights lighting their way through the black field. Rescue dogs bark as their handlers follow behind them. It's a disaster scene resembling those I'd only ever seen in a movie or on the news, and it's here in the town where I've lived my entire life.

Shoving my hands into my matted hair, I breathe in the fresh air and look up at the stars I thought I might never see again.

"West." My dad grasps my shoulder as he pulls me roughly into his side.

I haven't hugged my father since Mom's death. Not this way. Not like a small boy who's just woken from a nightmare. I hold onto him as though I never want to let go. Because, honestly, I don't.

"Where's Jules?" I ask with my face buried in his shoulder.

"They're loading her in an ambulance."

"I want to go with her. Will they let me?"

"There's no room; they have other injured kids with them. They're about to go."

From the moment the warning sirens sounded I've been on a roller coaster. My thoughts are all over the place and I have no idea what's up or down. I can't think straight, but I know I can't let her go without me. She's my one grounding force on this ride. We may be out of the wreckage, but our ordeal is far from over.

"Go? Dad, no. We have to go with them. I need to stay with her. I need to know she's alright" I argue, pushing out of his embrace when I spot a fireman slamming the doors to an ambulance shut.

"West, she'll be fine. Let's get you home and—" My eyes lift to his and he stops speaking. I don't know what he sees, but whatever anxiety I'm dealing with must be written all over my face.

He frowns at the ambulance before he nods. "Okay. We can follow them in the truck."

He plies me with question after question on how I'm feeling on the ride over.

"How's your head? You didn't hit it, did you?"

"No."

"Your breathing sounds shallow. Did anything hit your chest? Are you having trouble breathing?"

"No."

He must realize all he's getting from me right now are one syllable answers, so he stops asking. We listen to an emergency radio broadcast giving details of the storm. They mention names of landmarks—a street, the high school, a restaurant—that have damage or destroyed, and I hear something about the storm radius, but my brain is too numb to process anything. My eyes focus on the silent, red lights swirling ahead of us and the silhouettes moving around in the back window. In my lap, my fists clench and unclench as I wait to reunite with Jules again.

By the time we arrive at the hospital, find parking, and walk through the Emergency Room entrance, we've already lost sight of Jules. An emergency protocol is in place; the entire floor is set up for triage, and after looking at my shoulder wound once more, my dad insists on me getting medical attention. I relent, only after he promises me he'll locate Jules and stay with her until I'm taken care of. I join the others waiting to be seen with three words repeating in my head over and over. *She needs me.* My chest physically hurts at the thought of Jules waking up expecting me to be next to her.

"You're good to go." My nurse pushes her rolling stool away from me as she returns my soot and blood covered shirt. Her hair is pulled up in a haphazard ponytail, her eyes weary as though she's seen too much tonight.

"Thanks." I tug the shirt over my head, flinching at the tightness in my shoulder blade from the liquid glue she used to close the wound caused by a falling nail-covered two by four.

Her reply is a worn out smile as she moves to the next patient. The hospital is full of people waiting to be seen by her, and others. Head wounds, gashes in legs, dangling arms. There's blood and ruin everywhere. I don't have a particularly weak stomach, but I have to suck in a deep breath to curb my dizziness at seeing this much physical destruction in one place. This hospital is a war zone. Much as Grier field was.

I leave triage and make my way through the waiting area. My eyes bounce around the room, touching on the stricken faces. A dark head nods as I pass by someone from school, but I can't recall his name. He's holding his arm close to his body, and a second glance reveals his shoulder isn't where it should be. Bowing my head, I rush by, heading toward the last place I saw my dad. There's a semi-circle of curtained-off beds before me with a nurses' station in the center. The desk is three deep with people asking for help finding loved ones, but waiting isn't my strong suit.

"Dad?" I call out once, then once more, louder.

A hand pokes out of a curtain, then an arm, as my father's voice reaches me. "Over here, son."

Weaving through the crowd, I duck behind the curtain. "This place is crazy. Did you find—" my voice cuts off as a pair of baby blues stare at me, "—Jules."

"Hi," she sniffs, wiping tears from her face with her palms.

Shit. Heat rushes up my body as my eyes water. *Shit*. I have no idea how to contain the emotions coursing through my veins. I might as well be a twelve-year-old boy going through puberty all over again with the way I'm reacting at the sight of her. My thoughts go haywire. *What have you done to me, Jules Blacklin?*

Thankfully, I'm spared the need to speak by the arrival of a doctor.

"How are we doing here?" she asks with a bright smile. "I'm Dr. Metzger. I examined you when you were brought in. How are you feeling, Jules?"

Jules captures her upper lip between her teeth as her eyes flit around the small space between Dr. Metzger, my father, and me. "I guess all right. Um, my vision's a little blurry and my head hurts."

"Yes, that's to be expected. You have a concussion, so you're going to have problems with feeling dizzy, as well as spotty vision for a week or so. The good thing is you will heal, and you'll be okay.

You're very lucky. From what I hear, you were buried under a lot of rubble." Dr. Metzger looks my way, as though to confirm the story.

"Doctor?" Jules' voice is uncertain. Her hair, tangled and speckled with debris, falls across her face, and my fingers itch to push it away. "Um, I can't remember any of it. Is that normal with concussions?"

Can't remember any of it? Of what? Tonight? I draw a long breath. My father's arm drapes around my shoulders, his hand giving me a reassuring squeeze as I attempt to understand what Jules is saying.

The question doesn't faze the doctor. She pulls out a pocket light and moves to examine Jules. "Can't remember, huh? Okay, tell me what you recall last?"

"The last thing I recall is West," Jules sends me a small grin as she meets my eyes, "pushing me down and dropping on top of me as the house started to fall. It's all a blur from there. I remember my friends, and screaming, and I heard a siren and voices yelling, but nothing is clear."

Dr. Metzger flashes the light in Jules' eyes before picking up the chart on the end of her bed. She jots down some notes then looks at my dad. "Are her parents here?"

He shakes his head. "They're not here yet. I don't know if they've been contacted. The lines are down."

Jules' bottom lip quivers. She inhales. "Where did the tornado hit? What's going on out there?" she asks, covering her mouth.

I hurry to her side, then pause. My body is primed for pulling her into my arms, but my brain isn't so sure anymore. We're no longer trapped. The intimacy of holding her hand, of her body pressed against mine, is no longer appropriate. I stuff my hands deep into my pockets as I look at her small frame lying in a hospital bed and attempt to console her.

"Hey—don't do that, Jules. Don't freak out before you know anything. Don't worry; we'll see if we can get to your parents." I turn to my father; certain he can help. "Dad?"

Dr. Metzger issues her orders before he can reply. "I'd like you to stay for a while longer, Jules. Just to observe you since you were in and out of consciousness for so long. As for your lack of memory, let's try to stay calm and not worry too much right now. Amnesia is common with concussions. Sometimes people forget a few hours, and sometimes they lose a whole day. Usually the memories come back after a few days, at the most." Jules nods. The good doctor switches her attention to my father and I. "As for you two, I would suggest you stay off the roads and let the emergency crews do their jobs. We'll take care of Ms. Blacklin until her family can get here."

She's giving us the okay to go. I should be grateful, but I don't want to leave. I can't. Not yet. I stare at a streak of dirt on Jules' upper arm as Dr. Metzger and my father exchange words before she leaves, but I hear none of it. Kicking at the leg of a bedside chair, I tug it closer with the toe of my boot before lowering my body into it, all the while my eyes remain pinned on Jules' arm.

"How about I grab something hot for us to drink? West, how's your back, son?"

It takes me a moment to process what's happening around me. My dad said my name. *What? Oh, my back.*

"It's fine. They used that liquid glue like they said they would," I assure him as I look at Jules. "Coffee would be great right now. Jules?"

"Hmmm?" She's as lost as I am right now.

"My dad is going to get some coffee. Do you want some?" I repeat.

Jules frowns, her nose scrunching up in distaste, but she nods anyway. My father excuses himself, closing the curtain behind him. Once he's gone, Jules' shadowed eyes roam over me, searching for something. Something more than the physical sight of me. She's looking past me—through me—and I recognize she's not all here. A part of both of us is still partially buried beneath the rubble. I can feel it—the strange absence of something within me.

"What's wrong with your back?" Jules' eyes scan over my torso. "Did you get hurt?"

The worry in her voice shakes the darker thoughts, the weakness, from my mind. "Oh, it's nothing. I guess something took a nice slice out of it, but they glued me back up and I'll be fine. They did have to give me a mammoth tetanus shot, though." I hold my hands wide in exaggeration. "I swear that hurt like a mother." She shivers.

"I hate needles. Be glad you didn't need stitches," Jules points out, her face morphs into a look of mock horror. She's rallying, making light of an anything but light situation, and I admire her for it.

"Your dad seems nice."

"Yeah. You know he's my dad and all, but he's cool," I admit.

Her pale, dirt streaked face alters before my eyes. The joking act is exactly that—an act. It's as though the blinds closed and now she can let everything out while she's alone inside her head. The tip of her nose tints red as her eyes fill with tears. This time I don't stop myself. My hand bridges the gap between us and I touch her arm as I lean forward in my seat.

"Please don't cry. I hate it."

"Your dad kinda freaked out when I started to cry on him. He must hate it, too."

She has no idea. "It's been five years since my mom died. We've been a house full of guys and guy things. So yeah, he's not good with emotions."

"And you?" she asks quietly.

"I just don't want to see you cry." The question makes me uncomfortable. I smooth my finger over my brow nervously.

Jules shivers, goose bumps covering her skin beneath my hand. The hospital air is thick with humidity and the scent of medicine and chaos, but she's clearly chilled in her tiny cheerleading uniform. Swiping at her face, she leans forward, tugging at the hospital blanket covering her lower legs. Standing, I help her. I tuck the white material around her shoulders while she settles back and rolls to her side facing me. I return to my seat next to her bedside, leaning forward over the bed and resting my arms on the bedrail. I have to clasp my hands together to keep from reaching for her. It's torture. I want to hold her hand again.

"Does that thing move?" Jules' hand slips out from under the blanket and points to the metal rail.

"Uh, I would think so." I jiggle the railing, searching around for a lever to remove it. There's a button on the side and I press it, sliding the rail out of the way. Without the rail to lean on, I tuck my hands under my arms across my chest, leaning back in the chair as Jules gives me a smile.

"Thank you. Do you know what's going on outside? What condition the town is in?"

"My dad said from what he could tell, the twister went straight through town. Apparently where we were, at the Shack, that might have been its last direct hit. It's still chaos out there, though."

Her face loses what little color it had. Voices erupt on the opposite side of her curtained room and I rush to cover the sounds of panic to ease the alarm on Jules' face.

"Oh, I didn't tell you. We were rescued by Rossview EMS and Fire. They were closer to us obviously, so that's why we're here instead of at Memorial."

Her eyes roll around the area as she shrugs. "I didn't think about it. I've never been to Memorial, either. So they're bringing a lot of injured here?"

"I don't know. I'm pretty sure they're bringing people wherever is fastest. It's bad out there."

Idiot. I stop myself from saying anything else damning and study her instead. There's something so incredibly tiny about her as she lays here. She picks at the blanket, her fingernails black with debris. Uncrossing my arms, I look at my own hands. They wear the markings of our night as well. I rub them against my jeans in vain. As though ridding myself of the grime will rid me of the memories.

Jules stills and focuses on the ceiling. Air rasps in her throat as she breathes deeply, and I join in.

One . . . two . . . three . . . deep breaths.

"Hey, West? Do you pray? Like, to anyone or anything. I'm not saying it has to be God, but—"

"I have been tonight." I cover her hand with my own as moisture collects in the corners of my eyes.

Stretching nearer to the bed, I rest my arms across the top as Jules laces her fingers through mine and shifts closer. Once our faces are inches apart, she closes her eyes. I don't pray often. Since my mother's death, talk of God and prayer are far and few between in our house. It's not that we—my father, brothers, and I—are mad at God. We simply didn't understand, and we sort of fell away from religion. But now, sitting here with Jules, after having my life—and hers—spared, I wonder if prayer could be the answer. My mother believed strongly in her faith. She was the one who made us give blessings at meals and dragged us to church when Dad was out of town playing ball on Sundays.

Tonight, I return to prayer. I pray for Jules' family, for our friends, and for the town of Tyler. It's awkward hunched over this hospital bed praying silently when, all around us, people are talking and machines are clicking and beeping. Yet when Jules' grip loosens as she attempts to pull her hand from mine, I squeeze tight not willing to let her go. I'm not willing to lose this moment between us yet.

"I brought you hot chocolate. I hope that's alright. I saw the face you made when West mentioned coffee," my father offers softly, interrupting my silent vigil. My eyes snap open and I find Jules' tear-streaked face watching me. She's back into her former position, sitting up, but I have a feeling she was studying me as I prayed.

"Thank you so much, Mr. Rutledge," Jules says, wrapping a free hand around the cup my dad sets on the dinner tray to her right. He hands a brown cup to me as well, and something about the way he looks at me brings me to attention. I sit straight, dropping Jules' hand, and wait for whatever news he has.

"So listen, they're bringing in a lot of injured people. I ran into Chris out there and he said they could use help doing search and rescue. Since I have a four-wheel drive truck, I can get over debris."

I nod, of course he would want to help. That's always been his nature—something he's passed down to my brothers and I—similar to his love of football.

"Go then, if you can help others. Do you mind if I stay here? I'll—" I look to Jules for permission. "I mean, do you mind if I stay with you?"

She shakes her head, giving me a smile that clearly says I'm ridiculous for feeling the need to ask. "Of course not."

"I'll stay here. Then you don't have to worry about me."

I wonder if I'm being selfish, not going out and helping people in whatever way I can, then I look at Jules as she sips her hot chocolate, and I look down at myself, covered in debris and blood. I'm exhausted, both physically and mentally, and can't imagine seeing further destruction tonight.

"I think that's a great idea, son. Try to get a hold of your brothers if you can. They said the lines here are going in and out due to so much traffic right now." I nod, thinking of Austin and Carson. Surely they're completely out of their minds right now wondering if we're okay.

Dad asks Jules for her address, promising to see if he can get in contact with her parents, and Jules breaks down as she thanks him. Using the back of her hand to brush the tears from her cheeks, she mutters, "I swear I only cry like this at chick movies."

Her embarrassment at crying, yet again, causes my dad to chuckle lightly. "Your secret is safe with us," he says with a grin.

"She lives in Hickory Ridge, Dad."

"Hickory Ridge? Well that's good then."

"It is?" Jules asks on a hiccup.

"Everything south of downtown was spared, according to Chris. They should be safe, assuming they were home. They probably can't get to you or don't know where you are." Jules gives him her address and he enters it into his phone. "You know, chances are they're moving Heaven and Earth to figure out where you are and get to you. The emergency broadcast is telling people to stay in their homes and off the roads if they don't need medical care."

I stand. "I love you, son." He hugs me, applying extra pressure, something I think we'll both be doing more often for a while. "She's something special, huh?" he asks, and I nod.

"Take care, sweetheart," he smiles at Jules before he leaves us alone.

My dad leaves a crack in the curtain, and as I stare after him, my eyes catch the confusion all around us. I simply stand there and stare—as though I'm in a trance—as doctors, nurses, and others rush in and out of the curtained rooms. It's not until I take a sip of my coffee, the sting of the liquid burning my tongue, that I'm brought back to the present. A man wearing torn clothes approaches the nurses station begging for help, bringing me back to reality. Jules' voice brings me back to her.

"What made you run for the house?"

Damn her voice. Soft and questioning. Scared, worried, hopeful. "Sorry?" I ask, gathering my scattered thoughts.

"The house? You knew there was a basement. How?"

Turning my back to the chaos beyond the curtain, I return to her bedside.

"How sheltered have you been, Little Miss Cheerleader?" I ask. My intent was playful sarcasm, but I can't deny there's a tinge of bitterness in my tone as well. I have no idea where it comes from.

"The parties?" she guesses.

Lowering myself to sit in the chair again, I lean down and set my coffee cup on the floor. "Of course. Everyone's partied at Grier house at least once. At least, we did before the police caught wind of it and the place got boarded up." She presses the remote on her bed, lifting into a sitting position as I continue. "You never came to any of the parties there?" I already know the answer. No. Not Jules Blacklin, Tyler's princess. She's one of the good ones. Not that partying makes any one bad, but Jules is—I can't think of a word to fit her perfectly. It aggravates me.

"I don't party. Not like that, anyhow."

"You don't have to get stoned or wasted at a party, Buffy. More people than you think used to come. We'd have a good time, hang, dance. Some people would smoke weed or drink, but it was cool to just chill, too."

"Illegally, in an abandoned house? Do you know the crap I'd get in if I were caught doing that?" Jules asks, rolling her eyes.

Her tone fires me up.

"Oh, Miss Goody Two Shoes, that's why you make sure Mommy and Daddy don't find out. You know, your boyfriend actually showed up at one or two."

"What?"

Feeling smug, I bite the inside of my cheek to stop from smiling. "Just sayin'."

"You're full of it. Stuart never parties without me."

"Sorry to disappoint you, sweetheart, but like I said, a lot of people used to show. Ask Parker or Ya-ya," I counter, using a nickname for Jules' best friend Tanya that us guys came up with years ago. Jules snaps upright, her face full of anger. "Whoa. You're looking a little green, Buff. Sit back and relax. You okay?" I ask, reaching for her as she sways.

"Are you freaking kidding me? You don't hang with our crowd anymore, and here you are telling me you've been partying with some of my best friends. You called Tanya 'Ya-ya'. Where have you been for the past four years?" she asks, both anger and hurt appearing in her features.

"First, I was there the day Tanya was given the name Ya-ya, so I damn well have the right to call her that. Second, you're right. I don't hang with *your* crowd anymore, but I never left, Jules. I've been here all this time." My words come out harsh. I don't mean for them to hurt her, but my feelings are all over the place. And the way she asked about the parties at Grier, as though they were beneath her. *Damn*, her self-righteous attitude hit a nerve.

This conversation has somehow escalated out of control. Frustrated, I tug at my hair, grab my coffee, and stand. Intending to put some space between us, I say, "I'll be back."

I need to get a grip on my emotions right now. Jules hasn't done anything to me. We haven't talked much in years, but she's not the one who cut off communication. I was. I need air and I need perspective. *What is wrong with me?*

Eight

"If you didn't leave, then why did you stop being friends with us?"

I don't make it out of the curtain before Jules speaks, stopping me in my tracks as a swarm of people rush into the triage area. One man's voice rises above all of the other sounds as he speaks to the nurses manning the desk. "I was told my daughter is here—Jules Blacklin?"

Relief floods in, and I call to Mr. Blacklin, waving him our way as Jules gasps behind me.

"Daddy!"

"Jules!" Her father rushes by me, followed by a familiar couple. "Oh, my baby girl. Thank the Lord you're alive."

I press back, attempting to blend into the background as everyone talks at once. Tears flow from the woman's eyes and Jules' dad hugs her, running his hands over her face.

"Honey, where's Katie? Is she all right?" The woman asks, and I make the connection, recognizing her as Katie's mom.

With a shake of her head, Jules gives the spark notes version of our night. The crowd at The Ice Shack, the sirens wailing, the traffic jam and our running. Jules' eyes look past her father and Katie's parents several times as she speaks, almost in confirmation of what she relays. She finishes by explaining how we sought refuge in the house and how it collapsed, before she admits she doesn't know what happened to Katie next.

Her memory loss concerns me. She was awake, she spoke to Katie. She should recall them climbing out of the basement so they could find us help. I bite at the inside of my cheek, wondering what else she's forgotten. Can she not remember anything we talked about? All of the things I revealed to her, the things she revealed to me?

It's gone quiet and I glance up, finding four pairs of eyes watching me, clearly waiting for the answers Jules isn't able to provide. Mrs. Luther asks what happened to her daughter. I clear my throat.

"She was fine, Mrs. Luther." Her face visibly relaxes as I go on. "She climbed out of the basement with Jeff Parker to get help for us. I don't know what happened to them, I'm sorry. When they finally pulled us out, the others that were with us had already been taken away. They were worried about Jules, so they loaded her into an ambulance right away and brought her here."

Katie's parents spring into action, her mom furiously punching at her cell phone—which isn't working—while Mr. Luther rushes the nurses' desk seeking information.

For the first time since being reunited with Jules at the hospital, I think about Jeff and Katie and the others. I think about all of the other people in Tyler and the neighboring towns possibly hit by this storm. Deciding I might find some friends here and that Jules and her father might want some privacy, I move to leave. For a second time, I stop when Jules speaks. Forcing a smile, I face her attempting to catch up on what she's saying about me to her father.

"—I'm pretty sure he saved my life—and Katie's too."

I may have missed half their conversation, but I don't miss the way she sounds when she says I saved her life. The glow in her eyes is bright enough to light up my darkest days for months. I nod, my cheeks warming at her praise.

"It's been a long time, West," her father moves my way, his hand clasping my shoulder. "Jules says you're a hero, huh?"

I shuffle back and forth, my embarrassment growing. "Oh, no sir. No, all I did was grab her hand and run, sir. Anyone would have done it."

"He's being modest, Daddy. He threw me on the ground and covered me when the house started to come down on us."

"Oh. I can't imagine what you kids went through out there," Katie's mother sniffs. The woman's an emotional mess; large tears fall down her cheeks mixed with black mascara.

"There were only like, what, twelve of us in the house? Our friends scattered everywhere. We don't know what happened to them—" Jules' voice breaks. "Mrs. Luther, we lost Tanya, and Candy, and Tommy. I don't know where Stuart is, either."

Damn it. The crack in her voice, the tears in her eyes—I busy myself with tossing my empty coffee cup into a nearby trash bin to prevent myself from reaching for her. Thankfully, Katie's mom comforts her, pulling her into a hug. They cry together as Jules' father explains the details of their search for her and Katie.

"We were able to get to the edge of Grier field. We had to drive all the way around the town and backtrack, but we knew you were supposed to be there. The place was swarming with cops and Fire and Rescue, as well as a lot of civilian volunteers."

"What did they say?" I ask.

His eyes, so similar to his daughter's, meet mine, and something in them warns me to brace for bad news. "They said there were several fatalities there, but they're not done combing the wreckage. Then they told us everyone they found was sent here. They specifically knew Jules was here."

"Of course, everyone knows Jules," I smile uncomfortably. The quarterback's sweetheart of a girlfriend; everyone loves her.

"Steph, honey?" Mr. Luther returns, his voice abnormally loud and his face full of hope. "Apparently Katie's in the cafeteria. They finally set up a waiting area for people not needing medical attention and they have her name on the list."

Mrs. Luther let's out a strange whoop-cry and a whirlwind of hugs, praise, and 'love you's swirl around me as the Luther's rush away with Jules calling after them. "Give her a hug for me and tell her I'm okay."

Intending to use their retreat as a cover for my own, I inch closer to the part in the curtains. "Uh, I think I'll go too and check in. See who's here and all."

"Is your dad coming back here, West? Can I offer you a ride home when we leave?" Mr. Blacklin asks as he sits on the edge of Jules' bed.

"Thanks, but I'm good. He'll be coming back at some point. He went to help however he could since he has a truck," I explain. Then, playing the role of self-appointed guardian, I go over the visit with Dr. Metzger to Jules' father, making sure he knows she's supposed to remain admitted because of her head trauma. He nods as I let him know someone will be back to check on her soon. When I can think of no other reason to delay my leaving, I cock my head to the side in an attempt to grab Jules' attention. But I already have it, she's staring at my hands. They're clasped at my waist, my right thumb absently rubbing the palm of my left hand. I stop when I take note of her own hands, her fingers stretching open before fisting closed in her lap. Does she feel it too? The emptiness?

"I'll see you around, Jules." It's time to go, to end this— whatever this is—with her now before it gets any harder to walk away.

"Huh?"

"I said I'll see ya around," I repeat as her blue eyes rise from my hands to my face.

"Oh." She glances at her father. "Hey, Dad? Could you give us a moment?" Her fingers tap her lap restlessly and I bite back a smile. My need to get away is completely forgotten.

Mr. Blacklin glances between us before he presses a kiss to Jules' head. He walks to me and stops, offering his hand once again. "Thank you, son. We are indebted to you."

His offer of gratitude is filled with heavy emotion and I merely nod my reply before he leaves us alone. I feel sick. I don't want people to think of what I did as anything special. It wasn't. It was human nature. Wasn't it? I'm reminded of the temptation I'd had to leave Katie behind. The temptation to merely grab Jules and run. Did that make me a hero, my willingness to save one girl and not the other? My stomach turns at the thought.

Jules readjusts her position in her bed, sitting forward and pulling her knees to her chest. A visible shudder runs through her as she presses her forehead against her knees. I'm as inexplicably drawn to her in this moment as I was a few hours ago before this horror began. I move to the edge of the bed and lean my hip against it, watching her. Her hair conceals her face, but her jagged breaths attest to her struggle to maintain her composure. Whether it's for me or for her, I'm not sure, but I wrap Jules in my arms and inhale deeply, telling myself this is it. One last moment, then I'll leave, and Jules Blacklin and West Rutledge will go back to the way they were before tonight.

"You told me we weren't going to die. Thank you. I don't know what else to say, West." She sounds so achingly vulnerable. Her hands snake up and curl around my forearm that is draped across her chest.

I'm not entirely sure if I meant it at the time when I promised her we weren't going to die. They were merely words. From the moment the sirens sounded, I'd felt the need to protect this girl, to keep her calm. It was my purpose, perhaps one that bore out of the need to always help others as my father had taught me growing up. Who knows? It was instinct, a gut reaction, and maybe a little bit of an angel on my shoulder that drove me to do and say all I had tonight.

Wait, she remembered something! Hoping her memory is returning, I ask, "I thought you couldn't remember anything from the basement?"

"I don't, not really. That just came back to me all of a sudden." Her hands drop to the bed as I shift away. "Why? What happened tonight? I don't know how long we were trapped down there."

All the things we said. The things we shared. The bucket lists, the confessions. I smile at the situation. Those were the first honest conversations I'd had since my mom died and now Jules can't remember it. Figures.

"It doesn't matter. We made it out, and that's all that counts, right?" I want her to disagree with me. I want her to admit there's something special happening between the two of us tonight. I want her to admit that this changes everything for her, as it has for me.

I reach out, intending to push her hair back so I can look at her, when the curtain slides open and her father walks in with a nurse in tow. The spell broken, I spring from the bed, excusing myself as I give Jules one last look.

"Hey, Spike?" *The nickname slays me.* Her voice trembles as we hold our gaze. "Don't wait four years to get the nerve again."

Another memory.

There are no words. I nod. And I walk away.

I walk away from Jules' curtained room. I walk away from the triage area. I walk away from the voice in my head telling me to go back, to stay with Jules. The feelings are too intense, too gut-wrenching. Every way I turn there's another dirty face, another injured patient, another crying person. I push through them all and into a hallway. Rounding a corner, I lean against a wall in a relatively quiet place. My knees buckle and I squat, dropping my head and breathing harshly as I'm overcome with emotion.

"Shit." My hands cradle my head as weakness invades me. Weakness and tears. For five minutes I allow myself this moment crouched in a corner. Then I go in search of my friends.

The cafeteria is overrun with people waiting. Waiting for word on a loved one, waiting for a family member, waiting for a place to go. There are volunteers taking names and explaining procedures as you walk in, but I bypass them. I'm merely looking for Jeff, or Ruben, or anyone I know.

"West?"

I turn at my name, spotting two guys from school sitting at a table. They're both wearing the button-up white dress shirt typical of the uniform for Remington's restaurant in mid-town. Paul has a bandage taped to his forehead and Marcus cradles his left arm to his chest.

"Was Remington's hit?" I ask as I join them.

"Damn, man, the roof was pulled right off. Like it was nothing but a toy. Just sucked right off. We barely had the time to run," Paul says. A girl at the table covers her face and cries into her hands.

"But the sirens?" How could they have had so little time to find cover?

"A minute, two max. It drilled straight down main street and plowed right into us. It was chaos, we were packed with diners after the game. It could have been worse—"

"Worse?" I ask.

Paul touched his bandage. "Ms. Kathy—she didn't make it." Ms. Kathy was a fixture at Remington's my entire life. She is—was—a few years older than my parents. She used to drop meals at our house after my mom passed away. She had a son. "—There were two other deaths, I don't know who though."

"One was a student, he was in my Bio class last year," says the girl sitting with them. I don't recognize her as her bloodshot eyes meet mine. Her trembling hand swipes at her cheek. Biology? That means this student was most likely a junior, which means I might know him. Or knew him.

Reality sinks in. Much of my night and this storm has been wrapped up in what I went through with Jules, but there's so much more. An unseen weight presses on my chest, as though I'm back in the house under a pile of debris. I struggle to breathe normally.

"God," the girl breathes harshly, "was this night real?"

Paul and Marcus mutter. My gut churns as I feel myself tumbling into self-pity and fear. I don't want to wallow; I don't want to allow my emotions out again. I fear I may never stop sinking once I begin. Taking a sharp breath, I glance around the cafeteria to clear my head.

I locate Ruben standing at a table near the center of the room. Rising, I look at his group in an attempt to identify the dusty faces. When I spot the other guys—Mark, Jeff, and Tommy Wilson—who hadn't been with us at the house earlier tonight, my spirits lift.

"Hey, I need to check on some people. Hang in there." Winding my way through the tables, I hurry to my friends.

"You," Jeff points in my direction once he spots me heading for him. He gets up from his seat and we stand face to face. "I didn't know if I'd see you again. You scared the hell out of me," he admits.

Knowing the feeling, I grab his shoulder and pull him into the manliest hug I can under the circumstance. This is my best friend, my third brother, and the only person who knows me as honestly as anyone can. I turn to the others, slapping backs and exchanging hugs with each one of them before we sit.

"There were so many people, man," Jeff whispers. "So many bodies littered all over the field. I didn't know if Katie was going to be able to make it."

I push my mind elsewhere, not wanting to picture the images Jeff is describing. "Her parents are here. Did you see them?" I ask, changing the subject. Part of me is grateful for being trapped with Jules, as scary as those hours were; at least we were spared the views others witnessed.

"Yeah, they picked her up and told us you and Jules were here. How is she?"

"Concussion." I miss her like hell already. "But, she's okay. We both are. Correction, we all are."

At least I think we are, but as I look at the faces of the guys around me, I'm not so sure.

Nine

There are people—servicemen, chaplains, police—whose job it is to deliver what is referred to as death notifications. They are the ones who arrive on the doorstop of unsuspecting families to inform them that their loved one has died. As I step to the side of the Blacklin's foyer while my father comforts Jules' mother I wonder how someone can handle this sort of job day in and day out. How does one remove themselves from the emotional aspect of delivering the worst news they possibly can?

Maybe I'm affected more because the news we are delivering right now is personal. Perhaps it's easier when it's a stranger, though I doubt it. Seeing the pain on Mrs. Blacklin's face as my father breaks the news, hearing her cry, and knowing we still have to tell Jules—I wouldn't be able to handle this on a daily basis.

This is another item on a rapidly growing list of things I never would have seen myself having to do before last night—another way my life has changed.

"Mom?" Jules calls from above. I look to the top of the staircase as her head pokes around the corner of the hallway. Even from where I stand in the foyer I can make out the purple bruises on her skin and the dark circles under her eyes.

"What's wrong?" She steps into full view, grabbing the stair rail to steady herself as she descends. "West, why are you here?"

I can't tell her. I refuse to do it. I refuse to break her heart. It takes every ounce of my self-control to keep myself from turning and running from the house. I don't want to see her cry again, last night was enough. Her father called me a hero, but I'm just a coward.

"Oh, honey." Her mother rushes forward the moment Jules toes touch the bottom step. "I have some bad news."

My eyes focus on Jules' hand as it grips the newel post. Her knuckles turn white, her long fingers curling into the wood. Her mother wraps her in a hug as I work up the courage to look at her face again. When I do, I see resignation. She knows we're not here on a social call. I should paint on a smile, but instead I let my guard down. Removing the façade I swore I would wear around her, I let her see my pain; I let her see my need. I let her see that I'm not okay, because I'm not, and right now it's okay to not be okay.

I share in Jules' hurt by locking eyes with her as her mother delivers the nightmarish news into her ear. I use my eyes to allow her see into my soul. It's all I know how to do in this moment. Mrs. Blacklin's words scarcely reach my ears, but I know the news she is delivering.

Tanya is dead.

Jules' eyelids flutter, pain slashing across her features as she watches me over her mother's shoulder. Her blue eyes turn from confused, to hurt, to blank within seconds. Her feet shuffle as the color drains from her face, and I hurl myself toward the staircase just in time to catch her as she passes out. I sink to the floor with Jules limp body as her mother grabs for her hand.

"Jules?"

I sit on the ground and position Jules between my legs, her back and head against my chest. She stirs almost immediately and tilts her head up toward me in confusion. "What? What happened?"

I fake a smile as color returns to her bruised face. "Welcome back, cheerleader."

"Honey? Are you all right? You passed out, but only for a moment," Mrs. Blacklin, who is on her knees beside me, explains.

Jules blinks rapidly, her eyes scanning the foyer as she works to figure everything out. "You saved me again." Her face goes beet red. She shifts her gaze to her mother and sits forward, pulling her hand from her grip. Glancing around, Jules scoots up, putting some room between us as she places her head in the palms of her hands.

"It's this concussion. Man, it hurts so bad," she moans. I slide in closer, my hand resting lightly on the small of her back to support her.

My father stands beside us and clears his throat. "West, I think we should let them be now."

No. Not yet. My fingers graze her bare waist from where her shirt rose up when she fell, and my hand begs to explore her body at the feel of the soft heat of her skin . . . I shake my head. *Not helpful thoughts, West.*

"Why did y'all come by?" Jules asks as she massages her temples.

"Honey?" Mrs. Blacklin's tone tells the entire story. It reminds me of the way my dad would say my name when I was in trouble as a kid. I didn't need to hear anything but his tone and I knew I was in for it. Mrs. Blacklin's tone says it all; her one word contains every ounce of tragedy this moment holds. And after three heartbeats of silence, the truth sinks in and Jules' face crumbles.

"Oh, no . . . no," she weeps. "Tanya?" Her back trembles against my touch and she hunches forward, hugging herself as though she's attempting to hold all of her broken pieces together. Her mother leans into her, offering up her comfort in the form of a hug. I press my palms into the wood floor, prepared to slide backwards and give them their space when Jules' hand grips my leg and pins me in place.

"No!" she cries, her head lifting from her mother's embrace. She glances over her shoulder. "Don't go."

"Jules."

"Please? I need you here. I don't think I can do this without you."

The desperation in her voice robs me of all thoughts but one. *Jules.* If I knew what was best for me, I would leave.

"West?" my dad warns, his face is full of worry.

Too bad for him, I've never been the best at making smart decisions.

"I'm not going anywhere," I promise Jules while looking into my father's eyes. I don't know how to say no to her. I'm in for some serious trouble.

My heart is winning this battle: Heart: 1 ~ Head: 0.

Unpinning my shin from Jules' fingers, I grab her hips and slide her backward on the hardwood floor until she's in my arms again. She twists, curling into a ball and wrapping her arms around my waist as she cries into my shirt. Her mom offers my dad coffee, but I pay them no heed as they leave the foyer. My focus is on Jules as I rub circles along her back while she pours her grief into my chest.

Thinking of the death notifications again, I search for something to say. Certainly they have a protocol, some words they use to make the pain easier to stomach. But there's nothing. No clichéd comment about a 'better place' or how she should 'remember the good times' will erase the hurt she feels. I know this on a personal level and I hate it for her. There are no words of comfort when you lose someone you love so deeply.

Tanya Rivera. She'd been best friends with Jules and Katie since kindergarten; they were inseparable. Tanya was a feisty, free spirit who brought life and fun to the room the moment she walked in. I picture her golden skin, dark hair, and large, dark eyes that were always glowing with mischief. I recall the way she would jump into any game the boys had going on during recess in elementary school.

She was fearless, jostling and charging boys twice her size while playing soccer. I smile at the memory of the day she jumped off the diving board at a pool party and came up out of the water topless. She didn't cry or sulk embarrassed by the moment. She merely ducked under the water, slid her top in place, and threatened anyone who spoke about it. She was tough, but sweet. And she liked to party, so unlike my relationship with Jules, I'd stayed somewhat friendly with Tanya after I quit playing ball. At least on the social scene level.

"What happened to her?" Jules sniffles into my chest.

Clearing the mental picture of Jules' friend—my friend—I take a deep breath. "I don't know. My dad was with the crew that found her and two others." I fight hard to suppress my emotions as the pinpricks of tears form in my eyes.

"Two others?"

"There were a lot of casualties, Jules. All over town. People in midtown were caught in their cars," I admit tentatively, unsure of what her reaction will be. "Some were out to eat." I think of Remington's and Ms. Kathy.

She straightens, her face inches from mine. "That could have been us. We could be dead right now."

How many times did I think those same thoughts last night as I sat in the cafeteria with Jeff and our friends? I cup her face, feeling extremely grateful that I can deliver my next words. "But we're not. We made it."

"Yeah, we did." Her warm hand covers mine as she closes her eyes. She releases a deep breath and opens her watery blue eyes as she asks regretfully, "But who else didn't?"

I can't hold back my feelings any longer. "I don't know." We hold our gazes, and my secret thoughts spill out. "I'm just glad it wasn't us. I know that's selfish, but I was scared as hell last night."

Jules' chin quivers and she drops her hand from mine, tightening her arms around me as tears shimmer in her eyes again. Forming a small ball, she pushes her body back into mine and hides her face in my chest. Like a sponge, I absorb each tear, each waver of breath, each tensing of her muscles as her loss surges through her.

After my mother died, I would sneak into the game room and sit in her chair our chair after my dad and brothers were in bed. I'd cover myself in her blankets, press my face into her pillows, and I would cry. I was only thirteen. During the day, my brothers and I would put our chins up and act the part of the brave Rutledge boys for all to see. After a week, Carson returned to A&M for summer football workouts, and Austin returned to Hillsdale practices. I did nothing. I tried returning to football; two weeks after the funeral I slid into my workout gear and walked to the garage door while my dad waited in the car. I stood there dressed and ready to go, but my hand wouldn't let go of the back door handle.

"Maybe tomorrow," Dad says encouragingly, climbing out of his truck and walking me back into the house. Tomorrow came and went, and the next day too. Carson called from school to talk about it. Austin offered to come with me. Dad reminded me how much my mother loved the sport, how much she wanted us to return to normal once she was gone.

Normal: the typical, the usual, the expected. I no longer wanted to do the expected because what I expected—a mother to be there through my childhood and watch me grow up—was taken from me. Screw expectations. The next day I removed my pads and cleats from my room and set them in a box in the garage. Four years later, they're still there—a reminder of my defiance in the face of the shattering of my heart.

Sitting on the sun dappled floor of Jules' foyer, holding her while she processes the loss of her best friend, is a balm to my burning soul. I've been angry for so long—angry at God, angry at my dad, at my mom, and at myself—but at this moment the only thing my heart feels is overwhelming sorrow for Jules. And the longer I sit here, the more I understand. I don't hurt for Jules alone. I hurt for Tanya, and Ms. Kathy, and the others who lost their lives. I hurt for the town of Tyler.

The fire within me that's been fueling my bitterness with life for so long is being doused by the tears of the one girl I can't have. *Shit*.

I shift away from her, motioning to the staircase. We move to sit side-by-side on the stairs, and we don't speak for a good five minutes. I consider grabbing my father and hightailing it out of there, but Jules falls softly into my side, resting her head against my shoulder. And damn.

Right when I think I can work up the strength to walk away, she pulls me back. Ha, who am I kidding? I have no strength with her.

It's unsettling and makes no sense whatsoever. For now, I chalk it up to the stress and emotions of the last sixteen hours. I place an arm around her shoulders. Later I'll deal with the truth, whatever it may be, but for now it's:

Heart: 2 ~ Head: 0

"Did you stay at the hospital for very long last night?" she asks as my fingers trace up and down her bare bicep. She's wearing a tank top and small boxer-type sleep shorts. I hadn't taken the time to notice until now. *I need to stop touching her.*

I clear my throat. "Um, yeah. I stayed there pretty much all night. My dad was busy."

"We should have given you a lift home. I'm sorry."

She attempts to pull away and I tighten my hold. "It was fine, Buffy. I saw a lot of people come in. Jeff and I hung out for a while. I saw Tommy, Ruben, and Mark. It felt good to see people coming in and know they were safe."

"Tommy? He was probably one of the last people to be with Tanya before she—"

She breaks off without saying the word 'died', but that's not surprising to me. For months after Mom's death when we talked at my house, we always said that Mom "went away" as though she was on some amazing vacation.

"He didn't know what happened to her. He said they were separated in the crowd. I wish—" I sigh, wondering if I could have saved Tanya too. While I sat in the hospital waiting area with Jeff, he filled me in on what happened at The Ice Shack. According to him, Tanya was the reason for the fight in the parking lot right before the storm hit. That's why Katie came to get Jules and why Jeff wasn't around when the sirens sounded. He'd been too busy attempting to break up the fight between Tommy Wilson and Carter Cooper, a player from our rival school, Rossview High, and apparently a rival for Tanya's heart.

"What's this?" Jules' front door closes without a sound as Stuart Daniels steps into her foyer, confusion on his face.

Jules sits up and I drop my arm from her shoulders, settling my hand on the small of her back to steady her as she wobbles like one of those old school blow-up punching bag toys. There's this odd, slow motion type of moment as the three of us exchange glances before Jules stands and crosses the foyer.

Throwing herself at Stuart, a barrage of tears and broken words spew from Jules' lips. "Stuart! What happened to you? I sent you a text, but you never called back, and then the storm hit. I thought you were dead. Tanya's de—she's gone."

Stuart wraps his arms around Jules' waist and he smiles into her hair as he soothes her. His eyes, however, narrow thoughtfully on me. "I'm fine, Jules. You thought I was dead? Are you kidding me? I was crazy worried about you after hearing the radio reports, but my parents refused to let me leave the house last night. I finally told them it was too bad and left an hour ago. The streets are a nightmare. Thankfully I saw your dad on my way here, and he told me what happened last night."

Jules' mom shouts from the kitchen, the sound of chair feet scraping against their flooring pulls me to my feet. A moment later, Mrs. Blacklin enters the foyer with my father on her heels. "Oh, Stuart. I thought I heard you. I'm so glad you're okay. Jules was worried sick about you last night." Her mother gives him a side hug as Jules remains in his arms.

I contemplate puking.

"I'm fine. I was worried about her," Stuart reassures them both.

The five of us stand there awkwardly for a moment too long before I rub my hands together and say, perhaps a bit too forcefully, "Well, we better get going now, Dad."

I don't miss the scrutiny in Stuart's eyes or the way he tugs Jules to the side of the entrance, out of my direct path, as I walk to the door. I tell myself to walk out, to leave without offering another word, but I can't.

"Take care of her." It's a warning, and judging by the look on Stuart's face, he knows it. "She got a concussion last night and passed out again this morning," I add, as though her health is my real concern.

"Mrs. Blacklin." I offer a bob of my head as my goodbye and push the glass door open, stepping onto their front stoop.

"Thank you for making sure we got the news," Jules says behind me. I twist around, giving her a nod of acknowledgement, and taking the opportunity to get one last look at her.

I'm a glutton for punishment because, seriously, what do I expect to see? Jules chasing after me, begging me to stay? No. I get exactly what I knew I would—Jules and Stuart standing next to each other, their hands intertwined between them. My eyes focus on their hands, and I see red. I'm not typically a jealous guy; I don't own Jules Blacklin, but damn if seeing her hand in his doesn't burn me up. As though she's reading my mind, she pulls away from Stuart's and shoves her fingers through her hair.

"You take care, Jules," my father says before he walks out the door that I'm propping open. With another nod to the three of them, I turn and follow in his wake. I have to force myself to not look back.

○○○○○○○○

My dad and I don't speak until we're leaving the Blacklin's neighborhood. "Do you want to go home?" he asks, and I contemplate my answer.

"What, and sit around all day feeling like crap about everything? No way. What can we do to help?"

"West, you're exhausted. You didn't sleep last night and you didn't take much more than a cat nap after we got home this morning—"

"Dad," I interrupt. Sleep is the least of my concerns right now. I can't fathom sitting around doing nothing but thinking. "I need to be doing something. Please."

He nods and picks up the cellphone sitting on his dashboard. I watch out the window, taking in the random debris as he has a conversation with a buddy of his. There's trash strewn about everywhere—plastic grocery bags sway in the breeze as they hang stuck in tree branches, random pieces of wood and metal are scattered about the fields. We have to weave around a tire that is sitting in the middle of the road.

When we drive through the residential areas directly south of the high school, the debris becomes thicker. Three turns later, I understand why. The tornado made direct contact with the street behind where my father pulls his truck to a stop. As he parks, I look through the white picket fence of one lovely, untouched house and see nothing behind it but a foundation where another home should be. A foundation and a pile of rubble. Chunks of brick, bits of sheetrock, and a smattering of furniture—these are all that is left of someone's home.

"Okay, let's go help," Dad says as he opens up the door and hops out of the truck.

We pick our way through the wreckage, heading toward the destroyed houses. It's exactly what you see on the news after a storm, and yet it's different. The devastation is more in-your-face when seen in the flesh. The sounds, the smells, the sheer amount of damage—it's unlike anything I can describe.

My dad stops and puts a hand on my arm, holding me in place, as he waves to someone I don't recognize. "Listen, before we go any further, you should know there may be bodies in the area," he warns as he rubs the back of his neck. "I'd prefer you not see that."

"M'kay." I square my shoulders, readying myself. "I'm fine. Whatever I can do to help, I will." *Shit. Dead bodies. Shit.* I wonder what I've gotten myself into, but I paint on a brave face.

I spend the afternoon helping wherever I can. The street we're on used to have ten homes, yet it looks as though all of Texas emptied their doors and scattered their life belongings here. Books, papers, pictures, clothing, and toys are littered everywhere. I find a washing machine standing alone in the middle of a back yard. A car is upside down and propped up against a tree as though it's a matchbox toy.

As I work, the scent of food rotting in the hot Texas sun fills the air gags me. The smell mixes with the smoldering odor of an electrical fire that was contained hours ago but refuses to die, adding a hazy smog quality to the air. My eyes burn, my nose stings, my mouth is dry, but I keep working. Hour after hour, I find something to do or someone to help.

A few hours before dusk, my father learns of several missing people in the area so he moves me away from the heavily impacted homes and puts me to work helping secure the less damaged houses on the neighboring road. I help board up broken windows for an older couple and secure tarps for a single mom whose home sustained heavy roof damage.

I join others in helping clear limbs and random pieces of furniture, bikes, and lawn equipment from the neighborhood streets to provide access for vehicles. I find myself comforting a woman whose home wasn't touched, but can't find her family pet.

And I sit next to a boy, about ten years of age, and talk sports because he tells me today was supposed to be his first game of the season. Late in the afternoon, I sift through the life of a young family we've been told didn't survive.

I work until my hands are bleeding, my heart is shattered, and the sun is setting. Then, after a hot shower, I fall into bed and wonder how Jules is doing as I come to grips with what we survived and what we lost.

Ten

I'm hovering between wakefulness and a nightmare. I'm in a box, the air around me thick with dust. My hands probe the space, searching for a way out of the blackness. Pushing the ceiling above me, the top gives, allowing me to sit up. Light blinds me as I spot freedom yards away; all I have to do is stand and walk. My lungs burst with the need for fresh air as I pull my body up. The touch of a cold hand on my leg stops me. Twisting around, my pulse quickens as I find Jules below me. Her eyes meet mine, a tear slipping out at she speaks.

"Please don't leave me."

I'm confused, she wasn't here a moment ago. Was she?

"Jules? Come on, we can get out." I reach down, offering my hand. "Let's go."

"I can't." Her gaze flicks to her legs; she's pinned. She's not leaving this box.

I look out at my escape, at the light calling to me, at the fresh air beyond this box. Then I back up and squirm into the spot next to Jules.

"Save yourself," she whispers, jerking her head up to the opening as she grabs at my hand.

Rolling to my side, I touch her face. "I can't. We're in this together and I'm not leaving you."

Closing my eyes, I tilt toward her lips for a kiss. Our foreheads touch, my lips part, and a puff of air brushes across my mouth as something knocks into my head. *What the . . .*

"You're damn lucky you're alive, dude, cause now I don't have to kill you." I open my eyes to find Austin hovering above me. Reaching over my body, he grabs a pillow and smacks me across the back of my shoulders.

"Damn it, Austin. What the hell?" I growl, pushing blindly at his body.

"I'm happy to see you too, baby bro." He punches my side as he sits on the edge of my bed, and I groan.

"Yeah, I can tell by your oxymoronic statement, you jack wad." I scooch over, making room for him. Austin remains silent as I lie face down, waiting for the remnants of my strange dream to clear away. My mind is slow to let go of the way Jules' spoke, the way her hand grasped mine, the way I refused to leave. I will it all away; it was only a dream. When the pull of Jules' blue eyes is the only thing lingering in my memory, I flip over and face my brother.

"When did you get here?" I ask, sitting up and scrubbing my hands over my face.

"A few hours ago. Dad forced me to let you sleep. He says you've been through the ringer." His voice is tight with concern. The big brother, always worried about me.

"You could say that."

"I can see it," he counters.

I follow his eyes and look at what he's staring at. My shirtless torso is covered in bruises, cuts, and scratches. Add the injuries to the all-around weariness my body feels today and it's as though I've been hit by a truck, or I'm back at football camp doing two-a-days and being tackled at the line over and over. I'm a mess both inside and out.

"Do you want to talk about it?" he asks as his eyes bore holes into me. He's trying to size me up, trying to figure out what's going on in my head.

I consider sharing, for a moment. Only two years older than me, Austin's more of a best friend than a brother. I can tell him anything, but I'm not sure I'm ready to share this yet. I clap my hands together and paste on a grin. "I want food."

Worry mars my brother's features before he smiles and stands. "Then get yo' ass up, punk. Food we've got," he says all gangster-like. I bust out laughing, the rush of air making my ribs ache as I roll out of bed. "Although, you're looking a little out of shape, maybe you ought to back off the donuts."

I roll my eyes as I throw on a pair of sweatpants. "Dude, you wish. I can outrun your sorry ass, tornado hangover and all."

"In your dreams," Austin laughs, slinging his arm around and placing me into a headlock.

"Challenge accepted." I lean against his side, taking his weight on my shoulders. "After breakfast," I add, elbowing him in the gut and slipping away from his grasp before he can get me back.

"You look better this morning," Dad says as I slip into the kitchen with Austin on my heels. "Finally get some sleep?"

"Yeah, I feel better. Just sore." I stretch my arms over my head, feeling the tightness of skin around the gash I received Friday night. It seems to be holding with all of the movements I've been making, though. Next I roll my head from side to side, working out the kinks. Dang, everything is stiff.

"Are you heading out again?" I ask Dad, noting his clothes and empty breakfast plate.

Swallowing his coffee, he shakes his head. "I'm spending the day with my boys." He looks back and forth between Austin and I. His eyes are dull with weariness, but I don't dare suggest he get rest. I know where us boys get our stubbornness from.

"Speaking of, where's Carson?" I ask.

"He wanted to be here, but he was busy at work, and Mindy has some project due at school that she's not finished with." I frown at Austin's explanation.

"Uh, work and school won out over seeing if his family is alive?" I'm more than a little surprised to not see my oldest brother standing here this morning.

Austin snorts as my dad shakes his head. "Don't insult your brother. I spoke to him late last night and ensured him we're good."

Austin bumps into my side. "I'm totally telling Car you doubted him."

Ignoring Austin's gibe, I ask, "Cell service is up then?"

"It's spotty, but yes. I've been making calls this morning." Dad's face is somber and I read between the lines into what he's not saying. He's checking on people and getting news.

"And?"

"Forty-five."

Holy . . . my chest tightens. It's as though the oxygen is sucked out of the kitchen and my hand goes to my throat as Austin and I exchange glances.

"Forty-five deaths?" Austin clarifies.

Dad moves in between us and places a hand on each of our shoulders. "Forty-five. Eight of them were students at Hillsdale. It's people we know, guys. Ms. Kathy, Steve Conners, the Jessups."

The blood drains from my face. "The Jessups?" I repeat. "As in all of them?"

"The whole family. Their house—" Dad's voice wavers and Austin moves in for a hug. I join in, but I'm numb. Another family gone. I was the lucky one. Jules, Katie, Jeff—all of us trapped in the house were lucky. Thank God for a basement that saved us from a house falling on our heads.

"There's a candlelight vigil tonight, at Center Park."

A vigil. The urge to shudder is strong, but I resist.

The small town of Tyler is broken in two. One half is the clean, quaint southern Texas town it has always been and the other is a disaster zone. Shredded landscape, flipped cars, buildings tagged with spray painted warning signs from FEMA, body counts.

As Austin, my dad, and I talk with people at Center Park we hear implausible stories of the storm's strength. The force of the wind was so immense that it threw cars over one hundred yards. Concrete parking stops with rebar were ripped out of the ground and tossed. Steel beams became paper, mangled into nothing, while trees were debarked. Everything mere children's toys to a storm of this magnitude

We hear more tales of death, too. North of town, a nursing home sustained severe damage, killing multiple residents. Bodies are being identified in parts. Half of the deaths were people in their homes; trapped and crushed on a Friday night while watching television or sleeping. I shift back and forth on the balls of my feet, my knuckles rapping into the palm of my left hand, as we listen.

I don't want to hear this.

My dad looks at me. He reaches over and clasps my shoulder, and I still. Trying to contain my emotions, I stuff my fists deep into my pockets. When a family friend begins retelling the tale of a toddler ripped from her parents' arms as they ran for a backyard shelter, I can take no more. Excusing myself, I wander aimlessly through the crowd gathering at the park as the sky darkens.

"West!"

I crane my neck, looking for the body attached to the voice calling my name and I spot Melody Wade approaching through the crowd ahead of me. Melody's a friend of a friend. A random hookup from last year, but we're on good terms.

"Hi." She hugs me tightly. "I heard about what happened with you. I'm so glad you're okay."

I'm unsure of how to respond. Thanks? Do you thank someone for telling you they're happy you're alive? A young girl grabs my attention. She's clinging to a framed photo and wearing an oversized men's shirt as she holds on to a woman, probably in her mid-twenties, dressed in all black. Somehow I can't consider saying thank you as they walk by.

Melody waves for me to follow her, and I find myself joining a small group. I stand there pretending to be a part of their conversations as they take turns talking about where they were Friday night when the tornado struck. I have the feeling this conversation thread will be repeated for years to come. "Where were you when the 2013 tornado hit Tyler?" someone will ask. What will I answer? The person next to me coughs loudly and I refocus on the circle.

Most of these teens go to Rossview and live across city limits, so they weren't in Tyler when the storm hit. They speculate about the horrors we lived through, but they have no idea what it truly felt like. One of the guys, a stoner I've seen at a few parties, has the balls to ask me about Grier house. My reply is a glare. Melody changes the subject.

Restless, I scan around the park. Each time I spot a red head, my pulse quickens.

"I wonder where they'll put the Hillsdale students," someone says.

"I heard it's completely destroyed," Melody says, although it sounds as though she's asking me for confirmation instead of stating a fact. Eyes turn my way. This is not where I want to be right now. I fight the urge to glare at them all again as I shrug their questioning glances off.

"Hell if I know."

I hadn't thought about the school; I hadn't even realized we didn't have a building anymore. When I spot people passing out candles, I bend close to Melody's ear. "Hey, I'm going to find Austin and my dad. It was good seeing you, Mel."

She nods, squeezing my forearm. "You, too."

Ignoring every glance sent my way, I make it back to Austin within ten minutes. He's chatting with some girls, but the moment I arrive, he excuses us and we walk deeper into the crowd.

"Are you okay?" he asks when we find ourselves blocked in by people on all sides. The crowd has doubled in the last few minutes as people make their way closer to the front of the park where town officials have set up.

I'm handed a box from behind and stand there clueless as to what to do. My mind is shutting down. There are too many people, too many sad faces. I want to block it all out.

"West?" Austin says my name as he removes two candlesticks with small white cups around them from the box I'm holding. "Are you okay?"

Nodding my head, I pass the box to the person next to me. "Yeah."

I take a candle from him. My fingertips dig into the taper, etching a groove into the hard wax as I stare blankly ahead. "No," I admit after a moment. *I don't think I'm okay. How can anyone be okay?* "I don't know."

My brother moves closer, our shoulders brushing as he speaks low, "What's going through your head? You can lie to Dad all you want, but I know you."

What's going through my head? Wind, a house, blood, screams, Jules . . . I lift my eyes to his. "I thought a lot about Mom during those moments." I think back to the voice I heard. "When Jules was knocked out and I only had my own thoughts to deal with it was Mom I heard the most." I didn't necessarily mean to speak the words aloud, but I did. I spoke them and Austin closes his eyes.

"I'm not surprised." He nods as the stranger beside me extends her lit candle to mine, igniting the wick. "She's always with us, isn't she?" Austin asks as he borrows my flame and lights his candle next.

A hush extends over the crowd so I lower my voice. "Yeah, she is. I screwed up, man. I've—" I cut my explanation short as I spot Jeff on the other side of the park, facing in our direction. I'm a dog in the park who's spotted a squirrel. My conversation with Austin is forgotten by the sight of Jeff because wherever Jeff is, Katie will be close by. And where Katie is I'm positive Jules will be found. *Squirrel!*

My eyes survey the heads and faces near Jeff. No red hair or soft blue eyes. Skimming the empty space beside him, I lower my gaze and spot Katie. She's kneeling on the ground in front of the memorials that have sprung up around the huge tree at the end of the park, and next to her is Jules.

I see her hair before her face and it's as though she's a damn magnet. Everything within me longs to go to her. She lifts her head and her eyes roam over the crowd much as mine have been, and as though we truly are a set of magnets destined to constantly attract each other, she finds me. In a crowd of thousands of mourners, we connect. A conversation is spoken without saying a word. Her eyes remind me of my dream this morning; they have the same pleading look she had when she asked me to not leave her.

Austin says my name as he knocks into my side, and I reluctantly look away from Jules. "I need to go," I nod toward the tree and my friends, "over there." Without bothering to wait for his reply I move.

I haven't fully explained Jules to Austin yet. I'm not sure if he'd understand our tie or what he'd say about it. Apologizing to the people around me, I snake though the crowd on my way to reach Jules. I make it to the tree where the memorial is set up for victims as the speeches begin. While the mayor talks about perseverance and finding hope, I stop and take in all of the items left for those who died in the storm. The flowers, pictures, and mementos remind me of my mother's funeral. I hurry on, unable to face these memories tonight.

I locate Jeff in time to watch Jules hug Katie and walk away from them. *Where is she going?* I wonder, following behind her. Her petite stature makes her difficult to track and I lose sight of her before I make it to the edge of the crowd. Breaking through the wall of people I search for Jules.

The unnaturally bright light of a camera crew draws my attention to a news team. Standing in the spotlight, her face stricken, is Jules.

"Can you describe your experience Friday night?" a reporter asks Jules. "I understand you were with four of the victims at The Ice Shack on Friday, and that you were almost a victim yourself as you took refuge in the old Grier house with other classmates of yours. Can you tell us about that?"

Jules' hand goes to her face. Her eyes are wide. She looks terrified and frozen to the spot she's standing in.

Move away, I will her.

She shakes her head as she answers the question. "No, I can't. I got a concussion and have very little memory."

"You've lost your memory?" The female reporter gasps over dramatically. This woman sounds thrilled to have found Jules.

She asks another animated question and Jules mumbles, her head falling, her face miserable now. I've heard enough. White hot anger pushes me forward to save her.

"Well, Ms. Blacklin, who else was with you that night? Maybe they would like to talk to the cameras."

"I—"

Slinging my arm around Jules' shoulders as I reach her side, I pin the news team with a scowl full of disdain for their tactics. "She was with me, and no, I do *not* want to talk to the cameras. Excuse us."

Reining in the urge to go 'caveman West' on the woman, I tug Jules closer to my side and lead her away. Tucking her head down and into my chest, I steer her past the crowd forming around the news team and into a small clearing.

Once we're alone, I let her go. "Are you all right?"

"I'm fine; I was ambushed, that's all. How do the reporters know about the house?" she asks. I wondered the same thing when both Melody and the stoner mentioned it. Evidently people talk, and of course the news is everywhere. My answer is a shrug and Jules sighs in resignation.

She looks at the unlit candle in her hands and her forehead creases as though she's deep in thought. Her face is better tonight. The cuts and bruises are barely visible, or maybe the cloak of night and makeup help hide the truth.

She lifts her half-melted candle into the space between us and I realize I dropped mine somewhere between Austin and Jeff. A surge of guilt runs through me.

Her eyes move from the extinguished candle to my face. "Do you think this helped?"

There's such despair in her tone. "Here." I hold out my hand, taking her candle and looking around for a way to light it. There's a guy behind us holding a flame and I tap his shoulder, thanking him as his flame lights the wick. With a smile I bring the flame level with Jules' face for a better look at her. The glow reveals the bluish stain of a bruise high on her right cheek and the dark circles of her tired and puffy eyes. The make-up couldn't quite cover up the marks from our time spent together Friday night, but she's beautiful regardless.

We both watch the flame flicker between us before Jules asks, "What's it supposed to do for us? The whole lighting-a-candle thing?"

"Dad?" I ask as I walk into the game room late one night two weeks after Mom's death. My father is sitting in the dark, except for one candle lit on the table next to his chair. He's hunched over, his elbows resting on his knees, with his hands deep in his hair. At the sound of my voice, he looks up, his face a picture of grief as shadows flicker across it.

"Hey, champ. You can't sleep either, huh?" he asks, rolling his shoulders back as he sits up and attempts a smile.

I nod, not bothering to tell him how I've been sleeping in Mom's chair. I point to the candle as I come closer; it's a pink one with a floral scent Mom loved. "What are you doing?"

I get the feeling he's debating his answer. His eyes stare intently into the flame as though he's looking for something within it. "Your mom loved candles."

"And fires," I recall with a grin, and he nods.

"Yes, fire. Remember how she used to challenge us to find things in the flames of the fire pit? She was mesmerized by the way fire moved and changed every time we built one." Some people find shapes in clouds, my mother found them in the fire pit.

"Yeah, I can still picture the dragon she pointed out when we went camping two years ago. The way those red hot coals made up his fiery eyes," I chuckle.

"I didn't understand the game until I saw him. She was right; if you stare long enough, you can make out pictures."

"Exactly." He smiles, tipping his head, and I get it. He's seeing her, remembering her, in the flame.

The memory provides me the perfect answer for Jules' question. "I know there are a lot of religions that use candles to remember spirits of the dead, but I don't really know why. For me, I think it's a nice way to remember. I look at it as a metaphor of the light that a person once was. It kinda brings me strength."

"I don't feel strong. I feel alone and empty, like I want to crawl into a dark space," Jules says as she reaches across her body for the candle in my hand.

I concentrate on the flame between us. "You're not alone," I tell her as I cover her fingers with my own when we touch. "I'll be your strength, Jules."

"West?"

We are magnets. Because the moment she says my name, I turn toward her voice. Toward her. Each second lasting and pivotal as my right hand touches her left one. As our shoulders brush. As my eyes meet hers. Until we are inches apart, face to face, with only a candle and flame separating us.

I shift my feet and Jules' eyes slide beyond me; something she sees causes her to jump almost imperceptibly, pulling her hand from mine. Her tiny flinch breaks the spell. I step back, blinking, and release the candle and her hand.

"You know what? I need to run," I tell her as the need to escape presses in on me. "I'll see you around." I brush her upper arm with the back of my hand because I can't help myself, then I walk away.

Eleven

"Damn, I need a drink." I throw myself on the couch upstairs once Austin and I return home from the vigil. The vulnerable look in Jules' eyes is seared into my brain and her hesitant voice saying my name burns my ears.

"Seeing how you're underage, I think it's unlikely," Austin deadpans as he falls into the chair across from me. I hiss my displeasure and debate the wisdom of pulling a beer out of the refrigerator anyway.

"Wanna tell me what happened back there?" Austin asks after a few minutes of quiet. "First you walk away without a word, then you return with a damn chip on your shoulder and force us to leave. Now you're bitching about needing a drink?"

He has got to be kidding me. I don't respond to his line of questioning.

"West—"

"Shut it, Austin."

"I can still kick your ass, little brother," he warns.

When I remain quiet, he leans forward and slaps my shin, grabbing my attention.

I shake my head; I'm completely dumbfounded by his attitude. "Are you serious? You're giving me the tenth degree right now. Dude, you have no idea what I've been through."

He dips his head, working hard to maintain eye contact with me. "Then tell me."

"I can't." My fingers dig through my hair as I sit up, cupping the back of my head and releasing an angry grunt of frustration. "I can't explain any of it because I don't know. I don't know how I feel or what's going on."

"What's up with Jules Blacklin?"

My arms drop to my sides.

"West, you've gotta tell me something. You're not talking to Dad, and I know you won't go to counseling again. So you've got me or you can call Car, but you're not bottling it all up. Not this time."

Not this time. That's the kicker. Austin gets me, he knows how I box shit in and let it fester.

I give in. "What did Dad tell you about Friday night?"

The tension leaves Austin's body as he sinks deeper in his chair. "The basics."

I take a deep cleansing breath, blowing it out slowly as I replay Friday night in my mind. "When the sirens went off, there was this moment when everything stopped and the only thing I could think of was finding safety. I grabbed her hand and I ran. That was it."

"Her? As in Jules?" he verifies.

"Yeah." His eyes go wide, an unspoken urging to continue, so I ask, "Do you remember her?"

"The Princess of Tyler?" he smirks. "Of course I do, she was my pep girl Junior year. Plus, she was quite popular with the guys on the team."

"Anything in a skirt was popular with the guys," I counter, and he doesn't disagree. "How ridiculous is it for me to want her?"

"Want her? Dude, is this the storm talking or something more?"

"This is such a chick thing to talk about, Austin. I like her. I've liked her since seventh grade, before—"

"Before Mom," he finishes for me with a nod.

Looking up at the ceiling, I admit the truth to him. "I can't be with her. She's with Stuart Daniels. She's this perfect girl and I'm— I'm the screw up."

"What the hell?" A throw pillow skims across my face as it flies past me. "A screw up? What is wrong with you, man?"

"No wonder I was the QB in the family," I mock, grabbing the pillow from where it landed on the arm of the couch two feet away.

"Enlighten me. What makes you a screw up?"

I'm saved the need to answer by Dad walking into the game room carrying a couple bags of chips which he tosses our way from the end of the couch. "I just hung up with Coach Randall."

"Crap," Austin groans, reaching for his cell in his back pocket. "Did I miss a call?"

"You did, but you're not in trouble. The team is heading down tomorrow to help with clean up at the school. They want to support the town and give back. He called to let you know and asked for my help clearing it with Coach Thompson and the town officials."

Another day of sifting through wreckage. I know it needs to be done and I'm lucky I'm alive, but looking at the faces of those who lost so much yesterday was hard as hell. Hopefully being at the school will be easier.

Dad props his hip against the side of the couch. "What were you two talking about so heatedly?"

I look at Austin, my eyes asking him to not say anything and he plays along. "Oh you know, I was ragging on him about how soft he's become. You might not play ball anymore, but that doesn't mean you shouldn't keep in shape, bro." He flexes his biceps, sending me a ridiculous smile.

"And on that note," I fake a yawn, jumping to my feet. "I'm going to call Jeff and let him know about tomorrow, and get some sleep. I'm wiped out."

Their eyes follow me out of the room. I don't have to see them to know. I feel their silent judgment and worry drilling holes in my back with every step I take. It's Mom's death all over again. Everyone watching me, analyzing my decisions, playing want-to-be shrinks to get me to talk about my feelings. I resolve to handle myself better going forward. I don't need them hassling me. They've got enough on their plates without worrying about the baby in the family. I'm fine.

I'll be fine.

There's something to be said about manual labor. Working a twelve-plus hour day—hauling junk, chopping wood, sifting through piles and piles of debris searching for salvageable items—these things wear me down on Monday. I don't have time to think during the day and I'm too exhausted to do much more than have a quick bite for dinner and shift into a comfortable position before I'm sound asleep.

While my body rests and recovers, my heart is tortured, and I wake up thinking of Jules. Her body pressed against mine, her raspy breaths warming my neck, the feel of her silky hair wrapped in my fingers. Her hand clasped in mine. I wish I could say my dreams of her were sexy, but they're not. Instead, I relive the one from Saturday night where we're trapped in a box and she begs me not to leave her.

By the time I'm dressed the next morning and ready to attend the first funeral for one of the Hillsdale students killed in the storm, my body feels as though it's been stretched tight on one of those medieval torture racks. Every muscle I have has been put to work between Saturday's volunteering and yesterday's cleanup work at the school.

I'm beyond eager to see Jules, to speak to her and see how she's doing. She has Stuart, I remind myself over and over. I replay the way she ran to him in her foyer when he showed up Saturday as we delivered the news about Tanya. I remember the way she pulled away from me at the vigil Sunday night and the strange look she gave me. God, everything warns me to get over it, over her. But I won't heed the warnings. I debate skipping out on the grave site service, but Jeff insists and I give in—because I want to see Jules, and again the heart scores a point.

Heart: 3 ~ Head: 0.

"You cool, man?" Jeff asks when I arrive at his house so we can ride to the funeral together. Like my dad and Austin, he's watching me, although he is less Dr. Phil about it.

"Sure," I tell him with a smile, and that's that.

We head to the funeral for junior Mary Lee O'Connor. An honor student, Mary Lee wasn't in my circle of friends, but I saw her around. She was pretty with light hair, light skin, and light eyes—ethereal. The picture her family uses on the program is of a smiling girl in a white dress on the beach. She looks incredibly fresh and innocent, and I become angry looking at it. According to her eulogy, she had so much she wanted to do, to be, and now she's gone. *Such a waste.*

"There are the girls," Jeff says, pointing out Katie standing toward the front of the crowd.

"You go ahead; I'll be there in a minute." I know seeing Katie means seeing Jules, and as much as I need to see her, I don't want to. The conflicting thoughts within me grow stronger each day, maybe my head is going to win one. Maybe I can resist the urge to be with her today.

Stuart is out of town. I heard this news in passing while at the school doing clean up with the football team yesterday. According to Mark, he's in Houston visiting his grandparents. Of course my first thought was of Jules. Who is comforting her if not her boyfriend? Jeff has spent all of his waking hours with Katie since the storm. He did come to the school for a few hours yesterday to help and to see the A&M players and staff since he's committed to them for next season, but otherwise he's with Katie. He says she's a mess, crying constantly, worrying about some fight she had with Tanya recently, feeling guilty.

I wonder if Jules is taking Tanya's loss similarly. I remember having many of the same feelings when my mom passed away. I feel for her. Losing someone you love is brutal. One day they're there and the next you're left with this gaping hole. You can't touch them or hear their voice. You'll never smell their scent or have a long conversation with them again. I miss Mom's laugh the most. And her hugs.

Pushing those thoughts away, I steel myself and move forward within the crowd headed for Jeff's head which sticks out above those standing around him. I weave around three sniffling girls linked arm-in-arm, I bump shoulders with a former teammate, nod to a friend, and side hug another before I find myself behind Jeff, Katie, Tommy, and Jules.

Jules might be standing next to Katie, but she's alone. So many of the girls I walked by are holding onto their friends, hands clasped or arms linked. Jules is standing by herself. Katie's leaning into Jeff, her arms wrapped around his waist, and for a second I see red. Why isn't Stuart here to support his girlfriend? Why isn't Katie supporting her? Where are all of her other friends? Jules Blacklin, the "Princess of Tyler" as Austin called her. The popular girl everyone loves, and yet she's standing here, dressed in a simple dark blue dress, looking as though she's stranded alone on a deserted island.

Her shoulders rise and fall as though she's breathing deeply. I watch as her left hand moves, lifting and fisting her hair, scooping it up and away from her back before dropping it again. I inch closer, standing in the space directly behind and between Katie and Jules.

Jeff catches my movement and his eyes slide my way. He bobs his head, acknowledging my presence before he returns his attention forward again. Katie doesn't budge, and Jules, as close as we are, doesn't either.

The sun shines on Jules' golden, reddish blonde head of hair in front and I simply stare at it. I'm ridiculous. I have no idea what's going on at the grave site. I should feel bad, but I don't, or I can't. I cannot seem to feel anything except for this growing demand to touch Jules. So I do.

I reach forward, my hand taking hold of hers and squeezing once. She doesn't flinch or pull away—I suspect she thinks it's Katie's hand she's holding, but when her head turns and she looks to her side, her eyes widen. Shining blue eyes follow the length of my arm up to my face and her mouth forms a silent 'O' before she wets her lips and gives me an unsteady grin. *Every time our eyes meet I swear I see my soul. There's magic in being with Jules Blacklin, magic and . . .*

Our moment is broken by soft wave of chuckles moving through the crowd, and Jules returns her gaze to the person speaking about Mary Lee. But her fingers remain in mine and we remain hand-in-hand in complete silence until the service ends. As the hush of the crowd breaks, I walk away without a word.

Two hours later, at the second grave side service for another student, I repeat the gesture. This time I don't last halfway through the service before I reach for her. Again, I try to stay away. I use my head and start in the back of the crowd, amongst some of the people I typically hang out with at school, but as the service progresses I find myself drifting forward.

When my hand touches hers I'm content. *Yep, magic and . . . something. I can't pinpoint what else it is that I see and feel when I'm with her. My head tells me it's danger, but I kick that word in the ass, sending it back to the dark recesses of my mind.*

Once the burial wraps up, I withdraw from her side and retreat to the back once more. I don't stay and speak with her or any of the others standing around; I'm not sure why.

Before Friday night, I rarely spoke to the guys from the football team at school. When I quit football, the summer before eighth grade, I quit a lot of my friendships too. I'd hang with them at parties occasionally and talk smack in classes, but we don't hang out on our own—as friends—anymore. I found a whole new group of friends. It was easier to hang with the people who didn't remind me of what I gave up.

It's why Jules accused me of not being friends with her, with *our* group, when we were in the hospital Friday night. She was right. I told her I never left, and I didn't; but I wasn't there anymore either.

Jeff is the one person I've remained close with, although our friendship is maintained outside of school social circles.

"You want to hang for a bit?" Jeff asks when we return to his house after the funerals. "I'm not going to Katie's until later."

"What's up with you two anyway?" Their relationship has been on and off forever and I'm more used to Jeff complaining about their arguments than this happy couple vibe they've been sending out the past few days.

"It's hard to fight when you're so damn happy to be alive, you know?" He smiles halfheartedly, and I nod. "She's having a hard time with Tanya's death. You know the three of them have been best friends since the first day of kindergarten. I know you remember how close they were, but you've been out of the loop for a few years. Her death is tearing them apart, West. Both of them."

He says "both of them" as though he's trying to tell me something. Jules, Katie, and Tanya—most people don't speak of one of them without including the other two. Jeff is right, they've been the best of friends forever. Same as Jeff and I, probably closer, because they do—or did—everything together up until Friday night.

"It sucks. I wish I could do something. You know I get it all too well."

"I know you do," Jeff agrees. We throw ourselves into chairs in his living room. "Uh, I saw you holding Jules' hand. I'm not going to ask you about it, not yet anyway." His eyes pin on mine as he unbuttons his dress shirt collar. "Stuart's my teammate, West."

"So, are you putting me on notice?"

His face changes as though he's not even sure what he was saying. He shrugs with a smirk. "Hell no. He's my teammate, but you're my best friend. Look, you know Jules and Katie and their history with Tanya. Daniels doesn't get it, or he won't." He takes a moment, messing with his shirt and checking his cell before he says more.

"I do have to deal with him, though, and while I have no idea what football is going to look like this year since we don't have a school anymore, I do know that I need him to be on my side, man. So do things right, if you're going to do anything."

We stare at each other a full minute. He's encouraging me to go after Jules. I wonder if I have the guts to do it.

Jeff cocks his head and gives me a strange look. "Why didn't you drop me when you dropped everyone else?"

"What?" He's never asked me to explain myself to him before.

"Answer the question and then we can do some manly shit, like watch Sports Center." He laughs and grabs the television remote as proof of his intentions.

"Uh . . ."

The truth is I might have stopped talking to him too, if he would have let me. He wouldn't. His mother drove him to my house every day after my mom's death. He would sit in the kitchen and simply be there, waiting for me whenever I came downstairs. Like a puppy, he followed me from room to room or sat on the floor in my bedroom as I lay on my bed and stare at the ceiling. He didn't ask me questions or beg me to get up. He was simply there until one day I was able to ask him some random question about something that had nothing to do with my mom.

"Don't hurt yourself thinking so hard," Jeff laughs. "It's okay, you don't have to answer me. I'm just curious. Sometimes I wonder if I could have said something to change the way things turned out."

"What things?" I ask. It's not normal for Jeff and I to have these deep meaningful conversations. We're high school guys; we talk sports, food, and girls.

He diverts his gaze. "You. I've spent the last four years pretending my best friend isn't my best friend, I've watched you come to every football game and sit in the shadows when you should have been on the field—"

"Dude."

The television clicks on, the music and commentary of a commercial filling the room as Jeff groans. "I know, I know, take away my man card."

We share a good laugh as he flips the station to ESPN, then we sit in silence as we watch four commentators argue the individual merits of different baseball teams making it into the playoffs.

"In the hospital the other night Jules asked me the same question," I tell him during a commercial break. "Well, not the same, but she asked why I stopped being friends with her, and told me not to be a stranger anymore."

Jeff tips his head. "Good advice."

"There's nothing you could have done, Jeff," I say seriously. "You were my friend when I didn't want one. You did enough. I have to live with my choices."

He shakes his head. "You act like you killed a man."

I don't reply. Thinking about how I handled my mom's death has crept up on me, before the tornado and Jules I hadn't thought about it in a long time. I spent the summer having fun, being chill. Now every time there's a moment of silence I'm bombarded by the past.

I might as well have killed a man. I feel as though that burden would be no heavier than those caused by the thoughts of my mother—which is a completely ridiculous thought.

Jeff slaps the arm rests of his chair, jumping to his feet. "Want to shoot some hoops?" he asks in an extra deep, manly kind of tone.

"Hell yes," I agree, leaping up and following him to the backyard where we strip off our dress shirts and engage in a testosterone-boosting, manly game of hoops until we're both too exhausted to speak of this conversation again.

Twelve

I wake up Wednesday determined to talk with Jules. Something from Friday night insists on replaying in my mind and it is time to get answers. Slipping on dark pants and a navy button up, I slick back my hair before heading out.

Today's funeral is for a sophomore. Quinton. I didn't know him, but it doesn't mean I don't care. It seems as though the entire student body of Hillsdale cares. A good deal of them have made it a point to attend the student funerals thus far and I expect them to be at the others. Eight funerals. Eight students lost. Two were seniors, Mike Brown—whose private funeral was Tuesday—and Tanya. Tanya is the only one of the eight I knew on a more personal level.

Locating Jules in the crowd takes longer today. She's not with Katie and Jeff, nor do I find her among the other cheerleaders and jocks. She is on the outskirts of the burial site, standing among faces I don't readily recognize.

I work my way between the students until I'm behind her, watching her intently the entire time. Her gaze is fixed on the awning-covered seats beside the gravesite where the family sits and I follow her stare. The outward expressions of grief on Quinton's parents' and grandmother's faces turn my head away; I feel as though I'm intruding on a personal moment.

When Jules' attention returns to the front, I make my move, reaching forward and sliding my hand into hers. Today she doesn't move. She doesn't turn back to verify it's me; she simply squeezes my hand back.

As the service ends, my body twitches, ready to take flight, but I shake it off. Today I'm staying. *I'm talking to her.* Jules remains still while the people around us send sad eyes and smiles as they walk away. Curious glances take note of our hands, but I don't let go and neither does she. I'm waiting for her to make the next move.

"Jules." Katie waves a hand as she weaves her way through the throng of mourners with Jeff at her side. I loosen my hold on Jules' hand, fully expecting her to move away as Katie comes in for a hug. "Sorry we lost you in the crowd on the way to the site."

Instead of releasing me, Jules hugs her back with one arm. Katie's jaw drops open as they separate and she spies our hands. I haven't spoken to her since the night of the storm so I smile as she turns and shocks me by hugging me as well.

"Hey, West."

When she lets me go, I stand beside Jules for the first time, instead of behind her, and exchange a slap on the back with Jeff. He nods, his eyes smile knowingly in silent approval. I want to punch the smug look off his face.

I comb my fingers through my hair as the four of us stand in silence long enough for it to become awkward before Katie speaks again. "You ready to go? Jeff's parents invited me and Mom over for dinner, but we can drop you off at home on our way," she offers.

Shit. I stare at Jules, waiting for her to say goodbye to me.

"Ummm." Jules' teeth scrape at her lower lip as she looks at the grass.

Step up, West. Now. My brain screams and I shift closer gaining her attention. "I was actually hoping we could talk. I'll take you home, if you want." My gut churns as I wait for her answer.

"Oh," she nods, but it's not a yes. It's this confused nod; it tells me she heard me and she understands me, but she looks as though she has no idea what in the hell she wants to say.

Both Jeff and Katie study us as though we're something curious they've found. A social experiment of massive proportions—the loner and the cheerleader. I prepare myself to let Jules off the hook.

Then her eyes brighten, as though she's made a decision and she's happy with it. My pulse quickens. "Yeah, sure. I can hang around." *Sweet relief,* I think as the pressure leaves my chest. To Katie she asks, "You good with that?"

Katie laughs, then slaps her hand over her mouth as the sound carries. Her face is beet red as we glance around. Thankfully, no one is near enough to have heard her. The best friends hug again, and I notice Katie whispering into Jules' ear.

"Yes ma'am." She grins at her best friend as they stare at one another.

Next, Katie stands in front of me and stretches up, kissing my cheek. "I still haven't thanked you for that night." Her voice cracks. "I don't know how."

Tears gather in Jules' eyes at Katie's comment and I release her hand, hauling her best friend into a hug. "You don't need to. Ever."

I fix my eyes on Jules, willing her to hear my words because they're meant for her too. There's no reason to thank me for what I did Friday. Or for what they think I did. It was nothing. I ran, they followed. End of story.

Setting my hands on Katie's shoulders, I bend forward so we're eye to eye. "Okay?"

"'Kay," she sniffs, a tear running down her cheek.

I pass Jeff his emotional girlfriend with a nod and watch as they leave. Beside me Jules tugs on her dress and I run my hands through my hair again before stuffing them in my pockets. *We're alone, now what?*

"How are you?" I ask, kicking at a weed with the toe of my boot.

"I'm good." Her eyes look past me as she waves to a group of girls from school as they pass by. "I mean—well, you know."

"Yeah." Geez, this is awkward. Everything about this girl makes me lose my mind, my thoughts. Her strappy sundress shows off her smooth shoulders to perfection, my lips ache to kiss them. My fingers itch to tangle in her thick hair, to pull her face to mine. I want to get lost in her eyes, her lips, her scent.

Working hard to suppress my lust, I turn her way. "You ready to leave this place?"

Her face falls. "You mean, go home?" I grin at her disappointment as an idea takes root.

"No, I'm not taking you home. I said I wanted to talk, didn't I?" I look around the cemetery and attempt to tell her how I feel. "I'd just like to get away from all this—this death for a bit."

We hold eye contact for longer than necessary before I reach out my hand. "You game, Buffy?"

"Absolutely."

I don't realize my mistake until we reach the parking lot. "Uh, I didn't really plan this," I admit as we come to a stop in front of the motorcycle I rode here.

Jules steps back, holding her hands in the air. "Oh, no. I can't ride that."

"Sure you can. Come on. I promise I'll go slowly," I coax. I've got the chance to get her alone, I'm not letting her out of this now.

"West? I'm wearing a dress. Freaking A, you're serious, huh?" she shakes her head, horrified.

Hell yeah, I'm serious, Jules Blacklin, I grin as I hand her a black helmet without a word and slide onto the bike. I don't allow her time to think, I merely twist around, pat the seat behind me, and silently dare her to get on.

Buckling the strap under her chin, Jules steps closer. "You really are Spike," she groans, eyeing the bike warily.

Her use of the nickname drives me equal parts crazy and physically insane. Her thinking I'm the bad boy can be infuriating, but every time she says it my heart rate jumps in a good way.

She settles behind me and I avert my gaze as her dress rides up; as much as I want a peak, I was raised to be a gentleman. Once she's situated and covered properly, I point out the pegs for her to set her feet on.

"Hold on tight, cheerleader."

"Where?" Her lips press against my ear as she shouts over the rev of the motor.

I find immense pleasure in shifting her hands from where she's set them on my hips to around my waist. I tug her forward until her chest presses against my back. I cover her hands with mine, pausing for a moment, breathing deeply before I let go, kick the stand up, and take off.

Riding clears my head. It's the reason I didn't balk when Austin asked to borrow my Jeep. I would prefer to ride the cycle everywhere. I love the feeling of flying.

We turn out of the cemetery and head away from Tyler. The farther we go, the less the landscape resembles an apocalypse movie and the more it becomes the small southern town it is. There are no high rises this way, no stoplights or shopping centers. This is country; farms as far as the eye can see. The stress of the last week eases away as Jules' hands cling to my waist and her thighs press against mine.

We're not far from our destination when Jules' grip alters subtly. She tenses behind me, her arms tightening as her forehead lowers to my shoulder.

"Everything okay?" I shout over the road noise, brushing her forearm to gain her attention. She doesn't answer. Another few minutes and I lean to the right, turning off the street and into a parking lot. "Jules?" I pat her arm again as I kick the stand down and twist in my seat. "Hey. Seriously, what's wrong?"

She loosens her grip and shakes out her arms. Her expression is closed off as she attempts to scoot back and climb off the bike. Her act doesn't fool me. She's trying to be nonchalant, but I tug on the hem of her dress and stop her.

"Did I drive too fast? What's wrong? Tell me, please," I beg.

The face shield on her helmet is driving me mad so I reach up and unbuckle the chin strap. My fingers brush her jaw line and linger before I remove the helmet so nothing is between us as we speak. I hate the way she looks right now, something spooked her.

"No, nothing like that—" she looks at the ground. I push her helmet-head hair back, tucking a piece behind her ear. "Um, it was the wind."

"The wind?" *The wind*. Damn, it never occurred to me. "Shoot, I didn't think about that. I'm sorry."

How could I not have considered it? I know why, because the wind and feeling of freedom has always comforted me. Angry with myself, I take a moment to turn and hang the helmet on the handlebars. As I do, Jules climbs off the bike. She flips her head over and messes with her hair. My mouth goes dry as my eyes follow her movements.

"Seriously, Jules—"

"That's the second time in under two minutes that you've used my real name today." She sends me a smirk as she continues to comb her fingers through her mass of hair.

The return of her humor helps alleviate a portion of my guilt and I swing my leg over the bike. Standing, I catch Jules' hand as she continues to primp. "Don't get too used to it, *Buffy*. You look great, come on." I tug her into motion.

Her eyes go wide, as though she's just now bothering to look at her surroundings, as recognition dawns on her face. "South Berry Farm? Why are we here?"

I jerk my head in the direction of the field and lead her into a maze of cornstalks. We walk deep into the field until we see nothing but greenish-brown rows of stalks in every direction. I go a few more yards then veer down a wider path made for the farmers to drive through the crops.

Releasing her hand, I untuck my dress shirt. Jules' curious stare turns confused and I chuckle when she steps back as I unbutton my shirt. She smooths her skirt nervously as her eyes go wide. She looks as though she's afraid I'm planning on attacking her.

I continue, saying nothing as her eyes follow my fingers with each button I pop. I catch sight of her tongue as it darts out and wets her lips and now I'm the one who has to step back. Oh, what this girl does to me. I'd feel guilty about the dirty thoughts I'm having if it weren't for the disappointment I see flash across her face when she realizes I have a tee-shirt underneath the one I'm taking off. I'm apparently not the only one struggling to contain their thoughts today. I'm not here to maul her, though, as pleasurable as it would be. We need to talk. We need to straighten out our feelings and discuss the things we've said and done over the past week.

If I'd planned this better I would have brought a blanket, but since I didn't I do the next best thing and I lean down and spread out my dress shirt in the middle of the dirt path.

"Have a seat, Buffy." I bow in a flourish to the shirt before I sink to the ground.

Jules eyes me, then the shirt, before she takes her time sitting in her dress. Once settled, she looks at me with an expectant smile. "Now what?"

"Do you trust me?"

Her answer comes without missing a beat. "Of course."

"Lay down. Stretch your legs out and lay on my shirt."

"Ooooo-kay."

Her hesitation has me reconsidering this whole thing. I wonder if she's going to think I'm crazy, but when she scoots down and situates herself with her head on my shirt and her dress tucked between her thighs, I forge ahead. Joining her, I move to lay close enough for our shoulders to touch.

Jules' brows draw together. "Share the shirt. You don't have to put your head in the dirt."

She immediately slides over, making room for me. I chuckle because I certainly don't care if my head is on the dirt or not when she's this close to me, but I move because she asked me to. I angle closer to her. If I roll my head to the right, our foreheads would touch. Our lips would touch. It's reminiscent of how close we were while we were trapped.

"And?" she asks.

God, she's impatient. I sigh, closing my eyes and forcing myself to relax as my hand searches for and locates hers. "Now we breathe."

I wait for her to pull away, to sit up and tell me I'm crazy or to ask what I'm smoking. I don't open up this way to anyone. Vulnerability comes in different forms, and for me it comes in the form of sharing myself. To lay in this field, taking deep breaths and enjoying the peace, that is a West Rutledge no one knows.

When my mother died, I searched for peace. I missed her terribly and nothing filled her void. So one day I did something she loved. I lay in the grass under a tree at the park and simply listened. My mom loved the quiet; she was always getting onto us about turning off the television when we weren't watching it or asking us to turn off the music and be still. She loved simply sitting in a quiet room and thinking.

I imagine that's where her appreciation for staring into the fire came from. She would sit quietly with a book for hours by the fireplace. I can't count how many times I'd heard my father tease her and ask if she was truly reading her book or watching the fire. After that day in the park, seeking a peaceful place became my thing too, but only mine. My brothers don't know, my dad doesn't either. Finding quiet is for me and me alone. Until today.

Tilting my head sideways, I open my eyes curious at how Jules is reacting to this odd request. She's facing me, her eyes closed, her face relaxed and soft. Her free hand rests on her stomach, rising and falling with each breath she takes. I could stare at her all day. I want to stay her with her and forget everything waiting for us back in Tyler. Thoughts of funerals, and rebuilding, and nightmares of being trapped—these things fade away as my thumb caresses her palm and my heart falls harder and harder.

When her sleepy blue eyes open and meet mine, I finally decide to ask her the one question nagging at the back of my mind since the moment I stepped into Grier house and saw her standing there Friday night. "Why did you wait for me? At the house, when you were inside and safe. Why did you wait for me?"

I hold my breath. I didn't realize how important her answer to this question is until I ask it. It's the one thing I haven't been able to figure out since it happened. I know why she followed me when we ran from The Ice Shack. Hell, she didn't have much of a choice, I dragged her along. She followed me and she helped break into Grier house because those things saved her. But standing there at the window inside when everyone else was heading for the basement and seeking refuge, waiting to be sure I was inside and safe?

Mark told me he'd tried to pull her to safety, but she wouldn't leave. She put herself at risk, for me. Why?

Jules' eyes fill with tears. "I don't know. Standing there, all of a sudden it was like—like the thought of anything happening to you wasn't something I could live with."

Her confession draws the oxygen from my lungs while my body demands I lean forward and kiss her.

". . . I'd kiss you right now if I could."
"I'd let you," she says, "cause I—I want to live too."
"If you'd let me, I'd fall in love with you, cheerleader," I whisper in the dark.

The memory from Friday night assaults me. I'm already falling in love with her, she didn't have to let me. It's happened, and I'm so screwed because she's not mine to love. She has Stuart Daniels, she's sunshine and light, the peppy cheerleader, and I'm dark and misery, the brooding guy who walked away from everything. We're no good, and yet everything tells me we would be amazing together.

Jules' parents thanked me for saving their daughter that night. Little do they know, their daughter is saving me with every word, every touch, every moment. Sometimes the things you thought you knew are completely wrong. For so long I thought I didn't want anything to do with the West I was, then Friday night happened and now all I want is what I once had.

Thirteen

"Why did you speak to me that night?" she asks, as though she can read my thoughts.

Sitting up, I look away as answers whirl around in my head. I miss football, I miss my old friends, I want to go back, but I can't. *Damn, why now?* The words are loud and clear, but I can't speak them. I pull a knee to my chest, resting my arm upon it. My other hand doesn't leave hers; I don't want to lose contact yet.

Her lips press together. "You all but slammed the door shut on everyone when we started back to school in the eighth grade. Why?"

Do I have the guts to tell her how I feel? I pick up a rock and throw it into the crops as I work up the courage.

"A lot of things changed back then," I say with a shrug. It's the truth, but a copout too.

Jules releases my hand as she sits up next to me. "I remember the last time we talked. I mean really talked."

Though I'm facing forward, I catch her grin out of the corner of my eye. She scoots around, situating her skirt as she tucks her legs beneath her. When she's settled, I take her hand back in mine. She's wielding a powerful weapon over me right now and she doesn't even know it.

She chews on her bottom lip, looking at me as though she's waiting for me to guess the time she's remembered. "Yeah?"

"Yeah. Karen Wade's going away party, July before eighth grade started," she says.

I turn my head and chuckle. "You remember that night?"

Karen is Melody's cousin. How strange life is. First, I run into Melody on Sunday night and now here I am talking about Karen, someone I haven't seen since the summer after seventh grade when her family moved to Georgia right before my mom died.

Jules' skin flushes, a peachy tint, coloring her collar bone and creeping up her neck. "Of course. You were my first real kiss."

"No way. I call B.S. on that."

Her face twists into mock severity. "You can't call B.S."

I'm completely taken aback. "There is *no way* I was your first kiss, Jules Blacklin."

Her flush grows into angry splotches as she attempts to pull her hand away. "Yes there is, and you *were*, West Rutledge." Her voice rises as she mocks my tone. "Gimme back my hand if you're going to call me a liar," she pouts.

Not on your life, I think, but instead I respond with a simple, "No."

"No? Damn it, West, let go of me."

"I can't."

The moment I spit the words out between clenched teeth I know I have an admission to make. I hate it and yet I have to. I have to get these feelings off my chest.

"I can't seem to let you go, Jules. I can't stop thinking about you, and about those hours we spent trapped together." My voice breaks. "Your hand was an anchor. *You* were an anchor. I had you to keep safe, and it kept me focused," I admit on an unsteady breath as her eyes fill with tears.

I rub my palm across my eyes, attempting to cover the tears welling up. I admitted my feelings. *Shit*. I can't do that. I can't keep going back and forth with her.

"Man, this sucks."

Jules leans forward, stopping me from hiding my tears as hers fall freely now. "It does suck," she agrees. Her hand lingers as her fingertip brushes across my cheek.

Her touch shreds my resolve. Releasing a harsh breath, I haul her against my chest. She sinks into me, not fighting the embrace as our arms wrap around each other. Jules rubs her cheek against the soft cotton of my shirt and I set my jaw against the top of her hair.

"I spoke to you that night because I was tired of pretending to ignore you. I've never truly ignored you, Jules. Never," I admit, because I don't want her to think that's ever been a possibility.

Jules Blacklin can't be ignored. Small shudders roll through my body and I ride them out, taking in deep breaths of Jules as I do. She smells like flowers, something summery and light, and candy. So feminine.

As my emotions flow through me, I work at burying the memories of Friday night. I need to change the subject. I want to talk about the past, our past, but not the tornado. For a few minutes I want to remember us, Jules and I, as we were when we were young and happy. Before my mother's death, before Stuart Daniels, before the storm.

Jules sniffs in my arms and her breathing wavers as she continues to cry. When she regains control, I clear my throat and smooth my palm over her hair.

"So," I say. "I was your first kiss, huh? How is that remotely possible?"

She giggles into my chest. "I don't know. I mean, I never paid much attention to boys back then."

"You've *never* paid much attention to boys," I argue.

"What? Sure I have."

"Ha." Jules leans back in my arms and looks up at me as though she's challenging me to prove her wrong. "Not since Mr. Football moved here. Stuart had your attention from day one." I work hard not to roll my eyes as I point the truth out to her.

Two lines crease her forehead and I wonder which is more infuriating to her: the fact that my comment is true or the fact that she doesn't want it to be.

"Whatever." She waves her hand in the air; a Princess making something unpleasant go away. I chuckle at her superiority. "What? Were you stalking me or something?"

"I noticed you." It's not the same thing.

"Creeper," she teases, crinkling her nose. "Besides, that's not true. I went on dates before Stuart."

"Everyone knew those were mercy dates, Buffy. We all knew you were biding your time, waiting on Stuart." A thought strikes me and I laugh. "He's your Angel."

"What in the world? You're so weird. What's up with you and *Buffy the Vampire Slayer*? You're a guy. Where did you learn all this Buffy talk anyway?"

Maybe the Angel mention was too much, I realize too late as my neck burns in humiliation.

"Oh. Don't answer that, I already know—Carley," she says, doing a little dance in her spot. She's adorable with her cocky smile and teasing, and I reluctantly confirm her guess. "Your little goth girlfriend made you watch it, didn't she?"

"Oh, shut up. It was tenth grade. What's your point?" I nudge her with my shoulder.

Jules falls back to the ground giggling and I'm not sure if I should join her or walk away out of complete embarrassment. Enduring Carley's love of *Buffy the Vampire Slayer* won me a lot of boyfriend points, and when you're a sixteen-year-old guy that's what you want. That hot slayer got me lucky, more than once. I don't regret it; Carley's a great girl. It was fun when we both needed fun, and now we're friends.

"Let me clarify things." Jules lifts her hand, popping up her thumb. "First, the guys I dated before Stuart weren't 'mercy dates'. Second," her index finger pops up next, "Stuart is not my 'Angel', whatever *that* means."

She obviously doesn't know the show. "You guys have been together for, what, two years? He's your Angel; the guy you're hopelessly in love with. Whether he's right for you or not," I add.

"Why would you say he's not right for me? You don't know him."

"Forget it. Sorry." I should keep my mouth shut when it comes to Daniels.

"Forget it? Tell me what you meant."

Ignoring her, I get to my feet and walk away. "I should get you home. I don't want your parents to worry about you." My hand swipes at the cornstalk in front of me.

"Did I do something wrong?"

Bracing myself for an argument, I bury my hands in my pockets and face her. "What?"

As though she's remembering something, her eyes glaze over as she looks at me from her spot on the ground. She gasps softly, focusing back on me, and I feel my muscles tense.

"Wow, I can remember it so clearly, yet I haven't thought about it in years." She shakes her head as her mouth curves into a strange smile. She stands and brushes the dirt from her legs.

Curiosity gets the best of me. "Remember what?"

"My first kiss."

Our first kiss, my mind corrects her as I stand my ground. I rub my arm restlessly to prevent myself from going to her, but she apparently has no intention of letting this go. She walks to me, placing her hand on my forearm as she looks directly into my eyes as if she's willing me to remember too. But I could never forget . . .

The dark closet and a childhood game.

The way she wiped her palms against her skirt as the door closed behind us.

The way she blurted out a question about my dying mom, then sank to the floor in an apology.

The way I touched her forearm, how she is touching mine now, and told her it was fine.

The way my cell phone cast a soft glow on her face before it went out and I leaned in.

"You held my hand back then, too," Jules whispers as her hand slips around mine.

"I know. There's something magical about your hands."

Jules leans closer, rising on her toes as her free hand closes in on the hem of my tee shirt. For a moment I wonder what it would be like to kiss her again. Hell, twenty minutes ago I was lying next to her on the ground forcing myself not to do it. One kiss, maybe two, what harm could there be in that? Just . . . one . . . stolen . . . kiss . . .

I curse and pull away, shaking my hand loose from hers.

"Let's get you home." I return to my shirt on the ground, scoop it up, and continue on, heading back the way we came.

Jules eyes me miserably as she climbs onto the back of my bike again, but she doesn't speak. Neither of us do. I'm sure she's angry with the way I pulled away so abruptly. I feel the daggers burning into my back all the way to her house.

Once there, I shut down the engine and lean forward over the handlebars as Jules climbs off and removes her helmet. She stands there, helmet in hand, and I ignore her as she hangs it from the handlebars and turns away. I stare at the ground, counting slowly in my mind to keep me from saying things I shouldn't say. She takes two steps and stops. Her back may be to me, but her deep breaths reach my ears. She reminds me of me and I know exactly how she's feeling right now. We're both fighting the need to say and do things we have no business thinking about.

Not until . . .

"Where's Stuart?" *Idiot.* Why can't I keep my mouth shut? If not for him this would be simple, wouldn't it?

She faces me again. "His parents freaked out and took him to his grandparents' house in Houston for a few days."

"You're still together, right?" I know the answer, but I need her confirmation so I can force myself to shut this down once and for all.

She nods. Only she doesn't seem happy about it; in fact, she seems as sad about it as I am. I run my hands through my hair, at war with myself, before I slide off my bike with determination to set her straight.

I take her hand again and I study the look in her eyes. I imagine I have the same look. Need, want, pain, longing, hope. How can so many emotions be conveyed in a single stare?

"I won't mess with what you have with him, Jules. That's not my style. But—" I sigh.

Stop talking, West. Do not tell her things you have no business telling her. You're not ready. My internal voice is wreaking havoc on my emotions. I stop myself from another admission of feelings.

"I don't know if I can stay away from you. Can we be friends at least? I can't imagine not being able to look at this hand, even if I can't hold it again." It's such a bald-faced lie. Friends. I don't want to be her friend, but I don't want to lose what we've found. Stuart will be back in a day or two and I imagine he'll want his girlfriend's full attention again.

Jules nods and I ask for her cell. She fishes it from the purse strapped over her chest and hands it over. I enter my number by texting myself before I drop the phone back into her bag for her. She looks a bit shell-shocked, so I give her a reassuring smile. "My number, in case you ever need anything. You know, since we're friends and all." I grimace as I say the word 'friends', as though it's a dirty word, but it's better than the alternative.

"Thanks," she replies in a shaky voice.

"Tomorrow is going to be hard for you. Will he be there?" I ask, thinking of Tanya's funeral in the morning.

"He's supposed to ride with me and my parents. He'll be back in the morning."

Of course he will be. I bend down and press a kiss to her cheek. "Okay then. I'll be there too. I'll be the one mentally holding this hand." I can't stop myself from lifting her fingers to my lips and kissing them. *I'm so messed up right now.*

"The magical hand?"

"Yeah, the very magical hand. I told you it was my anchor." If only she knew how much truth my words hold. If only she knew how hard it is for me to be the bigger man and not take what she offered at the farm. What she's offering me now. I step back, keeping her hand in mine as I do. "I'll see you tomorrow, Buffy," I promise.

○○○○○○○○

I'm restless as I leave Jules. Every word spoken and every look we exchanged replays as I ride through town. Spotting my dad's truck on the main drag in midtown, I decide to park behind him, thinking a few hours of hard work could be a good way to bang out my frustration.

The road is littered with dumpsters and piles of debris as I walk along. The street front stores along this area were all hit in one way or another by the storm. Remington's, the restaurant Ms. Kathy worked at, sustained the most damage. The roof collapsed, the windows were blown out, equipment and furniture is strewn about every which way. Next to the restaurant are various retail and office spaces: gift shops, a boutique clothing store, a salon, and a realtors' office. They all have minimal damage. I throw myself into the fray, asking anyone with a hard hat how I can help.

Before I know it I'm dumping my third trashcan full of broken glass into a dumpster when a familiar voice speaks behind me.

"Since when did West Rutledge become such a productive member of society?"

Wiping the sweat from my forehead with my arm, I turn and smile at the tall blonde watching me.

"Well you know me, I prefer to keep everyone on their toes."

She throws her head back and laughs before she steps closer and tugs on my shirt, pulling me in for a hug without balking at my sweat or odor. "I heard about Grier. That must have been crazy. You okay?"

"Hi, Lauren," I breathe, hugging Austin's ex with one arm. "I'm surviving." *Barely.*

"Melody said she ran into you at the vigil the other night. She said Austin was with you too." Her eyes scan behind me as we pull apart, and I shake my head.

"He went back to school Tuesday," I tell her. She merely turns her head, as though she doesn't know who I'm talking about. Any time Austin comes up, her face falls; she's living with the brunt of breaking his heart years ago.

"So what are you doing?" She kicks at the trash can I set down. "I mean besides the obvious."

"Honestly? Working off steam."

"Uh oh, who pissed you off?"

My arms lift to encompass all around us and I raise my brows.

Lauren sighs. "This is crazy, huh? I never thought I would see something like this with my own eyes, you know."

I laugh bitterly. "Try being in it."

She flinches and looks away, combing her hair back with her fingers and pulling it into a ponytail as we stand there. "You don't really want to talk about it, do you?" she asks.

I've always enjoyed her bluntness. "No more than you do. Do you want to come help clean up? I'm sweeping up over at Kat's Salon right now."

"Um, actually I was heading down to the barn. I saw the bike and was hoping to find a Rutledge boy." She winks. "Why don't you come?"

To the barn. The party hut. With school delayed for a week or more, I should have known everyone would be hanging there. I think about the last few days, about today with Jules and everything she makes me wish for. The idea of hanging out with my people, the friends I made after my mom died, sounds like the best way to clear my head.

"Let me take this back to store." I motion to the trash can between us. A few drinks, a girl, and some chilling might be all I need to get back to being me.

Fourteen

Note to self: Jules Blacklin cannot be washed away with alcohol.

It's past midnight and no matter what I do I can't stop thinking about her. It doesn't take me long at the barn to realize I'm hopeless. Two beers and several offers of companionship be damned, my brooding soul wants what it wants and right now my soul wants Jules. I stay long enough to ensure the beer is out of my system before I head for the door.

I call Austin as I climb onto my bike, not surprised when I get his voicemail. "I didn't miss it until her. She makes me miss everything. It pisses me off."

Hitting the end button, I shove the phone into my pocket and rev the engine, heading home where I can wallow in peace.

I can't figure myself out. How could a few hours with Jules change me so much? We survived. Sure it was scary as hell and there were a few times I wasn't so sure we'd get out, but we did. I should have shaken her dad's hand in the hospital when he thanked me for keeping his daughter safe and I should have walked away unscathed. Why didn't I?

Mom.

Being with Jules made me think of my mom. More than I have in a few years. I'm not saying I don't think about her at all. My brothers, Dad, and I talk about her often, but it's always the good memories. The ski trips for winter breaks, the late night video game tournaments, and movie nights. The way she'd force us guys to watch black and white classics, telling us someday we'd thank her for it. With Jules though, I was reminded of Mom being sick and how the sicker she became the more she pushed us to be better men.

Climbing the stairs when I get home, I stop in the hallway where a collage of pictures hangs. There's an old one, from when Dad played ball, in the center with my parents smiling and looking at each other. They were romantics. Madly in love and never afraid to show their affection around my brothers and I. Dad brought her fresh flowers weekly, and he showered her with cards and presents all the time.

The practice rubbed off on Carson whose relationship with his girlfriend Mindy makes Austin and I green with nausea every time we're around them. For a while I thought Austin would be the same way, but his breakup with Lauren changed him. He became a player, different girls all the time, no relationships, all fun.

Then there's me. Sharing a kiss with the girl I was crushing on only a couple weeks before my mom made a turn for the worse and passed away. Afterwards I didn't express interest in anyone until Carley during my sophomore year. Carley showed me what I'd been missing, but it was all for fun, there weren't any true feelings involved between us. It's why we ended. When we did, I became like Austin, fun loving and free. No one tempted me to change my ways. No one, until Jules.

Her face enters my mind and I pull out my cell. Finding the text I sent myself from her phone earlier, I save her info and start a new text, "I can't stop thinking about you." My finger lingers over send before I close it as a draft with a curse.

I quickly open another, "You're with Stuart. I need to stop thinking about you" I type, closing it as well before tossing my phone onto the bed. I laugh at myself. Finally, my head has won a battle.

Heart: 3 ~ Head: 1.

I fall back against my pillows. I can feel the way Jules felt wrapped around me on the motorcycle today, the way her arms held me tight, the way her legs . . . *shit*. I sigh because I've already lost it. I've lost the battle to pretend I don't want her. I pick up my phone again.

"I can't believe you remembered that kiss. I bribed Karen to pick us. Convinced Wes Gruber to make out with her in exchange for seven minutes with you. I'm not even sorry." I smile at the memories. I recall Wes telling me he got to second base during their make out session, so his end of the bargain worked out well. As for mine?

New text. "You smelled like strawberry shampoo. To this day I love the smell of strawberries. It's because of you"

Damn, I'm going crazy. New text. "Why am I texting and saving messages I'm not going to send?"

I roll my eyes at my question and open another text to answer the previous one. "I'm crazy, that's why. Whatever. Where was I? Oh, so strawberries and spearmint. You'd eaten a mint. I saw you pop it into your mouth the minute your name was called."

My fingers hover over the screen as I recall the tentative touch of her tongue against my lips as our mouths moved together. She didn't attack me the way Jenn Ribicheck did when she accosted me by the lockers earlier in the school year. No, Jules was timid and shy, her mouth testing out its new power over mine. I should have known it was her first kiss, except a first kiss should never take your breath away. "Best damn mint I've ever tasted." I finish the text.

"I was going to ask you out . . ."

"My mom died two weeks later, Jules"

For almost an hour I lay in my bed thinking and typing each thought I have into a new text. I don't know why. I think about what I've revealed. My fingers type thoughts without my head considering what I'm saying. It's freeing in a strange sort of way—cathartic—so I type another.

"So, yeah. Life changed after that. I dropped out of football. I was stupid. I miss football."

Mom died, I dropped football, I dropped Jules, I dropped my friends . . .

"This is crazy."

Yes, this is crazy. Admitting these things in a strain of texts. I should delete them and yet—

"Anyway, Stuart moved to town that same summer and took my spot on the team like it was nothing and you were a goner. I don't care what you say everyone knew you had it bad for him."

Funny how his arrival to Tyler continues to aggravate me four years later. Stuart Daniels, surfer Cali boy, shows up to school and takes my spot on the football team without a second thought. I hated him for it, but I didn't want it. I'm the one who quit.

"Whatever, past is past. Then you sat on that bench Friday night and you were alone for a change. Do you know how often you're alone? Not very. I couldn't help speaking to you"

"Side note: I think it was that sweet little skirt. Whose idea was it to make cheerleading skirts so short? I need to thank them. Your legs look so sexy in that skirt"

"So there you were, alone and sexy, and I spoke. Then . . . well you know"

Sirens went off, a storm blew in and I grabbed her hand.

"This is like a confessional. Maybe I need to write in a journal or something." I laugh. "Wow. Did I just think about writing in a journal? Grief Counseling 101."

Maybe I should go to therapy. Dad's asked me every day if I want him to set an appointment. Maybe I need it. Sitting in the dark at 2 A.M. typing texts to the girl I like while never intending to send them is most likely an indicator of someone who needs help. Keeping track of how many points my head scores versus my heart is also an indicator of my being a crazy freak.

I stop typing and close my eyes. I'm not crazy, I make good grades, I have a great relationship with my dad and brothers, teachers like me, I'm a damn fine upstanding citizen. I'm okay, I'm normal. This is my one thing, my one quirk. Jules Blacklin.

Okay, and the lingering issues I harbor over my mom's death.

This thing with Jules will go away. It will, we need to let some more time go by. When the town gets some sort of normalcy back, so will we. Until then . . .

"So, I miss you." Admitting it, even in an unsent text, makes me feel better.

"I swear my hand tingles waiting to touch yours again." Typing this admission makes me want to drink shots and punch someone so I can prove I haven't lost my man card. I tell myself getting these feelings and words out of my head is better than swallowing them down. No harm, no foul this way.

I release a drawn out exhale. "What did you do to me, Buffy? I'm not that guy."

I type the words and sink lower, covering my head with a pillow. Several words come to mind for the way I'm acting. None of them are kind. My brothers, especially Austin, would have a field day with this.

The unexpected vibration of my phone in my hand startles the crap out of me and I jump, swiping the screen unlock and clicking on my text messages.

Jules: My hand misses your hand

"Oh, shit." Sitting up, I fumble with the buttons, reassuring myself that I didn't send any of the texts I'd written. I see that they're all sitting in the draft box right where I left them and I release a relieved sigh. What the hell? She sent me a text about my hand at 2 A.M. while I was creating a string of texts to her. *Shit*. Before I have time to consider what I'm doing I'm calling her. I can't plot this shit out; I can't ignore the signs.

For once I'm not sure if it's my heart or my head making my decisions. I want to hear her voice—that's all heart. We're thinking the exact same thoughts at the same time—that's my head knowing this is fate. I'll call it a draw.

The call connects and Jules picks up almost immediately. "Hi."

"My hand misses yours more." I slap my forehead, groaning inwardly at the admission. *So smooth*.

"Did I wake you?"

"Nah, I couldn't sleep."

"Me either," she replies.

I grin because she was thinking of me. She texted me.

"So, your hand just wanted to text me? Let me know she missed my big, tough grip?" I ask playfully, feeling infinitely better than I did only moments ago.

"My hand's a little whack these days." She sounds a little disgusted with herself. I know the feeling well; I have twenty or so texts hiding in my phone to prove how "whack" I am.

I don't admit to my crazy, though. "Why's that, Buffy?"

"Two A.M. texts to your hand? C'mon, that's whack."

"First, stop saying 'whack.' You sound like Ruben, and it's strange. Second, you can call me at any hour. You, or your hand," I offer.

"Yeah?" she asks uncertainly.

"Yeah." If she's whack, then I'm whack too. I've spent the last twenty minutes telling myself I was normal, only to hear Jules' voice and go back to thinking I'm crazy. Yet, speaking to her brings clarity to the events of the last few days. "I think going through a near-death experience together has earned us the right to be a little needy," I admit, perhaps more for myself than for her.

She's silent for a moment. "I think you're right. Thank you."

"Don't thank me. I only said it so I'd feel better about the twenty or so text messages I've typed up but didn't send."

As Jules gasps at my admission, I suppress a groan at my big mouth.

"Twenty? What did they say and why didn't you send them?"

"Jules—"

"Send them now and I'll reply back." Her tone conveys her excitement. I close my eyes and picture her face, her blue eyes bright—

"Come on," she begs, her voice crashing through my picture of her. "We're both up, anyway. You chicken, Spike?"

I can't, I tell myself again and again. *She's got Stuart. Get over yourself, Rutledge. End this now.*

"I don't think we should go there right now, Jules." My frustration is clear in my voice and my chest ache.

"Go where? Come on . . . I'm hanging up and I want a text in one minute, or my hand will be very mad at yours," she says smartly.

How could she not guess what types of things I've been thinking? Does she not see the trouble this conversation could cause? She ends the call before I can stop her. *Apparently not*. My fingers fly over the screen as I type her a new text and send it.

West: I can't send you the texts, Jules. It's not right

Jules: I want to know what you were thinking. How can your feelings not be right? They're yours

Well okay, thank you, Dr. Phil. Propping my pillows against my headboard, I lean back and pull the texts up. What if this changes everything? What if I admit how I feel? I could tell her and then I could remind her of what she's forgotten—remind her of our conversations from when we were trapped. How she told me she didn't truly love Stuart anymore. How she told me she would let me kiss her, how she said she wanted to live. Isn't going after what you want living?

Live, West—I swear I hear my mother's voice in those two words. Screw it. I send the first text.

West: I can't stop thinking about you

Jules: Is this one of the 20? I had a dream about you. Well about us and being stuck that night

West: Hey Buffy, don't reply. Just let me send them okay? And yes, that was the first one

One by one I send her each text. As I requested, she doesn't reply and every time I press send I wish I hadn't told her to keep quiet. I want to know what she's thinking right now. Is she laughing her ass off at me? Is she angry I've admitted these things? I send her twenty thoughts, and when I'm done and my draft box is empty, I inhale sharply and I wait.

Jules: You're not what guy??

That's her first question? Pick a trait and I'm not him. I'm not the type of guy who types his thoughts out for a girl, the guy with regrets, the guy who falls hard, the guy who falls at all, and most of all I'm not—

West: The guy who makes a play for someone else's girl
Jules: Oh
Jules: What if I wasn't someone's girl?
West: You'll always be someone's girl
Jules: ?

Say it, what the hell. I type the words out without allowing myself to think about the repercussions. I grin. This is an easy question to answer; I know I want her, but I shouldn't want her.

West: If you're not his girl then you'll be mine!
Jules: . . .

No reply. Is this a good or bad thing? I re-read my words and explain.

West: Like I said you'll always be someone's girl. I'd prefer you were mine but I won't steal you from him
Jules: I need time
West: Remember Buffy and Spike?
Jules: Yeah, enemies. At first

West: Exactly

There's a pause in her replies. I can't say I regret what I've told her. She needs know I want to be with her and she needs know I won't sneak around behind her boyfriend's back. I won't cause her to cheat. I ignore the guilty voice telling me we've already pushed the boundaries of cheating. Our circumstances aren't normal.

Jules and I didn't ask for this; we were put in a spot we never expected. The ending result is a mixed bag of emotions neither one of us seems to be handling well. My phone lights up with another text.

Jules: Never in my life have I read twenty text messages that made me feel the way those do
West: I feel like a girl
West: No offense
Jules: Ha, none taken. West . . .
West: Yeah?
Jules: I miss you too

My mind races. How can we miss something we didn't have a week ago? It's been bugging me all week so I ask her about it.

West: How can we spend four years barely speaking and it doesn't matter but we spend one night in hell and suddenly I want to be with you every moment?
Jules: Stress, ptsd?
West: Uh oh, did they get you into grief counseling too?
Jules: Not yet, but it's been mentioned. My dad was talking to my mom about ptsd. Apparently a lot of people have it right now
West: Do you think that's what this is then? With us?
Jules: ?

West: So we take time then?

Jules: Okay, time

West: I'll see you tomorrow

Jules: You better, I'm going to need you

West: You'll have Stuart

Jules: Yeah, I know and he's great but I figured something out today

West: What's that?

Jules: YOU are my anchor

And she crosses the boundary again. Damn her. I'm only human. My heart pounds as I hit the call button on my phone, the need to speak with her is overwhelming.

"Are you kidding me, Jules? Do we have to take time? Dump him and be my girl." To hell with right and wrong, I'm ready to beg.

She sighs my name.

"No, don't you 'West' me. Ask Jeff—he'll tell you. I've been crazy about you for years. I don't want to bide my time anymore." Anger seeps into my voice. I can't help it. How am I supposed to hold back when she says these things to me?

She doesn't reply. I attempt to gather my senses, rolling off my bed and pacing my room. Who the hell am I, calling her this way, being uncontrolled and crazy? I need to calm down.

"Damn it, I'm sorry."

"No, don't be sorry. I shouldn't—"

"You just," I blow out a long breath. "You can't *say* things like that to me." Closing my eyes, I inhale, attempting to maintain my control. "I'm trying to take the high road here, but I don't really owe Stuart jack, so if you press too hard I *will* break."

"I'm sorry. Truly, I shouldn't have—"

"Jules, don't apologize for your feelings," I interrupt, hating the way her voice shakes.

I'm an ass, tearing into her for being honest with me. I'm the one who crossed the line with those texts. I'm the one who keeps taking her hand, who needs to walk away. It's on me. I have to be better.

"You're stressed. Take some time and things will get back to normal."

Time and normal. Two words with new meanings after this week. We were reminded at how little time we could have, and as for normal . . . Well, we might never find normal again, but we need to try. Frustrated and knowing how hard her day will be tomorrow, I tell her to get some sleep.

"I'll try. You too," she says.

"Goodnight, Buffy."

"Goodnight, Spike."

My cell flies across the room the moment the call ends as I growl with infuriation. I hate this. I hate wanting her. I hate knowing she feels it too. She feels it, I don't care how much she wants to deny her feelings. And worse than that is what scares me the most about our conversation isn't thinking Jules would say no when I told her to dump Stuart. What scares me is the idea she might say yes.

Fifteen

Mortality isn't something a normal eighteen-year-old thinks about, not that I know of anyway. We're supposed to be the kings and queens of the world, the strong, the fearless. We have our whole lives ahead of us, college, parties, jobs, marriage, kids.

My first dose of reality was served the day my mom died. That day I realized I might not achieve everything I want in life. Hell, I might not make it to the end of life, let alone see the dream ending. The one where I'm sitting on a porch with my wife surrounded by grandkids and telling stories of the good old days.

The second glimpse into my mortality came Friday night when those sirens sounded and life flashed before my eyes. Only it wasn't my life, it was hers—Jules'.

As I sit in the crowded chapel listening to Jules and Katie talk about Tanya—about how they met on their first day of kindergarten, how they cheered together—I know I will never regret the moment I took her hand and brought her to safety.

Maybe she would have been fine had I not pulled her with me into Grier house. Hell, she probably would have run the other way, avoiding being trapped altogether. A lot of our friends ran in the right direction. Only four people died in the field so the odds were in her favor. But had I not reached for her, had I run one way and her another, where would I be right now? No, I won't ever regret that moment. I won't regret holding her hand, talking to her, falling for her all over again—because today my life has more color than it has since my mom's death.

Today, I'm the guy who wants to text this girl my thoughts. I'm wanting to find my old life. I'm wanting to be in love. I'm wanting the future my mother made me promise to work for before she died.

I came to these realizations in the middle of the night when my mind wouldn't stop processing. I lay awake in bed until the sun colored the sky with pink and orange streaks and I thought about life. I want all these things now, but I'm unsure how to go about obtaining them. And if I do get them, I'm terrified I'll screw it all up.

Jules stops speaking, looking up from the podium in front of Tanya's casket and peering into the crowd. She looks five years younger today, with her face void of makeup and her hair pulled back and curled around her shoulders and face. It's easy to discern that she's in pain. Katie looks the same, young, vulnerable, and hurting.

In a moment of weakness before the funeral Jeff told me he doesn't know how to comfort Katie anymore. All of her crying makes him feel helpless and the sound of her pain tears him apart. Then he told me if I repeated those words he'd kick my ass. He doesn't have to play the man card with me in this instance, though. I get it.

Jules' eyes scan past the occupants in the chapel until she reaches mine. I swear I see her intake of breath as she closes her eyes. Once they reopen, I nod, acknowledging her and sending her a touch of strength through my gaze. She wets her lips and continues her speech.

"Tanya was our third. We were more than best friends, we were sisters. And now there are two where there should be three."

"Tanya hated goodbyes," Katie steps in, taking her turn. "She told us after her grandfather's funeral several years ago that she never wanted to say goodbye again. Said it was too sad, too permanent. So today instead of saying goodbye to our beautiful friend, we'll say, 'Until we meet again.'" Katie finishes and turns to Jules.

Beside me, Jeff shifts and I catch him sending an encouraging smile to Katie as Jules wraps up their memorial.

"How lucky we are to have you watching over us. I'd rather have you here with me, but if we can't have you here, there's no one we'd rather have on our side up there than you. I love you, Tanya. I miss you, my best friend, my sister."

The girls walk around the podium and to the casket where they stop as their music selection plays through the chapel. They chose the theme song from Tarzan and my sight blurs as tears fill my eyes. I recall watching the movie on repeat as a kid, I imagine the girls did, too.

My eyes follow them as they share a hug at the casket before joining Tanya's family. They move down a line of people in the pews, hugging them all and sharing words before they take their seats. As she sits, Jules glances over her shoulder and smiles at someone behind her before she returns her focus to the front. She doesn't move again until the service is over.

"Katie said she and Jules are supposed to sit with the family at the grave site." Jeff leans his elbow on the window ledge of his car as we follow the procession from the funeral home to the cemetery.

"Good, at least I won't have to watch her hang on Stuart some more." A tremor runs through me as I think about the scene Jules made with Stuart in the chapel once the service ended. She'd been making her way down the aisle, hugging friends and giving the appropriate solemn smile to others. Until she spotted Stuart. He was standing at the back of the sanctuary in one of the last rows as though he'd arrived late, and when she saw him she essentially threw herself into his arms and cried. The sight of his arms holding her to his chest as I walked by is forever etched in my brain.

Jeff scoffs. "What did you expect her to do?"

"I don't know." I can still hear the sound of her sobs. I scrub my face with my hands. "Ignoring him would have been a good start though."

"They're a couple. I know you're hoping for something to happen between you two, but don't you think now isn't the best time?"

"You don't get it."

"Why? Because I wasn't trapped under the debris? Because I wasn't scared shitless, too? I get it, West. I lost a friend, too. I live here, too. We all do. You don't own the rights to feeling screwed up and sad around here anymore," Jeff snaps. My lips part, but nothing comes out. I'm speechless.

"Shit." Jeff smacks the steering wheel. "I don't mean to sound like a jackass." His eyes flick between the road and I.

I simply nod. He's right. "I suck. I'm the one who should be sorry. I only meant you don't get Jules and I. She sent me a text last night."

We turn into the cemetery and follow along the winding road into the back of the massive grounds where a small pond is situated among the acres and acres of grass, trees, and tombstones. Jeff pulls to the edge of the road and parks, along with the other cars in the processional.

He removes the keys from the ignition before he speaks. "What did she say?"

"There's something there. Between us, I mean. She asked for time," I tell him, thinking about everything we said last night.

"Time for what?"

"She said something to me, something and it made me confess how I felt way back in the seventh grade. I told her she could ask you for proof if she doesn't believe me about my feelings." I blow out my cheeks as I push open the car door. "I also told her I wanted to take the high road. I'm not going to steal her from Stuart; she has to break it off with him. Honestly, I figured she would thank me for Friday, tell me we could be friends, and then go back to the golden boy, but she admitted she's confused. We both are."

I jam my hands into my pockets as I make my way to the burial site with Jeff on my heels. "Confused?" he asks once he's at my side.

Stopping, I turn and truly look at my best friend. "What did you think about in those moments, when the house was coming down?"

Jeff studies me before he scratches his head and kicks at the ground. "My parents." He looks at me again. "My future, Katie, football, school—everything, I guess."

"Everything," I repeat and he nods. We move into step with the other mourners again. "Me too. I'm sure we all did. We all thought about all the things we would miss out on if we were gone. The difference is you only had to think about it for a few seconds, minutes at the most. I'm not belittling your or anyone else's feelings, I swear. But Jules and I—" I shake my head. "We were stuck under a pile of debris for three hours, Jeff. She went in and out of consciousness for three hours in my arms with me promising her she would live. Do you think that's why I can't walk away now? Maybe it's not my place to be here for her now that we're out. Maybe I need to step away from her and let her go back to her life."

I shake my head as the realization hits me. It's almost as though I feel guilt where she is concerned. I've made it my job to make sure she's happy, to make sure she accomplishes all those things she told me she wanted while we were under the house.

God, we're seniors in high school; we're teenagers. There isn't supposed to be so much pressure here, but every time I look her way, my stomach twists and my heart leaps into my throat.

Jeff doesn't have the answer any more than I do, and as we stand respectfully through the burial service, we exchange several looks. We're at Tanya's funeral. Tanya, our friend, not just Jules' and Katie's friend. Ya-ya kissed Jeff in the ninth grade after homecoming—I doubt Katie knows—and she sat next to me at a party last year and pretended to be my date when "Randy Candy" Crenshaw wouldn't stop coming on to me. She was a fun girl. Loved to party, loved her family and friends, loved life. The preacher at the grave says the same things I'm thinking, minus the party part, and Jeff and I share a smile with those nearby.

The entire Hillsdale football team is around me, the cheerleaders too. It's the first time I've been with these guys as a group since I stopped playing before eighth grade. I noticed Stuart make his way over as Jules goes to sit with the family, but he's staying on the other side of Ruben and Tommy, and as far as I can tell, hasn't looked my way.

I slide my arm around the blonde next to me when she starts crying. I don't look at who she is, it's automatic. Comforting others has become routine for all of us in Tyler over the last six days. It's so instinctive that when the service is over and people are dispersing, I find myself pulled to the one person I shouldn't be pulled to—especially when her boyfriend is standing nearby.

Oddly enough, Jules is all alone at the casket, sort of staring into the sky. I check over my shoulder and find Stuart engrossed in conversation with his teammates so I make my move. I walk up behind Jules, intending to merely breathe her in and be there if she needs me, but her hand lifts my way.

She doesn't look at me as her fingers reach for mine. "Do you wonder why we lived? Why we were saved, when in all honesty we should have been crushed to death?"

"Every day," I say honestly as my fingers weave between hers.

I admire the view from Tanya's final resting place as I hold Jules' hand. I feel her eyes turn to me, but I don't meet them. Knowing this isn't the time or place, I clear my throat and attempt to pull away.

"Don't." Her head shakes as her teeth catch her bottom lip.

Stuart is nearby, her parents are nearby, anyone and everyone could be watching us, but when she inches closer and leans into my side, her head resting against my arm, I forget them all.

"This is why," I say under my breath.

"This is why, what?"

Everything about this moment causes me to smile. "*This* is why we're alive, Jules," I tell her, lifting our hands up between us and grazing her knuckles with my lips. She and I, we were thrown together for a reason. Call it luck, coincidence, accident, fate, whatever you want; I don't care. I'll call it meant to be.

If it weren't for Stuart showing up right then, I think I would have told her my thoughts. Instead, as Jules pivots on her toes, nervously stepping away from me, I swallow down every thought I have and simply tell her I'll see her later.

Sixteen

"Hey, man, you think you could drop me home?" I ask Jeff once I catch up with him.

"I thought you were coming to the reception at the Rivera's house with us?" Jeff asks, pointing out Katie who's leaning against his car fixing her smudged make-up. She looks up from her compact with a tentative smile. "Did something happen?" he asks over the hood of his car.

Jeff's eyes squint as though he's trying to read between the lines with what I'm saying. He knows me too well. I'm in no mood to be subjected to Jules hanging on Stuart for any length of time.

I make a subtle shake of my head, clearly telling Jeff not to push this while I answer aloud for Katie's benefit. "Uh, I'm just not into crowds today."

Katie's forehead creases as she attempts to decipher our conversation. Jeff has the gall to chuckle low and shakes his head. "Nah, you should be there. For Tanya."

"For Tanya, huh?" Unless I want to open up a discussion about Jules and Stuart with her best friend standing there I'm going to have to go along. Jeff won't give in. "Whatever," I concede as I slide into the back seat and Katie takes shotgun.

"How are your brothers?" Katie asks, breaking the tense silence once we are halfway to Tanya's house.

"They're good, thanks."

"Good."

"It's crazy they have an off week so early in the season," Jeff chimes in, referring to A&M football.

"Right? It sucks for the team; the rest of the year is going to be jam packed with games. But, it means they can come home for the weekend since we don't have to go there."

Katie circles in her seat and looks at me with a frown. "This is weird. Is it because I'm in the car?" she asks. I meet Jeff's eyes in the rear view mirror.

"Weird, how?" I ask.

"This," she points her finger between Jeff and I. "Obviously you two are better friends than I knew, right? I mean I've seen you around more this week than I've seen you in the last two years, West. What's up with that?"

"You're most definitely Jules' best friend," I laugh.

Her eyes widen in surprise. "I'll take that as a compliment."

"I meant it as one," I assure her. "Jules ripped into me at the hospital on Friday night and said the same thing."

Katie grins. "That's my girl. So what's the deal with you two?"

"Me and Jules?" I nearly choke.

"No, you two," Katie signals to Jeff and I once more. "But now that you mention it, what is going on with you and Jules?" She plops her chin on the back of her seat, her face all wide and innocent looking as she waits for me to answer her.

Shit.

Jeff frowns, rescuing me, "I never knew I had to explain my friendships."

At his irritated tone, Katie angles back to the front and smiles prettily at him as she touches his arm. Whatever anger her question provoked thaws at her smile and touch. Damn, she might as well flutter her lashes too, she owns him. I'll remember this exchange the next time he gives me crap about being hung up on Jules.

"Sweetie, I'm not asking for you to explain your friends. I'm just curious. You two act like brothers, but I've never seen you hanging out. I just—I didn't know you were friends still, that's all."

Jeff pulls into a parking space on a side street in the Rivera's neighborhood and turns off the car. Turning to Katie, he runs his hand over her hair. "West is a brother to me, okay?"

She nods and faces me again. "Okay, can I expect you to be hanging around more then?"

"Is that a problem?" I ask, worried Jules has spoken negatively about me to her.

"Really? We were friends once, you know. Of course I don't care. I'd love for you to be around more. I could use all the help I can get keeping Parker in check," she teases with a wink in my direction. "Plus, I miss those jokes you used to tell me in English."

I laugh. A full belly laugh. It's the first genuine laugh since Friday night, and Katie joins in. "Man, I forgot about that. Mr. Fuller was such a stiff. He never laughed."

"West and I had freshman lit together," Katie explains to Jeff when he looks at us both in confusion. "He helped make Chaucer interesting by telling me jokes. Horrible jokes," she clarifies.

"Horrible? I'm offended by that notion. My jokes rocked."

"You're offended?" she asks with a laugh. Focusing on Jeff, Katie thrusts her chin down and lowers her voice, "Did you know I'm like a sleeper sofa . . ."

"Oh my—dude, you hit on her?" Jeff bursts out laughing as Katie finishes the pick-up line.

"—Because I pull out," she groans as the car fills with our laughter.

"And of course you know it too," she frowns as Jeff's arm drapes around her back.

He pulls her across the front seat, placing a kiss to top of her head. "I've never used that line in my life."

"I wasn't hitting on her, by the way. Not that you should care, it was way before you two hooked up," I point out once our laughter subsides.

"Dude, I don't want to envision my best friend and best girl hooking up. Ever."

Katie and I share disgusted looks and burst into laughter once again. I look between Katie's face, red with hilarity, and Jeff's mildly aggravated scowl, and something within my chest eases. I think back to our middle school days. Remembering all of the team events and parties with these two, along with Tanya, Jules, Mark, Tommy, and so many others. I'm brought back to happier times. It feels good.

"I'd forgotten how much fun we had in his class," I admit once we're settled down.

"That's the last time we were friends," Katie whispers. "Or I guess the last time we talked as friends."

As with Jules on Friday night, my guilt creeps in. I hate how I turned my back on the people I grew up with. Classmates walk by the car, casting curious glances at the three of us sitting there. I straighten in my seat.

"I guess, we can't stay in here forever," I hint, running my hands through my hair and preparing to exit. I crack the door open, then stop. "Hey, Katie."

"Yeah?"

"I'm sorry," I reply as I finish pushing the door open with my foot.

"Don't be sorry, unless you plan on ignoring me—us—again."

I seriously think about it. I wonder if I can go back to being another guy in the hallway at school once classes start. It's not as though I was anti-social; I have a lot of friends, I hang with everyone, and yet, with the exception of Jeff, I don't hang with anyone. What would it be like to have deep relationships again instead of surface friendships?

Katie climbs out of the car and stares at me, waiting for an answer as Jeff walks around to meet us.

"Our lives have changed, K," I reply, smiling when I say her nickname. "You're stuck with me now."

Katie's smile grows as she clasps hands with Jeff and ropes her other arm through mine. "Nope, you're stuck with *us*, Rutledge."

As we make our way to the Rivera's house I feel as though a weight has been lifted from my back. It's a strange feeling to know that I'm attending a memorial reception for a friend, but knowing I have Katie in my corner changes me. I'm another step closer to the old West.

This realization helps me remain calm the longer I'm at the Rivera's house. Instead of searching for Jules when we arrive, I tell myself to stay cool and make it a point to socialize. We make the rounds inside, hugging Tanya's older sister and parents and grabbing a snack and warm punch. I lose Jeff and Katie when I get backed into a corner listening to Tanya's extended family share stories from the past.

After what feels like an hour, Jeff pops into the dining room and waves at me. Excusing myself, I follow behind him and out onto the front porch where Tommy, Katie, and a few other guys are hanging out.

"Hey guys," I say, leaning against the porch rail after giving Tommy a fist-bump. "What's going on out here?"

Katie shrugs and Jeff looks a bit like the cat who ate the canary. "I heard you were at the barn last night."

I simply roll my eyes. Katie leans into his side and looks up at him. "The barn?"

"It's nothing," says Tommy, who's sitting on a rocking chair, snorts into his cup, causing Katie's eyes to narrow suspiciously.

"It's where a lot of the Rossview kids hang," Jeff explains. "Bonfires and drinking. We had the Shack, they have the barn."

My ears perk up at the way he used past tense. We *had* the Shack.

"So, is that where you spend your time when you're not with me?" she asks Jeff, nudging him in his ribs as he shrugs. "You're a bad influence, Rutledge."

The guys around us snicker. They've all been to the barn for a party or two. In small town Texas you need variety after a while. Jeff and I trolled Rossview parties when we wanted to hook up with someone we know we wouldn't have to see on a daily basis. Katie's right, I am a bad influence—or I was.

I'm mentally forming a reply when Katie shouts over my shoulder, "Jules? You're leaving?"

My apology for my wayward ways flies from my mind at the mention of her name. Where has she been?

Turning and leaning against the porch railing, I see Jules and Stuart coming from around the side of the house. Jules tosses a set of keys to him as she stops and searches for Katie. Even from twenty feet away, her eyes appear tired.

I watch in curiosity, attempting to maintain indifference, as Katie hurries down the steps and wraps Jules in a hug.

"You guys are leaving already?" she asks again.

My eyes meet Jules' as she pulls out of the hug and answers. "Um, yeah. I'm not feeling well. My head is pounding."

"Daniels isn't giving you a friendly look," Jeff mutters beside me, so I stand taller, preening my feathers like a peacock. My eyes flick to Stuart who immediately turns his head away. *So subtle, douchewad,* I think as I turn my back on them determined to ignore them until they're gone.

"I'll call you later, 'kay?" Jules offers.

I listen for the engine to crank, clenching my fists to distract myself from watching her drive away. I would have made it too, if it weren't for Katie's shout.

"Wait!"

Jules hops out of the running car and meets Katie halfway up the sidewalk where they hug again. It's reminiscent of a scene from a chick flick. I can practically hear the top 40 power ballad playing as they speak to each other.

"Hey, K. Let's do girl's night Tuesday," Jules calls out. *Will they ever leave?*

"Yeah, we should," Katie agrees.

"I've been in the mood to watch something old school . . . maybe some Buffy."

Buffy. My head snaps to the car where Jules stands half-in, half-out, and I smile. I nod subtly, hoping she sees it, hoping she knows I caught what she said. She might be trying to look unaffected by whatever this is between us, but she's not. She admitted it, even if I'm the only one who knows. Her hand lifts in a small wave before she slides into the car and leaves, taking a piece of me with her.

Seventeen

My dad is sitting on the back patio drinking a beer and watching the sun go down when I make it home. "Hey." I grab a football in the bin near the open back door of the garage and step outside. My mouth waters at the scent of meat he's got cooking on the grill. "Burgers for dinner?"

"How'd ya guess?" he asks with a smile.

I make a beeline to the grill and lift the lid, taking a long whiff before walking along the patio and tossing the ball in the air.

"Long day?" he asks.

"Yeah. She was there that night, Dad. Tanya. With Jeff and Jules—I—" I break off, irritated that my thoughts keep going there.

"You what? Could have saved her?" he asks as he stands. "There's nothing you could have done. Had you run the other way, you might not have made it." His jaw clenches as he flips our burgers. "Sometimes things happen, son. We can't prevent it."

Mom.

I know he understands the guilt I feel more than anyone. When Mom became sick, he was so angry with himself because he travelled often between his radio job with A&M and our family franchises. One night, I overheard him tell her that if he'd been around more he would have known she was ill. He said he would have seen it in her eyes, or in the way she had less energy and more aches and pains. My mom hadn't seen it in herself, so I don't know how he thought he would have.

Guilt is a damn ugly feeling—guilt and regret—and he had a lot of both after her death.

I also understand regret these days.

Dad claps in cadence three times. "Toss it here," he calls, holding his hands out.

"Go long," I challenge, throwing him the ball with a perfect spiral.

"I think maybe we should go down to A&M for the weekend, get away from here," Dad suggests, motioning for me to back up before he tosses the ball back.

"I thought they were coming here since there's no game and all?" I ask.

"They were—"

"But?" Hunching down, I fake as though I'm taking a snap from a center before I step back and release the ball again. The movements are second nature for me and the football spirals straight on target to my dad who catches it, pulling it to his chest with a smile.

"*But* I figured you could use a break." His eyes narrow as he adjusts his hands on the pigskin. "I know I could."

"Dad."

"West, I'm not pushing you, son. You've been through a lot this week. It's been tough. You're tired, I'm tired. It reminds me—" he cuts off as he winds his arm back, and I tense, ready for his throw, but he pump-fakes and I'm left standing there.

He brings the ball back to belt-level as he spins it in his palm, and I get the feeling he's thinking hard about what he wants to say next. His eyes fall from mine and he inhales sharply.

When he looks up, he lets the ball fly—a laser tight spin, slicing through the air in my direction—as he finishes his thoughts. "It reminds me of when your mom died. Your eyes are the same. You're retreating."

Shit. The football grazes the tips of my fingers as my attention snaps to his face. Retreating? I've been trying not to act much different than I always do. Sure, I'm tired and maybe quieter than usual, but enough for him to worry? I feel his eyes on my back as I jog toward the fence to retrieve the ball. Tell him you're fine, apologize for sulking or whatever he thinks this is, and make him see his son.

"I'm sorry." *Act, act act.* "I regret it—the way I was back then. I'm sorry I didn't listen to you more. I was stupid."

The words sort of come out on their own accord and I chuck the ball across the yard to hide my discomfort.

My father, being the ex-player he is, of course has to run a route, faking to the left before darting right as he snags the ball from the air.

Seeing him this way, playing ball and smiling, makes me feel normal as I grapple with admitting thoughts that are so abnormal for me.

"I've been thinking about that a lot since Friday. My regrets."

"Yeah?" he asks, attempting to be nonchalant, but I'm sure inside he's anything but.

I shrug. "I guess when you think you're going to die, your life really does flash before you. Jules said some things that made me think."

"You didn't die, West."

"I know. Dad, trust me I'm okay. I'm mad at myself though." I want to admit the truth to him. Tell him I miss playing ball, I miss hanging out with my old friends and being the guy I was. But I can't. I don't know why it's so hard for me to allow myself to be me again.

We toss the football back and forth a few times in silence before the burgers are ready. As he scoops them onto a plate and we go inside the house, he clears his throat. "When you're ready to talk—" he offers without finishing.

I know the ending, though. I've got him, Austin, and Carson if I need them. They'll always have my back.

A vibration and knocking against wood startles me. "What the hell?"

Opening my heavy eyelids, I'm surprised to find myself sprawled on my bed. I'd eaten dinner, grabbed a shower, and sat down for what was supposed to be a few minutes. Grabbing the glowing, vibrating cell off my bedside table, I realize Jules is calling me.

I hit answer. "Buffy?"

"Hey." The sound of her soft voice draws the air from my lungs.

I manage a low 'hi' in return.

"I'm sorry, I know it's late. Did I wake you?"

Scrubbing at my face with my palm, I work to clear my head. "No, it's fine. Are you okay?"

Why is she calling me again tonight? She ran to Stuart at the funeral. She left Tanya's with Stuart. She has Stuart. She can't keep doing this to me.

There's a beat or two of silence before she answers me. "Um, not really."

Her sadness vaults me into a sitting position. She might have been with Stuart, but she held *my* hand at Tanya's gravesite. She forced me to stay, to not let go of her when we both knew I should. She told Katie she wanted to watch Buffy as she sent me the most heartbreakingly gorgeous smile. *Man, this back and forth shit needs to give.*

"I'm here, what's up?"

"Can you meet me?" She needs me? "You don't have to, it's just—"

"No, of course I can. I can be wherever you want." Or whatever you want. *Damn, this girl.*

"Whitwell Park?" she asks.

I'm already tugging on some ripped jeans. "Okay, give me ten minutes."

Yep, Heart: 4 ~ Head: 1.

As I turn into Whitwell Park, Jules' voice fills my head. I try not to speculate what she could possibly want, but it's difficult as my headlights pass over her car. The purr of my engine bounces off the trees that surround the empty park. As I turn off the main road, my tires kick up small stones and Jules comes into view.

She's sitting on the trunk of her car with her feet propped on the fender, wearing the same demure black dress she wore to the funeral. I swallow hard as I angle beside her and cut my engine.

"Hey," she greets me with a wide smile as I pull off my helmet.

My eyes study her, looking for any clues as to why she told me she's not okay on the phone. Seeing nothing, I return the smile. "Hey, yourself."

Climbing from my bike, I survey the park. It's just us two, a few parking lot lights, and the trees. Jules pats the trunk next to her and I wonder if I'm being punked. She looks different tonight somehow. It's off-putting.

"Is everything okay? What's going on?" I ask, keeping my distance.

"Can we talk?"

Attempting to remain neutral, I stride to her car and lean my backside against the taillights. Jules' smile wavers as I cross my arms over my chest. Her bare legs are two inches from my shoulder and I have to dig my fingernails into my palms to try to distract me from looking at them.

"Shoot."

She clears her throat. "I've been thinking about those hours we were trapped."

"I thought you couldn't remember anything. The concussion, right?" I ask, my pulse speeding up.

"Well, yeah, it's like selective memory loss. So, yeah, conveniently enough, I haven't been able to remember all of the horrifying moments after I hit my head." I shift uncomfortably as she adds, "It should all come back, though."

"Why would you want it to?"

"Well, why wouldn't I?" she asks, brushing the stray hairs back from her face.

"It sucked," I tell her honestly. I'm sick of thinking about and dwelling on those moments. The truth is that it sucked; every last minute did. The heat, the dust, the fear, the weakness she made me feel.

"I'm sure most of it did, but not all of it," she says, almost flirtatiously as her fingers brush my shoulder. *What the hell?*

I leap off the car as though it's on fire. "Look, Jules—"

"Why did you ask me if I was in love with Stuart?" she interrupts boldly.

I have no intention of talking about Stuart so I shrug, dismissing her question. Why did I ask her that? Why did I start all of this? Why couldn't I ignore her on Friday night when she sat down on the picnic bench next to me? I'm so pissed at myself for not walking away.

Of course, I'm full of shit and I'm lying to myself.

The lights in the parking lot illuminate Jules' face as she waits for more than a shrug. She arches a brow and her mouth tightens into an angry pout.

I relent. "I said a lot of things that night to keep you coherent. You obviously don't remember half of what we talked about."

"I keep having memories. They're slowly coming back to me."

"And why is this one important enough for you to call me at eleven at night?" I'm being an ass speaking to her this way, but I'm not in the mood to play games.

"I don't know—it was an awkward memory to have," she admits softly. *What does she mean?* She shrinks at the silent aggravation on my face. "I was at Stuart's house. I woke up in his arms with the memory of myself telling you I didn't really love him."

Whoa! I shake my head as I step back, raising my arms to ward off any oversharing. "Look, I don't need to know the details surrounding you and Stuart. I should go."

"Oh gosh, no! It wasn't like that!" she argues in frustration as I turn my back. I hear her hands slap her trunk and her feet hit the ground, so I'm expecting her touch when it comes.

"West?" she asks as her fingers skim my arm. While expected, the contact tears a chink in my armor and I grab her by the waist. I drag her into my chest, breathing her in as her soft hair tickles my cheek. I force myself to look over the top of her head and into the dark tree line beyond us. I force myself to follow my rules from our text conversation the other night as my hands slide to her forearms. I will not steal her from Stuart Daniels.

But right now the smallest request from her will break my resolve.

"Look at me."

Shit. I'm not in the driver's seat any longer where my body is concerned, and I lower my head to look into her soft blue eyes. Her lips part, hesitating as we stare at each other. Her body brushes against mine as she stretches on her toes. When her eyelids lower and her mouth moves closer, I shout a million swear words in my mind.

Tightening my grip on her bicep, I push her away and hold her at arm's length. "No."

My brusqueness causes her to stagger backward and she averts her gaze as she attempts to pull away. Regretfully, I tug her back into my chest. Staring down at her, I bring my right hand up to touch the side of her soft, flushed cheek as pure lust streaks through me.

"One of these days, Jules Blacklin, I'm going to kiss you again, but it's going to be when you're mine—" I pause at her wide-eyed Bambi innocence. It drives me insane. I run my thumb across her bottom lip; there's no way she can't see the hunger in my eyes. I study her face as I finish telling her exactly what I want. "Because when I start kissing these lips, I don't want to know he gets to kiss them after me."

Jules' entire body softens at my words. *I admitted the truth, I admitted how much I want her.* I want her all for my own and maybe forever and—*damn, damn, damn*! What are you doing, Rutledge?

"You know what? I shouldn't have come," I blink, pulling away. "You need to go back to your boyfriend, Buffy."

"We broke up."

I go still. My jaw aches as I clench it and I long to punch something. "Do you want to repeat that?"

"I said we broke up," she repeats, and I swear there's a smile in her voice.

I can't control my movements, I simply look over my shoulder, searching her body language for some sign, some clue telling me what to do. She's standing right in front of me, letting me know she's free, and I can't seem to grasp it.

I can't seem to process the idea that she would leave Stuart Daniels. For what, me? That can't be right. I'm a worthless fool, an idiot. I'm scared shitless by these monsters in my head constantly telling me I'm going to screw things up. I'm scared of Jules Blacklin; scared of being with her and scared of not being with her. I don't want to want her but God help me, I do.

"Why?" I ask once I'm facing her completely. This one word encompasses so many questions. Why did you call me? Why did you two break up? Why would you want me? Why do I feel this strongly about you?

Jules pales and her jaw drops as she looks at me. She can't believe my reaction. I imagine my facial expression is a mirror image of hers. "I told you underneath that house. I don't love him. Not the way he deserves."

Not the way he deserves? What is it she thinks he deserves? She didn't seem to care about her feelings quite so much before the storm, so why now?

"That didn't stop you before," I remind her.

"Really? Do you have to be such a jerk about it?"

"I'm not—"

"Yeah, you are. What's with the tone? The sarcasm?" she asks, her shocked face morphing to anger.

"I'm just speaking the truth. I'm not going to sugarcoat everything for you, cheerleader. That's not me."

"I'm not asking you to sugarcoat anything, West. I'm merely asking for a little compassion."

"Oh, that's rich. You want me to have compassion for you? For what?"

"I just broke up with my boyfriend of almost two years."

"And?" I ask tightly as Jules kicks the ground in frustration. Crossing my arms over my chest, I ask her what I really want to know. "What the hell does this have to do with me, anyway?"

"I did it for you."

Wrong freaking answer. I'm unsure of what I'd hoped she'd say, but that certainly wasn't it and an angry fire burns in my chest. "I didn't ask you to dump your boy toy, Buffy."

I've never seen someone so close to throwing a hissy fit in my life. I almost expect her to stomp her feet when she starts yelling at me. "First, he wasn't my boy toy, *Spike*. Second, when I say I did it for you, what I meant was that it's like I told you. I don't love him. I haven't been in love with him for a long time." Her eyes close as she hugs herself. "I simply didn't know it until you touched me."

"You're joking, right?"

My angry retort doesn't stop her. She draws closer and takes my hand, holding it between us. "No, I'm not joking. I don't know what this is between us, but I can't stop thinking about you. That's not fair to Stuart."

Seriously, his name again. "Stuart? What about me? You think this is fair to me?" I yank my hand from hers. "Hey, West, I dumped Captain America for you," I mock. "What the hell is that?"

"I don't—" she shakes her head wildly.

"You can't put that on me." I don't want to be her scapegoat.

"I'm not putting anything on you."

"No?" Sarcasm laces my voice now. She's liable to hate me for treating her this way but I have to push her to tell me the truth about how she feels. I should be kissing her now that she's free to be mine and yet somehow nothing she's said has convinced me that she wants to be with me. So I ask her point blank, "Would you have dumped him if it weren't for me?"

"He's changing schools. Leaving for Houston tomorrow."

Ouch. Her reply is a knife plunging though my chest and piecing my heart. "Oh, I get it," I sputter. "The golden boy is leaving, so why not, right?"

Her eyes darken. "Are you mental?"

Hell yes I am. It's as though I'm watching an accident happen. I know I may see something horrific, but I can't force myself to turn away. My mouth is flying down the highway with a devil-may-care attitude and Jules is about to get run over. I can't stop myself from pushing her away, from saying these things when I should take her in my arms.

I sigh as I run my hand through my hair. "I'm gonna go."

"You're gonna go?"

She stumbles back against her car as I walk away and throw my leg over my bike. Something within tells me to stop being stubborn and I open my mouth, prepared to apologize, but I pause. The moment passes and I crank my bike, turning from the look of defeat written across Jules' face as I kick the bike stand and leave.

I want to beat my own ass as I drive away. I make it as far as the park entrance before I pull over, take out my cell, and send Jules a message:

West: You need to head home. Please

Jules: What do you care? You left me here

West: I care a whole hell of a lot!

Jules: Then what, West? You flipped out on me. No worries, I'm sorry I misunderstood things so badly

No, she misunderstood nothing. That's what hurts. I want everything she seems to be offering me now. What I don't know is what she wants.

West: Don't be that way. I'm an idiot

She doesn't reply and I worry about her as she sits there alone in the dark. I'm tempted to drive back when a pair of headlights come into view, heading my way. Her car pulls to the exit, and while I know she must see me, she doesn't look my way. Instead, she pulls out onto the highway, turning in the direction of her neighborhood.

I text her one last time before stuffing my phone back into my pocket and following her, making sure she arrives home safely.

West: I'm a jerk . . . I'm so stupid, I'm sorry

Eighteen

Jules never responds to my last text. The following morning I'm working overtime, creating a mental list of all the reasons why her lack of response is a good thing, as Dad and I head to A&M for the weekend.

Our drive is silence punctuated with an occasional random question from my dad and one-word answers in the form of grunts from me. We settle in eventually and I stare moodily out the window while Dad taps his fingers against the steering wheel in time to a country station.

I don't care.

It's better this way.

I need to clear my mind of everything.

These are the thoughts winding through my mind. *I'm done with Jules Blacklin*, I lie to myself. I can't explain it—my feelings, her feelings—but I know it's far better left alone. I'm not the guy she needs. I'm not Daniels. I'm not—

"West?" Dad's voice breaks off my thoughts. "You going to answer your phone?"

What? My cell vibrates in the cup holder and my hand shoots out to catch the call before it goes to voicemail. I'm not able to stamp down the hope that it'll be Jules and find myself slightly disappointed when I see it's Austin. The ridiculous selfie he saved to my phone fills the screen, and once again I tell myself that it's better this way. If I think something enough it'll sinks in and become real, right?

"What's up?"

"Where you guys at?" Austin shouts into the line. The deep bass of music in the background nearly drowns him out.

"Uh," I look out the window at the scenery. "Thirty minutes out, I think. Where the hell are you?" My brother is at a party and the clock hasn't even made it to past noon yet?

"Sig house, man. Party all day long," Austin replies. A girlish giggle comes through and Austin murmurs something indiscernible. "West, get your ass over here when you guys get in, 'kay?"

"I'm not in the mood, Austin."

My side eye catches a glance from my dad. His eyebrows lift as he tries to decipher our discussion. My finger automatically slides against the volume button on my phone, turning it down a notch in case Austin's voice is carrying to our father. Austin groans and I brace myself for the rude comments I know are coming. I'm not disappointed.

"Bull, quit your moping and come party. I'm not letting you come down here for the weekend just to sit around and whine about how much you suck again."

I've steered clear of heavy conversation with Austin since I confessed my feelings for Jules. Of course he took it upon himself to pry a time or two by phone or text, but I'm a pro when it comes to the art of subject change.

"Have Dad drop you here. We'll take my car home later." Austin's speaking, but I barely hear his words as I debate the idea. A party? "C'mon, man. You're a Rutledge. I've got plenty of pretty co-eds to introduce you to, and if they don't work, I've got a cooler of beer."

Babes and booze. It's been Austin's motto since I was at least sixteen and most likely before then.

"Fine," I relent. "I'll see you in a bit."

Austin shed his booze and girls long enough to meet me at the street when we arrived, vowing to take care of his "little bro" as my dad pinned us both with warning glances. Our dad isn't naïve; he's lived through Carson's college years and of course had his own. He doesn't lecture us anymore. He merely told us to stay on campus if we couldn't safely drive back to the house. He drove off shaking his head as Austin made joking comments about securing us ladies for the evening.

"Nice, dude," I laugh, pushing him off me as we head for the party.

The house and yard are filled with people chilling. Reminiscent of one big tailgate with corn hole and ladder ball, some grills smoking up the air and alcohol flowing. After shoving a red cup into my hand, I make the rounds with Austin as my personal tour guide. Each time he introduces me to another sorority girl with tan legs, cowgirl boots, and perfectly constructed curls, I take a sip. Meet girl. Drink. My own personal drinking game. The music gets louder, the conversations dirtier, and the girls friendlier, but my heart isn't in it.

Note to self: Jules Blacklin cannot be washed away by alcohol. Still.

I thought I'd learned this lesson at the barn. Apparently not. Apparently I'm a glutton for punishment.

I ease onto my side on Saturday morning with a groan. My tongue is thick and dry in my mouth and my head is pounding. I throw an arm over my eyes as I try to think back to yesterday's barbecue.

The front door slams closed, hard, and I grumble at the lack of respect that my family has for sleeping. Next the doorbell goes off one, two, three—*oh my God*—too many times to count. When deep laughter fills the foyer, I get the urge to murder a Rutledge. Evidently my damn oldest brother and Dad think that making a shit-ton of noise to wake me is funny.

"Lunch is here!" Carson shouts, confirming he's behind the antics.

"You two are horrible." That voice is softer and comes from right outside my room. It's Mindy, Carson's girlfriend. She chastises Carson and Dad before she knocks twice. "West? Austin? We've got food."

Austin?

Forcing myself to roll to my other side, I find an Austin-sized lump beneath a wad of blankets on an air mattress. The room we're in is supposed to be mine next year when I attend A&M. The house has three bedrooms, one for Carson and Mindy, one that Austin uses when he wants to get off campus, and one for me. It's not fancy; in addition to the three bedrooms, there's a large open kitchen, dining and living room area, and a great back yard with a patio. Simple and perfect for three guys. Considering our combined nine years of college at A&M, it was a smart buy for my parents to make. Often times when Dad and I come for weekend games, Austin stays on campus so Dad can take his room.

I guess Mindy or someone set up a bed for him in here last night before we came home. Speaking of which . . .

"Austin?" I cringe as my voice reverberates against the walls of my skull like a bell chiming in a tower. It's not the worst hangover I've had, but it's not pleasant. "Dude, wake-up."

"Mmmm," he moans from under the covers, his feet fighting with the blankets around his legs.

"How did we get home last night? You didn't drive, did you?"

I'm not stepping foot out of my room until I know I can face my dad. If we drove home under the influence, then there'll be hell to pay. He'll be able to tell we were drinking; there's no way I can play off this hangover. Judging from the growling under the blankets, I seriously doubt Austin can either.

"Please tell me we got a ride." I'm thoroughly pissed at myself for not remembering much more than three or four rounds of beer pong.

"I know I got a ride," Austin laughs.

"Like hell you did. Do not tell me you screwed some chick while I was passed out somewhere?"

"M'kay, I won't tell you then."

"Seriously?" I flinch at the angry rise of my voice. I need some water and pain meds, stat.

"Nah," Austin chuckles. Brown hair pops out from the blankets. "I sweet-talked Amy into giving us a ride home. Her friend was way into you. Don't you remember?" he asks as he rises, balancing on his elbows.

Crap. I fall to my back and close my eyes. Was I wasted enough to—no way. I think hard, recalling climbing into a vehicle. I remember soft skin, a pretty voice, laughter . . . What was she saying? What did we do?

A pair of blue eyes and silky red hair pops into my mind and I want to be sick. It figures I would envision Jules at this moment. Damn it, if I hooked up with some random chick and can't remember it I'm going to be pissed.

"Nothing happened, don't worry." Austin's voice startles me. I open my eyes to find his face looming near mine and I sit. "You told me you wanted to forget her last night so Amy introduced you to her friend. Beth, I think. Then you wouldn't shut up about Jules. Beth liked you at first, but by the time they dropped us off I believe she was ready to kill both of us."

I drop my head into my hands. "I talked about Jules? To another girl? While drunk?" So not cool.

"I know. I really need to take away your man card, dude."

Austin leaves the room on that note. That's never happened before. I've never whined about one girl to another. I don't whine about girl problems with my brothers or Jeff either. Hell, after Carley and I broke up, I wasn't upset at all. It was the end and we were cool with it. Jules and I aren't even in a relationship and I can't keep myself together. I'm in for so much trouble.

"Must have been some party," Mindy teases once Austin and I join them in the living room after we've cleaned up.

Thankfully there's a college game on and it's holding my dad's attention as we grunt our greetings and walk toward the food choices. Lots of bread, meat, cheese, and salty chips. Bless them, this is perfect hangover food.

I make my lunch in silence all the while catching Austin shooting glances my way. Once we've piled enough food for an Army on our plates, he tosses a water bottle at me and finally decides to speak.

"Look, we both know I know a thing or two about being screwed up over a girl." He speaks in low tones meant for only my ears.

I think about Lauren. She broke his heart three years ago and he still carries the burden around with him. He says he went from being boyfriend material to hook-up material after her. He doesn't want to trust a girl with his heart again and I've always understood it, related even.

"West, every time I ask you about the tornado and what happened, you find a way to ignore me. That's cool, I'm just glad you're okay, but I hate seeing you so torn up over Jules. And yet I love it."

I still at his admission. "Excuse me? You love it?"

He grins. "Yeah, you can ignore it all you want, but you're whipped, man. You're whipped, and you haven't been passionate about something since you quit football. It's like I'm seeing the old West again. The real West."

"I'm glad my pain brings you such happiness."

I walk away with Austin's low laughter following me as I take a seat with the rest of our family. We spend the day the way so many

Americans spend their Saturdays: watching ball, eating, and being lazy.

Once I have food in my system and rehydrate, my hangover turns into a mild headache and I can enjoy the day. I miss being in the same house as my brothers on a daily basis. I'm looking forward to next year when we'll all be here together, and as I fall asleep, I resolve to spend Sunday not talking or thinking about Jules.

So maybe 'not thinking' about her was a bit of an overstatement. *I'll think about her less*, I tell myself when I wake with her fresh in my mind thanks to my dreams. My family keeps me busy all afternoon—I imagine it's their attempt at keeping my mind off of her or the tornado and mess back in Tyler. Dad grills with Mindy's help as my brothers and I play a little touch football in the back yard. Late in the afternoon, when the Texas heat pounds down and we're all dragging, Mindy pulls out a surprise.

"No you didn't," Carson shouts with laughter.

Mindy nods and removes a box from within a store bag, waving it in the air at us.

"What is it?" Austin asks from his place on the ground where he was last tackled. We play a very vigorous game of 'touch' football.

Shoving Carson's large frame out of my way, I look at what Mindy's holding. A Slip'N Slide. The old school, twenty-foot-long, blue slide with sprays along the side and a pool at the end.

"Holy—dude, I want to marry you," Austin whoops as he jumps up from the ground and rushes Mindy. In his excitement, he grabs the box from her hands and throws is at Carson, hitting him in the gut with a grunt. "Sorry, man," Austin chuckles as he playfully hoists Mindy into the air.

Mindy giggles and slaps at Austin's arms while he spins her around. "Sorry, I think your brother might have something to say about that."

"Damn straight I would," I object before Carson can, plucking her off her feet in a bear hug the moment Austin sets her down. "You're the best."

"Would you two stop pawing my girl and set this sucker up?" Carson orders, pushing us both as he hugs Mindy and kisses her cheek, mumbling something I'm positive neither of us want to hear.

I fetch the hose while Austin opens the box and removes the slide, then we both get to work scouting for the perfect site.

"Carson told me about how you guys used to love playing ball in the sprinklers when you were younger," Mindy explains, watching us as she takes a seat at the patio table next to our dad. "I believe there was a story about a Slip'N Slide in there too. Something about West the Missile plowing into his big, tough brothers. So I thought, why not?" she winks my way as she raises her water bottle in a mock toast.

"I'm never living that one down, huh?" I ask.

"Not in my lifetime," Carson laughs as I roll my eyes. Dad's laughter joins Mindy's and Carson's, and I look his way. He looks relaxed, leaning back in his chair with his legs propped up on the seat of another as he enjoys the youthful antics of his three sons. I wonder if he's sitting there thinking about Mom and wishing she were here. I know I am.

"I don't know what y'all think is so funny. He broke my damn arm," Austin points out, although beneath his bitter scowl is a grin.

"I had no idea how adding a drop of dish soap to my chest would change things. When I hit the slide I flew."

"Yeah, right into your brothers," Dad adds. "Your mother was livid."

"She was livid because Carson and I were screwing around in the pool and keeping her precious baby from taking his turn," Austin recalls, although I don't need the reminder.

I remember the day clearly.

"Mom!" I whine, watching Austin and Carson kicking at the water in the landing pool of our slide. *"Can't I go now?"*

"No, baby," her answer is soft and sweet as always. Then comes the shout. Not angry, but it's no longer her *"West voice"* as my brothers call it. *"Boys! Move out of the pool so your brother can go."*

I snuck liquid kitchen soap onto my chest before coming outside because the last time we set up the slide it wasn't fast enough for me. The yard is flat and I want more speed. Jeff said they put soap on their slide so I figured it's worth a try, but it's itchy, and the longer I stand here waiting on my brothers to move, the worse it itches.

"Yes, ma'am," my brothers singsong to my mother's back as she tends to the weeds in her flower garden.

Austin turns to me, waiting at the starting line of our orange slide, and sticks out his tongue and laughs as he toys with me by taking one step out, then back into the shallow water.

I glance at my mother's back and make my decision. I take three steps back, hold my breath, and run. Throwing myself onto my stomach, I fly down the slide, the soap removing all friction between my skin and the plastic, and scream as I plow into two sets of legs at the end. Carson topples over my back, landing with a splash on his backside, but Austin? Austin takes flight, falling forward with a face plant into the wet grass. I end up with a mouth, face, and nose full of water, choking as Mom comes running toward us.

"Ha, Mom was so worried about West she didn't even notice you until you sat up with your jacked up arm," Carson laughs at Austin as my face goes red. Oh, the joys of being the baby.

"That break ruined my football skills," Austin complains, inciting a groan from us all. We've heard this sob story a million times. "For real, Dad, you know I had a stronger arm before I broke it. I could have been a QB."

"Except you've never had the brain," I murmur under my breath.

"Screw you." Austin glares at me as he pounds the stakes into the ground along the slide and shakes his head. "Whatever, I was obviously blessed with all the speed in the family, so I guess it was a good thing."

Does he believe what he's saying or is he trying to make himself feel better? I'm not sure. He's a damn good tight end, NFL prospect good, but I remember him before the break. He did have a strong arm. Maybe he would have been a quarterback if not for me. Guilt sneaks up on me. I was a QB and I quit. As if he reads my mind, Austin hits me in the face with a shot of water from the hose.

"Dude, don't sulk. It wasn't your fault."

I'd like to tell him I disagree, but I don't. I know he'll tell me to shut up or he'll get Carson and Dad into the mix. Instead I pull off my shirt—the master of the subject change.

"Hook this sucker up and let's take it for a spin."

Nineteen

"Can I give you a word of advice?"

I'm sitting on the front porch, randomly scrolling through the apps on my phone, when Mindy sneaks up behind me. She scoops up her blonde hair, piling it onto her head as she takes a seat on the step in front of me.

"It's hotter than I expected it would be today."

"And . . . you have advice on the heat?" I ask, knowing her random comment is her way of putting off something uncomfortable. Mindy shakes her head with a grin and an eye roll.

"How am I ever going to put up with you Rutledge boys for the rest of my life?" she huffs.

I give her a wink; she loves us and she knows it. We love her, too. She's the first woman to come into our family since Mom's death. She's the whole 'sugar and spice and everything nice' package we've been missing for five years.

I wait anxiously for the advice she mentioned.

"I know I've only heard bits and pieces of the story, but I gather you like this Jules girl?" she asks, and I nod. "Then tell her."

Tell her. Ha! She says that as though it's a simple thing to do.

"Tell her? That's your big advice? And what is telling her supposed to do for me, huh? Let's say I go home and I tell her all the things I want to. I tell her I like her, and how I can't stop thinking about her, and how I want to hold her hand every day for as long as she'll let me and maybe even longer. Then what?" I ask as I lean back against the column flanking the front steps.

Mindy's jaw drops. Maybe I opened the door to my inner conflict a tad too wide this time?

"What are you afraid of?"

I shrug because I really don't know. I don't know what it is about being with Jules that makes me so crazy irrational. I keep asking myself why I'm scared. I ask myself why I ran away from her when she was standing in front of me telling me she was interested.

I'm an idiot.

That's one answer.

I'm a coward, a jackass, a boy instead of a man. Those are all possible answers, too.

I look over my shoulder and into the house; I'm looking for my subject change. I find it through the front windows. Dad is carrying his overnight bag as he stops and hugs Carson. That's my cue. I stand, offering a hand to Mindy.

"Honestly? I don't know," I confess as we hug goodbye.

Her light blue eyes hold mine as she takes a step back. "In the three years I've known you, West Rutledge, you've never been afraid of anything. Don't be afraid of falling in love. Stop waiting. Tell her what you just said to me and I guarantee she'll fall into your arms. Any girl would," she finishes in a whisper as the front door opens behind us.

It's not the falling in love part I'm worried about, it's the her 'falling into my arms' part that scares the shit out of me.

What are you afraid of? Stop waiting.

Mindy's words loop through my mind, causing my mind to work a mile a minute all the way back to Tyler. Why am I so afraid I'll screw up? What made me this way? I go back to five summers ago, the memory so vivid it's as though I'm still there. Trapped in the past, destined to relive those days over and over . . .

Sweat trickles down my temple as I pull my helmet off and jog off the field to the bench. We're working through drills at practice today and I'm running on empty. The late nights I've been spending with Mom have taken their toll. I'm exhausted physically, mentally, and spiritually. She had to force me to leave the house this morning. She's become so weak, none of us like to leave her side for much more than a shower anymore, but she hates for us to change our daily lives. As though her cancer isn't going to change the way we live.

In the end it's Carson and Austin who convince me to leave the house.

"We should give Mom and Dad some privacy," Carson suggests, offering to bring me to practice and forcing Austin to come with. "We've been huddled around her so much lately, I'm sure they could use time to talk without us in earshot."

It was nearly impossible to walk away from her, but we did because Carson was right. Our parents could use some time alone. Dad looks as though he's dying, too. His normally tanned skin is pale from being indoors so much, his eyes are dull, and his shoulders are slumped. There are lines around his mouth and eyes that weren't there only weeks ago. In the six weeks since school let out and summer began, we've all become shadows of our former selves.

I squeeze water into my mouth, pouring some over my head to relieve the heat, as one of my coaches makes his way to the bench.

"Nice moves out there, West," he offers as he grabs a drink of his own. "Your mobility rolling out of the pocket has become one of your true strengths. Duel threat quarterbacks are in high demand these days, especially when they have a cannon for an arm like you do. Your future's bright, kid." He slaps my shoulder as he turns to bark out orders to other players, and I nod, remaining cool as I guzzle my water, but inside I'm smiling.

His praise refills my empty energy tank like gasoline for a car, and I hustle back onto the field, ready to show them all just how good I can be. How good I will be. Being on the football field is my life. I live and breathe it. The cracking of pads as hits are made, the feel of my cleats tearing through the turf as I move, the smell of sweat, and a pigskin ball in my hands - this is my heaven, my home.

Then it became my hell.

There is something ominous about our house when we pull up after my practice. Carson insisted we pick up burgers for lunch since it's doubtful Dad bothered to eat, and as the three of us gather up the food sacks and my gear, a sinking feeling nags the pit of my stomach. Chalking it up to returning home after spending the morning smiling and laughing, I carry the drink tray to the back door and balance it against my chest as I push my way inside, my brothers following behind me.

Dad enters the kitchen the moment the back door closes behind us, as though he's been waiting, and one look at his red-rimmed eyes is all it takes.

The drink tray tumbles from my grasp, four large cups descend to the hardwood floors in a storm of dark liquid and carbonated fizz. The impact soaks my legs and sends cola flying across the kitchen as ice scatters before me, but I feel nothing.

"Mom?" I ask, but my body knows the answer. My eyes burn with tears and my chest is hollow, as though someone has punched in and ripped my heart straight out.

I rush from the kitchen, my sticky, soaked-through shoes slipping as I bolt for the stairs, taking them two at a time as I haul ass to the game room where, against all hope, I expect to see my mother taking a nap in her—our—chaise. She's there! My heart leaps in my chest.

From the entryway I can see the top of her head barely peeking over back of the chaise. Behind me I hear my father's deep, earth-shattering whispers. I hear my brother's murmurs and their footsteps as they follow after me. But they're all a blur, a cricket chirping in a forest. They barely penetrate my thoughts as I tiptoe numbly around the chaise to see my mother.

She's napping, my desperate brain thinks as I spy her tiny frame covered and surrounded by fluffy blankets and a mountain of pillows. Her hands rest at her waist. Her face is turned my way, the dark bruises under her eyes so at odds with the pale skin of her cheeks. She looks so at ease, so peaceful and beautiful, and my knees meet the floor because I know—

She's gone.

My mother is gone and I wasn't here to say goodbye because I was playing football.

Back in my Dad's truck I rub my fingertips over my eye, pretending there's something in it as I focus out the car window and concentrate on breathing evenly. All of the pain I felt as a thirteen-year-old works its way into my soul once more, and the need to curl into a ball and cry like a baby is nearly uncontrollable. Just as it was that day . . .

Carson and Austin drop to their knees beside me and we cry together. There's no way to describe the emptiness inside. For a moment, Dad stands back as though he's letting us say our own goodbyes before he joins us on the floor.

"It was peaceful," he promises, his hand covering hers as he looks at the three of us. "She wanted you boys to know how very much she loved you. She would have given anything she had to spend another minute with you, but she was at peace. You know that, right?" He touches the top of my head and I raise my eyes to his. "She wasn't ready to go, but she had faith and she's healed now." His voice breaks as his gaze skims over each of us. Carson leans into our father, hugging him as I jump to my feet, run into the nearest bathroom, and throw up.

Later in the evening, after the funeral home has carried my mother's body from her home, and after the select friends and family members we called leave, my father finds me on the hammock in the back yard. I'm staring at the clear sky that is littered with stars and memories.

"West?" He approaches me as though I'm a skittish dog who will run at the first opportunity I get. Or a huge mutt who might bite him at the slightest provocation. Neither are far from the truth.

I cursed him earlier when the funeral home came to take Mom away. When I returned from being sick in the bathroom, I sat on the floor next to the chaise, touching my mom's arm and resting my cheek on her blankets. They smelled like her, like flowers and lemons.

I didn't leave her side until Dad dragged me out of the room so her body could be removed. He didn't want us to watch them move her, but I didn't want to leave her side. I was frantic; the small cut on his lip where I head-butted him while thrashing about is proof.

"You made me leave," I accuse when his shadowed face comes into view in the dark backyard.

His sigh is audible. "I didn't want you to see her like that."

"No." I sit, my mother's blanket falling to my side. "You made me go to practice today. I didn't want to go."

In truth it was Carson who dragged me out of the house, and Austin who helped, but I know it was my dad who put the idea in their heads. He wouldn't let up about my practicing—I blame him for my not being home.

"Champ, if it wasn't today, it would have been another. I'm sorry—"

"Stop." I jump from the hammock. "I knew she was going to die, Dad. I knew that! But she didn't have to die while I was at football. I was out playing a game, having fun, laughing. All while she died." A burning pain rips through my throat as I speak. "I wanted to be here to say goodbye to her. I promised." The torrent of tears I've been holding back find their way down my face and my father grabs me.

"West—" I jerk in his arms and he puts his football muscles to work, wrapping me in a strong embrace. "Champ, your mother knew how much you love her. Don't do this to yourself. You couldn't promise her you'd be there when she passed away."

"But I did."

"You couldn't guarantee something like that and she knew it. She knew," he whispers near my ear as my body continues to shake with emotion.

He made perfect sense and yet I struggled with it. I was thirteen and in pain. I'd lost my mother and all I could think about was how I wasn't there. I wasn't there because I'd gone to practice. I hated football for taking me away from her when she was saying goodbye. It was irrational, but I quit anyway. I was angry.

Then I holed up in my room with only Jeff or my family to keep me company. I withdrew from everyone and everything, except for them. Why?

Again I hear Mindy's voice asking "What are you afraid of?" As we pull into our driveway I realize I may have no idea, but I know I don't want to be afraid of Jules.

"You've been awfully quiet," Dad says as he cuts the engine.

"Sorry. I was thinking."

"You okay?" He attempts to look nonchalant, but his crinkled forehead and tight jawline tell another story.

"Would you think I'm crazy if I told you I felt as though Mom was there with me when the tornado hit?"

His chest puffs out as he inhales thoughtfully before a knowing smile forms on his lips. "Not at all. I would expect her to be there."

"You would?" We rarely discuss her in this manner. The after death part, her spirit.

"Of course I would. I think she's the busiest angel around, watching over her four Rutledge men. I imagine we exhaust her."

I smile just thinking about it. I wonder how many times she's cursed us for the stupid things we've done since she's been gone.

"I think—I think I heard her voice Friday night," I admit. Cracking my knuckles, I think of how to explain myself. "I heard two voices in the moments immediately following the siren going off. I heard the static voice of the emergency broadcast system; you know the one, the warning that always interrupts us on the television?" He nods. "And I heard the word 'safety'. I think it was Mom telling me what to do, leading me to where I'd be protected."

We're sitting in the dark cab of Dad's truck in the garage. The overhead garage light is on and shines softly through the windows, casting shadows across my father's face, but not fully illuminating either of us. I watch his profile as I speak. He nods as he listens, a slight smile remaining on his face.

"I also think she's the reason I spoke to Jules that night. I never told you about Jules and I, but I liked her, or I guess I had a crush on her back in the seventh grade. I wanted to ask her out, but didn't get the chance before Mom—anyway, do you believe things happen for a reason?"

He shrugs. The hesitation makes me sad because it's something we all struggle with. I imagine it's something anyone who has lost a loved one struggles with. Fate, destiny—things happen for a reason unknown to us.

"I try to look at the bigger picture," he says. "I know things don't always happen the way we want them to, son, but I think there's a reason for it. I hope we'll find out eventually."

I swallow hard. I wish I could continue to have this conversation with him, but I can't. I can barely figure out why I do the things I do, let alone why God, or the universe, or whatever, works the way it does.

"I'm going to go over to Jeff's for a bit." I open the truck door, ready to get away. He nods without a word. He's lost in deep thought. He does this sometimes, gets all philosophical and spaces out. I assume he's thinking of Mom like I am. "Hey, Dad."

"Yeah?"

"I really miss her."

"Me too, West. Every day."

I find myself getting all worked up on the ride to Jeff's because I'm unable to think of anything besides what I said to my dad. Do things happen for a reason? Jules asked me at Tanya's grave site. She asked why we lived when others hadn't. Was my answer right? Were we meant to be there, to live through that night together?

At the first shrill ring of those sirens, my life changed. My thoughts, my feelings—everything is changing. Damn it. And here I thought I was fine the way I was before.

I don't bother knocking as I walk into Jeff's house.

"Dude, I'm so screwed," I shout as I head in the direction of the sound of a television and the only room with a light on. "This is so ridiculous."

I walk through the doorway cursing and mumbling about the whole situation.

"Shit." I stop in my tracks. Jeff's laying on the couch and beneath him is Katie. Thankfully they're fully dressed, but damn, what a way to break up the party.

"What the hell?" growls Jeff as he scrambles into a sitting position.

"Dude, I'm sorry. The door was open. Katie—" I backtrack as I apologize.

Katie sits up, fixing her hair as she adjusts her twisted shirt. Her cheeks are a nice, flaming red as she looks at me. "It's fine, really," she says as she touches Jeff's forearm.

He doesn't look as though he agrees, but her touch and silent nod appear to take some of the edge off.

"What's wrong? You look like you did that time Kyle Foley said those things about Lauren and we had to kick his ass."

"I—"

"You kicked Kyle Foley's ass? Lauren who?" Katie's gaze flicks between Jeff and I like a spectator at a tennis match.

"Lauren is Austin's ex, and a friend, and yes there was some mild ass kicking once upon a time," Jeff explains before looking my way. "So what's up? Didn't you party it up at A&M all weekend?"

"Ha, I'll tell you about the party later." I glance at Katie now that she's straightened her clothing. "I'm good, I'll leave you two alone."

"Not on your life, Rutledge. Sit your ass down," Jeff commands before I can back out of his living room.

Katie stands, smiling my way as she leans down and whispers something into my best friend's ear before exiting the room.

"Sit and talk," Jeff growls. "You sort of ruined the mood, so you might as well hold nothing back." He stretches his arms over his head before propping his feet on the coffee table.

Hold nothing back? That I can do.

"She's a spoiled little cheerleader, right? So why can't I stop thinking about her? Why can't I walk away? I've turned into a damn chick, texting love notes and baring my soul to my family. It's ridiculous and it's just going to end up a big damn mess in the end." I curse and throw myself into a chair.

"Love notes?" Jeff chokes back a laugh and I shoot him a death glare. "Uh, what happened?" he asks before clearing his throat.

"They broke up." I can barely believe I'm saying these words. I can barely believe I've spent almost the last four days ignoring this fact. They freaking broke up!

"Whoa, this is what you've been waiting for, man."

"I know."

"So why the 'I'm going to crazy town' act?" Jeff looks at me as though I've just turned down a million dollars.

Hunching forward, I rest my elbows on my knees and take my head in my hands as I think about Jules and the one fear I have. "She dumped him for me. Mr. Football, for me. What if I screw it up?"

"Dude, you need to stop—"

"No, I already messed up. She called me Thursday night, after they broke up, and asked me to meet her at the park. I was such a jerk. I completely freaked out on her and yelled at her for dumping him. I'm such an idiot."

"You're right, you are an idiot."

"I'm not good enough. I'm not Stuart."

"Mr. Douche Canoe? No, thankfully you're not!" Jeff laughs sarcastically.

I chuckle in spite of myself. "You know what I mean. I suck at this. I don't want to want this. I don't want to screw it up."

"I swear I'm gonna kick your ass if you keep saying those words. You're a broken record now. You have been for almost five years. Give it up."

"I kind of want to kick my own ass," I tell him. I'm ashamed of my weakness.

Katie clears her throat as she comes back into the room, and I'm relatively sure she's been listening to our entire conversation, but I say nothing.

"Hey, I'm sorry I busted in on you two," I tell her once she's sitting next to Jeff again.

"Seriously, not a big deal. Is everything okay? Should I leave so you two can talk?"

Jeff's the best friend I could ask for. He looks at me, a brow raised in question, clearly telling me silently that if I need him he'll ask his girlfriend to leave.

"No." I rise to leave, shaking my head. "I'm okay, I just had a moment there. Don't mind the crazy man," I laugh. It's a fake laugh, but it's a laugh.

The moment is awkward so I decide a change of subject is necessary.

"Hey, I'm going into town tomorrow to help with rebuilding and cleanup. You in?" I ask Jeff as I shove my hands into my pockets.

"Sure, call me in the morning."

Twenty

The site where a large Victorian farmhouse once stood is now nothing more than a hole in the ground. I sit near the gaping hole among chunks of plywood and slivers of glass, and I listen. In my mind are the terrified screams of students running from a black cloud pressing down upon them. Behind my eyelids are the people I've known all my life standing amidst the ruins of our town with shock written on their faces. In my heart is the plea of the one person who spent three hours trapped with me within this hole I'm sitting by.

"I don't want to die," she'd cried as the winds tore the house to shreds and deposited it down on top of us.

I'm uncertain as to why I'm here. When I woke up this morning my plan was to call Jeff so we could meet in town to volunteer. Last night Dad mentioned there were trucks filled with plywood and building supplies showing up this morning and those leading the cleanup and rebuilding efforts had asked for able-bodied helpers to unload.

But as I left my house, ready to throw myself into doing anything to keep my mind off of Jules, I found myself turning in the opposite direction. Taking a back road around town, I headed for the Rossview town line and straight to Grier house. Or what was formerly known as Grier house. I had to see it. I had to see the place where so much happened. The place where my life changed.

As I sit here, I reflect.

The day after the storm, when my dad and I went to the neighborhoods and pitched in wherever we could, I'd talked to the people I worked with. The faces were all different, but their stories were the same. Their homes were destroyed, clothing gone, furniture gone, wedding photos, baby photos, heirlooms, and valuables gone.

Like Dad and I, most hadn't slept since the storm hit. Unlike us, though, when the sun went down they were heading to shelters or friend's and family's homes for a place to sleep. They were homeless and I wasn't, and so I whispered my thanks for how lucky I'd been Friday night.

At the vigil on Sunday I was faced with a whole other loss. The loss of life. Before the tornado and before my mom, I'd lost three people in my life. They were all grandparents who, while loved, were old, happy people who lived amazing lives and whom I could scarcely remember.

Walking around Center Park before the vigil and seeing the memorial to the victims growing around the large tree, I felt the loss of those lives as though they'd each been someone special to me.

The little girl who walked by me wearing what I'd assumed was her father's shirt, the parents of a classmate, the classmate who lost a parent, they all wore a face different from those I'd met Saturday. They wore the faces of people who'd lost something you could never replace.

A person, a human, a heart and soul.

I felt their loss as I lit my candle.

I felt it as I offered Jules my strength while she struggled with her own pain.

I felt the loss, but I didn't own it the way the family members of the forty-five people who died did.

So why did I wake up today with this unfamiliar feeling? It's as though I've lost a limb and the spot aches and itches, and no matter what I do it'll never go away because my mind thinks it's still there.

Personally, I lost nothing Friday night. I mean people I care about lost their lives and my town is forever changed. I'm not soulless, this means a great deal to me, but at the end of the day I'm a lucky guy.

I'm a lucky guy who lived through one of the largest storm systems to ever hit this area of Texas, and yet here I am sitting at the graveyard of a house. A house that could have killed my friends and I, but didn't.

I could have died. My throat tightens and I swallow, wishing I had water with me.

I could have died. My ears ring as I stare at the blanket of debris Jules and I were covered with.

"Shit," I sigh as my eyes burn.

The Texas sun stings the back of my neck as, all around me, the air is filled with the sounds of recovery and rebuilding. Chainsaws hum, hammers pound. A dump truck near what was once The Ice Shack beeps as the driver goes in reverse.

I sit here right beyond the yellow 'Do Not Enter' tape. I drop my head into my hands as it hits me. And I cry.

I could have died. I don't want to die. My phantom limb is urging me to find it, but I don't know how. How do you find something you know you lost, but you don't know what it is?

Man, I feel it so clearly. Something is missing. Something is eating away at my insides and making me feel as though I'm withering away because I've lost that one thing that makes me not feel lost.

"What the hell is wrong with me?" I rub the stinging tears from my eyes. My pocket vibrates and I check my phone, reading the text.

Jeff: Main and Queens?

It's the intersection in town where I'm supposed to meet him. I pull myself from the ground, stomping off dirt from my worn jeans as I reply.

Me: On my way.

I give the hole where we were trapped one last look. I don't think I'll ever return to this field or this house. I may not have lost my personal belongings or my life Friday night, but standing on this field, huddled in that house and under that debris, something happened to me. I'll never be the same.

I could have died. Part of me did.

Twenty-One

A day full of manual labor followed by a sleepless night filled with a mind that won't turn off leads to me sleeping in on Wednesday. My arms protest every move they make. When lifting my toothbrush proves to be a difficult task, I seriously mull over the idea of returning to bed. When I consider a full day of doing nothing but contemplating the tornado and Jules, my choices are clear. Neither of these things is tempting in the least, so I'm heading back out to punish my muscles some more.

I promised myself I would do my best to move forward so my dad won't worry about me; getting out and staying busy has become my best bet. Jumping on my motorbike, I take my usual route into town in search of work. Judging by the construction traffic jam, there's no shortage of things to be done.

I swing around the 'No thru traffic' signs on Kenilworth to avoid the traffic, only to nearly run over Carter Cooper. He's standing in the middle of the street, so I pull to a stop out of curiosity. I flip my visor up and switch off my bike.

"Hey, man," Carter offers with a nod.

"Hey, you're doing some work too, huh?" I ask, taking in his paint-splattered shorts.

He points out the small storefront behind me. "Yeah, my mom's shop." The walls inside are half painted. A counter and various fixtures are pushed into the center. I consider offering to help, but a paper rustling nearby distracts me. Pulling my gaze from the storefront, I glance around Carter, nearly losing my shit at what I see.

Rising from the curb in front of Carter's black sports car is Jules. She's holding a crumbled lunch sack in one hand and a half empty water bottle in the other, and she's dressed casually, like

Carter, in work clothes with the same green paint from the shop splattered on her shins and the front of her shirt.

What in the actual—

I focus on Carter as I slide from my bike while removing my helmet and setting it on my seat. The moment I see Jules I go into over-thinking mode. Is my heart or my head making my decisions right now? I don't know and I don't care; I'm not keeping score right now. I don't think. I don't second guess. I don't ponder, question, or argue with the voice telling me what to do. I listen. I move.

"Do it."

Carter backs up a step, raising his arms in defense as I round my bike and stand before him. "Whoa, man. She was just helping me paint the shop. Nothing else."

He's blocking my view of Jules, and I'm torn between knocking him out of the way and being polite. Since I'm attempting to win Jules over, polite wins.

"Excuse me," I hint, and Carter hops to the side. Obviously he can read my expression and knows not to screw with me in this moment.

Jules, on the other hand, looks as though she might prefer to argue with me as she stands ten feet away. She doesn't have to say a word. Her ire is visible in the way her chin juts forward defiantly as she clenches her jaw. Her arrogance brings a smile to my lips.

Raising my hands, I absorb her angry looks as I whisper my nickname for her. "Buffy?" It's a plea of sorts, of forgiveness. I hate the way she seems so standoffish right now. I'd do anything to make her forget the way I acted on Thursday night.

So I do. I do anything. I do the grand gesture in the hundred romance movies I watched with my mom. The Clarke-Gable-lifting-Scarlett-O'Hara-and-carrying-her-up-the-staircase sort of gesture. The Richard-Gere-with-roses-hanging-out-the-sunroof-of-his-limo type of move. Mom used to sigh at every one of those scenes and tell me to take notes, as I groaned and sank deeper into my seat and complained of all the 'kissy junk'.

"Some day, baby," she says with a smile and a wink, "you're going to fall in love, and when you do, she will fall right back. You'll find the epic kind of love your dad and I have."

"Epic?"

"Yes, plain old love and romance won't do for my boys. You deserve nothing less than a sweeping love story made for movies and told over and over for generations. Your father has given that to me, and someday each of you will find it yourselves."

So with epic love stories and grand gestures in mind, I stalk toward Jules. I move in three strides as she retreats three. The bumper of Carter's car is my ally though, and I step forward again as she finds herself trapped against it. I push my body up flush with hers and she curves her spine back in an attempt to keep her personal space.

It's cute, but unnecessary. I'm not letting her go. She must realize this because her eyes go wide and her mouth drops as she attempts to protest. Attempts and loses because I slide my fingers into her hair and sweep in, claiming her lips for my own.

She doesn't fight me. Her body freezes; her hands, still holding her lunch, are down by her sides, but she kisses me back. It's unexpected, given her scowl one minute ago. I nudge my hips closer to hers as I kiss her deeply. My fingers massage the curve of her neck and into her scalp as the kiss shifts from hard demand to soft giving.

When I realize she deserves more than a public mauling, I pull away with a groan, mourning the temporary loss of her lips. I kiss her cheek right along the edge of her lips as I regain control of myself and my ability to form words.

"I'm not screwing this up again." I give her another kiss, a quick peck this time. "I'll be damned if I let another guy step in and get a chance with you before I do." I nod slightly toward Carter to make my point as my hand slides from the base of her skull to her lower back and presses her body as physically close to mine as possible as if to prove a point. 'You're mine,' my inner caveman wants to growl.

"I . . ."

"Shut up and kiss me, Buffy," I order softly into her mouth as my lips descend for a second time. I'll apologize for the crude order later. *Damn caveman!*

With this kiss, she participates 100%, dropping the bagged lunch and water bottle to the ground and fisting my shirt as she molds herself to my frame.

Behind us, Carter clears his throat. "Well I'll leave you two alone, I guess. Be careful of the paint job, Rutledge."

I should question him, get the full story on why I just came upon him shirtless with Jules, but my brain isn't computing rational thoughts right now. My brain is too busy loving the turmoil and the feeling that Jules' jaw under my thumb ignites within. It's too busy singing praises at the little sigh Jules makes when my teeth graze over her bottom lip and the way she shivers at the touch of my hand at her waist. There's no rational thinking here. Except, what was she doing with Carter?

Caveman West awakens . . .

"Why the hell are you hanging out with *Carter Cooper*?" I ask as I force my lips to stop kissing her again.

"You're going to let me speak now?" she asks. Her hands release my shirt and her tone is cold in spite of the kiss we shared. I'm gathering she's not a fan of Caveman West and his highhanded ways by the scowl on her face.

"Actually—" I tilt my mouth near hers again; I'm more than happy to keep her from talking if it involves her lips on mine. To my surprise, she laughs into my mouth. Yeah, her roller coaster emotions aren't confusing at all.

"I need air," she gasps, punching my side with more playfulness than malice. Her fingers touch her lips as she sidesteps me, attempting to put space between us.

"What was that?" she asks, sounding more confused than angry now.

"How come you're hanging out with Carter?" I counter, tugging on the hem of her shirt to keep her from running too far.

She shakes her head. "I don't think so, bud. I asked you first." She bends down, picking up the items she dropped. She appears so aggravated by our kisses, and maybe even a little unfazed, that I find myself covering up my own feelings.

"It was just a kiss." Such a lie. It wasn't just a kiss. That was epic. That was me stepping into the game at long last. That was fate.

"You kiss all the girls you know like that?" My lips twitch into a satisfied smirk before I can control them because I see it now. She's acting all cool and collected, but she's as bad at keeping her feelings in check as I am. Her brows knit together angrily. "Nice way to accost a girl on the street, Rutledge."

She goes to leave, knocking into me. I allow her one step before I tug her backward into my chest. Her spine straightens at the contact, but she can't fool me. I lower my mouth to her ear, grazing it as I point out the obvious. "You didn't seem to complain, Buffy."

So help me, she is a mixture of strawberries, flowers, and the most alluring paint scent I've ever had the pleasure of inhaling. I drop my hands, preparing for her to leave if it's what she wants, because if I touch her for another second I won't be able to fight this battle of whatever the hell it is we're fighting. I want her so badly, but I want her to want me too.

The moment she is free from my grip she rounds on me. There's anger, but I also sense her willingness to surrender to me beneath that angry facade. All she has to do is decide to forgive me. When her eyes soften as we stare at each other, I grin. She is raising her white flag.

"You and Carter?" I ask in a civil tone this time. I need to be sure it's nothing.

"I was riding by and saw him. Asked if I could help."

"You're friends?" I recall Carter being at the Ice Shack the night of the storm, but I also remember he was fighting with Tommy, so I don't know where he fits into all of this.

"No. Um, he went out with Tanya this summer. I guess, I don't know. When I saw him I just felt like I needed to stop and speak to him."

I relax, feeling somewhat placated by her clumsy explanation. I'd heard rumblings at a party over the summer about Carter and Tanya hooking up. There were some girls at the barn who wouldn't stop bitching about loyalty and shit one night, as though Rossview and Hillsdale were the Texas equivalent of the Jets and the Sharks.

"Well, um, thanks for that kiss, I guess," Jules babbles, skirting by me. She's damn jumpy today, and what the hell? Thanks for the kiss?

I turn, following her with my eyes as she tosses her lunch into the construction dumpster outside of Carter's mom's shop. I don't speak; I'm too curious about what she plans to do next. Is she really going to leave, just like that? And if that's her intention, will I let her?

She stops two steps from the dumpster and everything stills as I wait. Her stance changes and I smile knowingly as her fingers flex by her sides. We're not done here yet.

"Damn you!" she hisses as she stomps back to stand before me. "What the hell was that kiss for? Why did you walk away from me last week? You brushed me off after I opened up to you."

My smile grows with every wild arm movement and temper tantrum stomp she gives me. I can't help myself.

"Don't you dare kiss me ever again," she shouts, her fists landing on my chest as she pushes against me, making me laugh harder. My hands catch her wrists, yanking her forward as she continues. "You arrogant jacka—"

Her colorful noun is cut off by my hungry lips. I don't let up until her rage softens, and even then I only pull back enough to speak, keeping my forehead pressed to hers.

"I already established I was a major jerk the other night when I sent you texts saying I'm sorry, so let's not waste time repeating arguments or lying to each other. I'm a jerk, and you *sure* as hell want me to kiss you again."

I'm so sick of playing games. I'm tired of pretending I don't care, and I sure as hell don't want her pretending she doesn't. Her lips don't lie.

She stares at me silently, so I push her. "Am I wrong?"

"No." Her voice is a whisper.

My nose nudges hers playfully in an attempt to take some of the sting out of my earlier tone. "Oh, you wound me. I was hoping you would at least disagree with the part about me being a jerk."

Jules' head falls back as she laughs. "Sorry to disappoint you, but you *are* a massive jerk," she grumbles. I frown. "But—"

"I like butts," I tease with a wink at her olive branch.

Jules' mouth twists and contorts as she attempts to remain serious. It must have been the wink; these warm brown eyes work like a charm every time. I'm about to finish her off with another sweet move when she turns the tables and completely takes control with a single touch. Her hand cups my face, the warmth of her palm sliding over my jaw as the soft pads of her fingertips brush my cheek, and all of a sudden I'm no longer the player, I'm the playee. I'm the cartoon dog with his jaw dropping to the floor, eyes bugging out. Austin wasn't lying; I am totally whipped.

"But you were right," she confesses as I turn into putty in her hand. "I *do* want to kiss you, West Rutledge. Why fight it anymore?"

Stay calm, West, stay calm.

"So there's really nothing stopping us anymore?"

Jules shakes her head and I tilt mine forward, nuzzling at her jaw because I can't stop myself.

"Then can you come with me now?" I ask as I savor her salty, sweet taste on my lips.

"Where?"

Where? I want to take her everywhere and anywhere she'll let me take her. I want to bask in the glow of her blue eyes. I want to touch her soft skin and smell her strawberry perfume until I'm sick of it, as if that will ever happen. I don't care where we are. I want to be with her.

"Does it matter?"

"No." She takes my outstretched hand. She doesn't care where we are either.

This is the beginning of our epic love.

Twenty-Two

I have trouble suppressing my smile as we drive away from town and into the country. I have one place in mind—South Berry Farm.

This time I pull around the back of the farm to a well-worn gravel trail where no one will see my bike. The paths through the field aren't as wide in this back section of the farm, but we're less likely to be bothered by anyone working today, and that's what I want.

We hold hands as we walk through the maze of crops until I find a relatively smooth area of ground to sit on.

"It's so peaceful here," Jules sighs, settling herself on the ground and tipping her head back.

The sun colors her hair a fiery red and I prop myself on my elbows so I can soak up the look of her. The cut above her right brow is nearly gone, the scab reduced to a red line on her pale skin. The skin beneath her eyes looks too dark to me, as though she's not sleeping well, but otherwise her face has healed. Her eyes are closed as she rolls her neck back and forth on her shoulders. Her lips rub together and I sigh. Her bottom teeth catch and tug at her lips, stirring up my desire to kiss her again.

I puff out my cheeks, swishing the air back and forth before blowing it out in an attempt to keep my mouth busy. As though she's reading my thoughts, her eyes open and she cocks her head to the side, looking down upon me with raised brows.

"Can I kiss you now?" I ask, leaning closer.

"Shouldn't we talk?"

"I'd rather kiss you first. We can talk later." She's sitting up, so I throw my arm over her stomach and tug her backward and sideways until she rolls to her side and is facing me. My lips skim hers and she sighs into my mouth.

"Talk is overrated, I suppose." She scoots closer, rolling into my body and hovering above me.

My hand roams from her hip down over her ass. This amazingly strange machine gun type of chuckle releases from her throat and my hand stills as she sinks into me further.

"What?" I ask, wondering if I've uncovered a ticklish spot.

She laughs against my lips. "Your hand is on my, um, nether region."

"Oh, uh, sorry?" I remove my hand reluctantly.

Sitting up with a laugh, Jules returns to sitting cross-legged next to me and combs her hair back from her face. Her cheeks flush as she explains, "I wasn't complaining. It's just weird."

Okay, that is not something a guy wants to hear at the start of a make-out session. I sit up, guessing Jules has decided it's time for us to talk.

First things first, since I would like to be allowed to touch her ass at some point in our relationship, I dig for more info. "Weird, how?"

Jules has this look about her when she's thinking. I've caught on to it over the past ten days. It's as though her eyes go blank; she's looking at me, but past me. And her mouth, her damn fine, kissable mouth, tightens around the edges as though she's sucked on a lemon. It's adorable and highly appealing to every part of my body, although that may just be a Jules side effect.

"It's you and me," she admits after some thought.

Well, that's not an answer I can work with. "Could you possibly be a little more vague?"

And now she's nervous. Nervous Jules is a completely different look: the wary face, the glances around at her surroundings, the way she rubs her hands together and bites her lip. I reach into her lap, taking one of her hands and wrapping it tightly in mine.

"Jules? You can tell me anything."

I don't hear her deep inhale as much as I see it. I brace myself for her reply. I'm worried she's going to tell me she's changed her mind, that this isn't what she wants.

"You're Spike and I'm Buffy, right? Like fire and gasoline. The rebel boy who walked away from everything and the cheerleader who dated the golden boy. We are so cliché."

Damn, it's as though she's rummaged through my brain, picking out all of the reasons my mind told me we wouldn't work. I contain my laughter to a ridiculous snort.

"More cliché than the head cheerleader dating the quarterback?" Her mouth snaps shut. "What's your point? So we're cliché. I can't douse this fire any more than you can," I tell her.

"Fire?" she asks.

I contemplate waving the comment off. I look at Jules' hand in mine. "Yeah," I admit, gaining strength from the anchor she provides for me with those five fingers. She steadies my emotions and quiets my inner demons. The way I feel when I'm around her, when I think of her, it's as though there's a fire consuming me. I can't stop the flames, they're too intense.

"I want to be near you all the time. Like, freaking stalk-your-house-and-stand-outside-your-window near you."

Shit. My feelings are scary to me; I can only imagine how she perceives them. Jules moves closer to me and places her head on my shoulder.

"I get it, West, except for the crazy stalker issues. I meant it when I said that everything changed the moment you touched my hand."

"It changed for me, too. I need you." *And I hate needing anyone or anything.* I kiss the top of her head.

"Then why did you freak out on me at the park?"

"Because I suck?"

"Not good enough." Of course it's too simple of an answer for her. She lowers her voice as she continues, "After the twenty texts you sent me, the conversations we had, the moments we shared last week during the funerals, you walked away from me Thursday night when I was baring my soul to you."

Damn it, I really do suck. In trying to protect myself, I hurt her.

"Come here." I tug her arm, pulling her between my legs. I wrap her in a tight hug from behind as she leans into my chest

"You told me you dumped Stuart Daniels because of me. I know I may act like I don't care about much in this world, but I do. It freaked me out. I wanted you to be sure of what you'd done. I don't want to screw this up. You're too perfect for me to screw things up."

"I'm hardly perfect, and Stuart is far from being the golden boy everyone thinks he is."

I want to argue her view of her own perfection. Her perfectly smooth, slim neck is within my reach and I bury my face into the curve between her neck and shoulders. A content sigh leaves my lips. "I seriously didn't expect you. I don't like needing things, Jules."

She tilts her head, granting me better access to her skin. "Well you're stuck with me now."

"I am, huh?"

"Yep. Remember you said you weren't going to kiss me until I was your girl?" she asks, nudging my face from her skin and looking over her shoulder at me. She grins as though she's carrying a secret. "You've kissed me, West Rutledge. You're done for."

I steal a kiss from her smiling lips. "I was done for way before that kiss, gorgeous. Way before." She turns her body into mine and I touch her cheek before kissing her deeply.

The rustling of corn stalks in the absence of wind interrupts our kissing.

"Holy crap! What's that noise?" she asks, curling her legs into her chest and angling herself into my torso. Her hand grips my shirt, fisting it so tightly I have to pry myself loose.

Something is breaking through the stalks off in the distance. Unsure of what is coming, I get to my feet, dragging her with me. Pushing her behind my back, I peer into the dying vegetation.

"West?"

The cracking of stalks and slapping of leaves are too noisy to be a bird or squirrel, but they're too quick to be a person. Unless they're running. The likelihood of a crazed criminal racing through a cornfield in Tyler, Texas is low.

"It's okay," I insist when Jules lets out a squeak as the sounds edge nearer to us. "I'm sure it's—" Heavy panting and a deep snort reaches us, followed by a whine. "Bear."

Sure enough, Bear, the farm owner's Australian Shepherd, comes bounding through the stalks, a whirl of cream and red fur nearly knocking me over in his haste to lick my face.

"No, Bear, sit," I order with a laugh as Jules dances around behind me in her attempt to keep away from the huge, wet nose Bear is trying to sniff her with.

"Gah, is he friendly?" she yelps.

"Yeah, he won't hurt you. Trample you or sniff you to death, yes. But he won't eat you." I laugh as Bear's front legs go down in a ready to run position and he barks at us playfully.

I slap at his rear, riling him up as I skid around in the dirt, growling at him as he growls back. Jules plays my shadow, sticking to my back.

"Are you afraid of dogs?" I ask when Bear plops his butt on the ground and takes a moment to lick himself and scratch an itch behind his ear.

"No, not at all." I look at her skeptically. She shakes her head. "For real, I'm not. He's just huge and . . . energetic."

"Yeah, he is," I agree. "Bear. Bear," I taunt until the furry guy looks up from his personal pleasure licking party. "Home, boy, go home."

Bear jumps to his feet and spins around, giving us a bark before he takes off in the general vicinity of the main farm store.

Jules plunks her hands on her hips. "Sooo, you're a dog whisperer, huh?"

"More like former playmate," I explain as I sit back down. "My dad is good friends with the Owens. We've all helped a time or two during crop season. I've known Bear since he was the size of a Chihuahua."

"That huge beast was never the size of a Chihuahua. You lie." She shakes her head as she lowers herself to the ground. She takes a spot across from me so we're facing each other. Her bare legs cross in front of her as she leans back on her hands and smiles at me. "You've spent time farming and dog wrangling since we were last friends. What else do you do for fun, Mr. Rutledge?"

"First, Mr. Rutledge is my dad, and second, if you come closer I'll show you what I like to do." I crook my finger at her and waggle my brows.

"Naughty boy? Duly noted."

If only she knew how naughty I'd like to be with her. I'm forced to adjust my seating position at the mere idea. Reining in my dirty thoughts, I attempt to come up with a real answer. What do I do for fun? Nothing. I go to parties, hook up with girls, and chill. I'm sort of pathetic.

"How about an easier question. Favorite music, movie, or food maybe?" she teases as she draws a pattern in the dirt beside her.

"Okay. Indie rock and alternative, anything with action or sports, and anything with cheese." I tick each item off on my hand. "You?"

"I like all music. I've been into country lately though. As for movies, I guess I'd have to say romantic chick flicks. Or anything with Reese Witherspoon or one of the Jennifers, and for food I'm a sucker for Mexican."

"The Jennifers?" I ask, unsure of her meaning.

"Aniston, Lawrence, Garner, Lopez. You know, the Jennifers. There are so many of them."

"Huh. Are they in any sports films?"

"Not that I can think of."

"Then no, I do not know the Jennifers."

"Well, I'll just have to educate you then. I mean really, if you can watch all those Buffy episodes with Carley the least you can do is watch a few chick flicks with me." She throws a pebble at me.

"Of course I will, and you can watch sports with me." Turnabout is fair play after all.

"You don't think cheering for eleven years constitutes enough sports watching?" she asks as she falls to her back, her knees bent to the sky.

"You don't like it?" I ask curiously. "Football, I mean."

"Actually, I love it. Always have." I wish I could see her face from this angle. She sounds happy, as though this is a subject she could discuss for hours. "As a matter of fact, I was thinking about that the other night."

"Oh yeah? How come?" I ask, shifting so I can see her better.

Her head rolls to the side and she smiles at me. "My little brother, Jase, had a nightmare so he came into my room. For some reason it got me thinking." Her fingers pinch her bottom lip as she blinks away the emotions hitting her.

"Did you always love it," she asks. Subject change.

"What do you think?"

She nods. "Of course you did. Was there ever a time you didn't play ball?"

"Nope, I came out of the womb throwing a football." Jules' smile falters. She doesn't have to say anything, I can read her face. She feels guilty for what she just said. "Hey, don't look like that. I still throw the ball with my dad, you know. And when I'm with my brothers we play. I'll always love the game, it's just for fun now."

She sits up, stretching her legs out flat in front of her. "Sorry."

I grab the toe of her sneaker and wiggle her foot back and forth. "Don't be sorry, Jules. I don't play football competitively anymore, but it'll always be a part of my life."

She taps her shoe against my palm. "There was this one time, with Stuart" she stops. Her eyes search my face as though she's asking for permission to speak. Truthfully, I want to ask her to never mention his name, but that would make me look like an ass, so I nod, giving her an encouraging smile to continue.

"Man, he acts like the self-appointed God of football sometimes, doesn't he?" She rolls her eyes and I bite my tongue.

"Sometimes, the girls and I would hang around after cheer practice and wait for the team to finish. Sometimes some of the guys and their girlfriends would stick around for a scrimmage, just screwing around, you know? Well, Stuart would never let me play. So one day I got angry because he had the nerve to tell me to go sit on the bleachers where I belong and look pretty for him." She shakes her head at the memory.

"He was teasing me, but boy did it pissed me off. So you know what I did? I totally ran into the path of a ball he threw, intercepted it, and kept running."

She giggles as though she's reliving the moment. "Oh. My. Gosh. It was the best moment ever. I grabbed the ball and took off all the way across the field with a pack of wild guys chasing me. The other girls cheered, and of course Tanya and Katie joined me, shouting at the boys the entire time. They could have cared less about playing, but they loved getting one over on the guys."

God, I love the sound of her laugh. The way it bursts out of her mouth as though she's been holding it back until she can't stop it any longer. It's musical and magical.

"Did he let you play after that?"

Jules shrugs. "He almost broke up with me that night. He was pissed. I suppose I should've examined our relationship a little deeper after that."

I bite my tongue again. This may become a dangerous habit. Stuart is out of the picture now, so there's no need for me to speak against his character. No matter how much I would love to.

"I wish I could have seen it." I can picture the seething look on Stuart's face as Jules stuck it to him.

She smiles, tipping her head back to the sun. "It was glorious."

"Just so you know, I'd let you play ball with me anytime. In fact, my brothers and I will force you to play, and Mindy will absolutely love having another girl in the game. Plus, adding you will even up our teams to three-on-three."

"So what you're saying is it's a good thing I came into your life. You know, to even up the teams," Jules laughs, making a silly face.

"What I'm saying is that I can't wait for you to get to know my brothers and future sister-in-law. And of all the reasons I'm glad you came into my life, that doesn't even make the top ten."

"There's a top ten?"

"Yep, I'll tell you eventually, if you sit there and keep looking so pretty for me." I grimace as her foot kicks me in the side before our laughter fills the air.

We sit quietly for a while, enjoying the warm sun and peace. Eventually I lay back on the ground and Jules inches into my side and rolls over, blocking the sun from my view as she leans over my face.

"What prompted you to bribe Wes and Karen to put us together at her party?" she asks. Her face is like the eclipse, completely in shadow from the way the sun is beaming directly behind her as I look up.

"You."

"Me? What did I do?" I push her back lightly and roll onto my hip so we are laying side by side, the sun no longer blinding me.

"You were standing with Katie and Tanya by the food table and I remember getting this feeling like you three were staring at me. So eventually I made my way behind you, being all cool like I was just getting something to eat, and I kinda overheard you three."

Jules bites her thumb nail. "Oh gosh, what were we saying?"

"You said something like '12 is so cute.' Apparently I wasn't too bright back then because, after listening to you three for a little longer, I had to ask Jeff what you meant."

Jules collapses to the ground in a symphony of laughter. "12! It was your football number. You couldn't figure that out on your own?" She gasps at the look on my face and laughs some more. "We used to use code words for the guys we liked so people couldn't guess who we were talking about."

"Well obviously I had no idea the complexities of the teen girl's mind back then," I point out, laughing with her. "What I do recall was you complaining how you were too shy to talk to me. So I did what any smart boy would do and the moment Karen brought up playing games I made my move."

"You bribed them because you knew I thought you were cute? Would you have done it if you hadn't overheard us?"

"Hell no! You remember how it was don't you? Always waiting for all the signs before you could let the member of the opposite sex know you liked them? I wouldn't have had the guts."

"But wasn't the point of the game to make random people have to be alone in the closet?"

"Sure, and if I'd been paired with you I totally would have had no problem going in, but—do you remember Carrie Ann and Jeff when they had to kiss during spin the bottle that time?"

"Yes," Jules cries, slapping her hand over her mouth. "I felt so bad for them."

"Everyone egged them on and made jokes, and poor Carrie Ann cried, and Jeff got into a fight with Bryce. So much drama over a kiss." I shake my head at the memories.

Jules grins. "How about now?"

"How about now what?"

Out of the blue, she jumps up and clasps her hands behind her back. "Truth or Dare?" she asks waggling her brows.

This could be interesting. I sit, craning my neck to look at her face. "Dare. Always."

She grins. "Still the rebel, huh, Spike?" She retreats into a nearby row of cornstalks. "I dare you to kiss me."

"Really? Do I have too?" I fake whine.

"Mmmhmmm," she nods. "But first you have to catch me."

She dashes off into the stalks without a second thought, and I laugh as I jump up to chase the little cheerleader who once defied a team of football players because she wanted to prove a point to her boyfriend. When I catch her, five minutes later because *Damn!* she's fast, I happily fulfill my dare and kiss her among the dying fields of a Texas corn farm.

It's getting late. We're back to sitting on the ground face-to-face chatting when I realize I've lost her attention. She seems to be fascinated by a group of black birds hopping around from stalk to stalk near us. I stop talking and simply stare at her. It's been at least thirty minutes since I last touched her, too long, and I want her to know it.

Narrowing my eyes, I study the places I'd love to touch my lips to right now. Her soft lips; her smooth jaw line; her long, slender neck. I boldly flick my gaze lower, taking in her tight tank stretched across her chest. I catch the way her chest lifts and falls, and I know she's spotted me, but I play with her. Slowly and deliberately, I move my hungry eyes back the way they came, wetting my lips just as my eyes meet hers, making sure she knows how much I want her.

Jules scoots across the ground slowly, and maybe it would be sexy if it weren't awkward, until we're face-to-face and hip-to-hip. The sexy part is the way her eyes hold mine the entire time she slides her ass through the dirt. When she halts next to me, I turn into Caveman West again.

Grabbing her knees, I spin her around to face the same direction as me. I hope I didn't give her bare thighs gravel burn. I wrap one arm around her back and I push her to the ground, shifting her to lay in the crook of my arm and chest while I hover over her flushed face.

I kiss her temple first, sucking in a deep whiff of her strawberry hair. It's going to become an addiction of mine. Once I've had my hit, I move my lips over her face, kissing her forehead, the tip of her nose, her closed eyelids. Jules laughs as I take my time plying her with little kisses everywhere but her lips.

"Do you need help finding your way?" she asks as I near her lips then move back to her other temple.

Tucking her hair behind her ear, I look down at this beautiful girl who picked me and I tell her as humbly as I possibly can, "I found it. I'll just keep following you."

A low moan is her reply as she gives in to my lips when they land on hers, her fingers weaving into my hair and holding me to her.

I don't return Jules home until after the street lights have come on and the sun has gone down. After I drop her off, I worry all the way back to my house about her getting in trouble for being out all day without calling, but I can't regret the day. I can't recall a time when I've had such a perfect date. Being with Jules is better than I could have ever imagined and I can't believe it happened. I'm so amped about our time together that I call her as soon as I walk into my house.

"Hey," Jules' sweet voice answers. Before I can speak I hear her mother's voice through the line.

"Jules? Tell him no more motorcycles."

There are mumbles and silence before Jules returns to the line. "Hey, sorry about that."

"No more motorcycle, huh?" I laugh, not surprised.

"Oh, you heard that?"

"I didn't get you in trouble, did I?"

"Nah. She's cool, but apparently your bike isn't."

"I can live with that, although I like feeling you pressed up against me," I hint suggestively. The memory of her stomach, chest, and thighs against me stirs my blood.

"We'll just have to find other opportunities for me to wrap my arms around you," she replies.

"Again, I can live with that."

"Mmm hmm, I bet you can. So what's up? Didn't you drop me off like, um, twenty minutes ago?" I can hear the smile in her voice.

"Too soon?" I ask innocently, and she chuckles.

"Not at all."

"Good. I'd hate to know you were getting sick of me already. I just wanted to let you know I talked to Carter. He put your bike in the shop since you left it there."

"Oh my gosh, I totally forgot about it! Thank you for checking with him."

"Of course."

"Hey, I don't think I told you I had an amazing day with you."

"Did you let me kiss you? Or did I imagine that?" I ask. I'm still half-convinced today was a dream.

She giggles. "I believe I did."

"So you know what that means then, right?" I ask. "You're my girl, Jules. I told you if you weren't his, you'd be mine. I'm jumping on this train."

"Ha! The Jules Blacklin Express?"

Not my best line. "Well it sounded better in my head. I just meant that I let you pass me by once and it took me five years to get another chance. I'm not missing you this time. Can you deal with that?" I ask seriously.

"I can more than deal with that. I endorse it and will happily buy you a round trip ticket."

"You're cute, but I don't need one."

"No?"

"Nope, I'm not getting off this time."

Jules bursts out laughing and I'll be damned if I don't feel the heat burning my face. Jules Blacklin is making me sound like an amateur tonight.

"Dirty girl," I laugh.

"Blame Tanya."

"Shocker."

Tanya had a great dirty mind and she was always a blast to hang out with for that very reason. The guys loved how they could talk smack around her and how she would dish it out in return. She didn't get offended or act prissy. I'm realizing Jules has a similar mind frame and I'm liking it.

Muffled voices reach me through the line before Jules speaks again. "Hey, West, my parents want me downstairs. Can I call you later?"

"Anytime, Buffy."

"Okay, I'll call you soon."

"Jules?" Her name rushes from my lips before she can hang up. "I meant what I said. I'm in this, as long as you're interested in being in it with me." I need her to know this, to trust my intentions.

She's doesn't respond right away and I pull the cell from my cheek, checking to be sure the call didn't drop. I see we're still connected when she replies.

"I was in it the moment you finally spoke to me. The moment you called me Buffy," she admits in a voice so heartbreakingly soft that I want to run to her house and kiss her for hours all over again.

Instead I release a long breath and bite back words describing feelings I shouldn't be having about her. Not yet. Not this soon. "Call me as soon as you can," I tell her instead, my head winning out over the demands of my heart this time.

Heart: 4 ~ Head: 2.

I think I'm starting to get the hang of this.

Twenty-Three

I should have called first. I'm standing on Jules' front porch speaking to her little brother, Jase, through the side glass window because I didn't want to take the time to call first. Idiot.

"I promise I'm a friend of your sister's," I tell Jase through the glass. His wide eyes scan me before his head turns and he shouts behind him.

"He says he's a friend." His muffled shout reaches me through the door.

I tap on the glass to get his attention. "Tell her it's West."

"It's West!" he shouts behind his back again. Then he turns back to the glass and puts his face up close, his breath fogging it as he speaks to me. "She just got out of the shower, hold on."

Damn, I wonder if she needs help toweling off? Shoving my hands in my pockets, I glance around, feeling stupid for running over here without permission first. I missed her. She didn't call me back last night.

When I woke this morning, the nagging thought taking residence in my brain was what if she'd changed her mind, and I had to see her. I wonder if this insecurity will ever go away? My waiting for her to walk away. I hate it.

A flash of movement takes shape behind Jase and he disappears from the glass for a moment before the door opens. I smile, a little embarrassed at myself for showing up like this, as I look at Jules' dripping hair and hastily pulled on tee shirt and yoga pants.

Jase swings open the exterior glass storm door with a huge smile on his face. "You like *Star Wars*?" he asks incredulously. "I like *Star Wars*, too."

I look down at the vintage *Return of the Jedi* tee I'm wearing. "You do?" I ask. "I still have all of the Lego sets from when I was your age." I hold the glass door open, waiting for an invitation to enter as Jase gasps in delight at our mutual fandom.

"I collect them. I have almost all of them. I have this book with all of the sets, and I check them off when I get them," Jase rushes to explain, his face filled with excitement. "Jules thinks it's silly. She says Legos are *stupid*." He rolls his eyes, his face twisting into a look of shock.

"What?" Jules squeals.

Laughing, I switch my attention from Jase to Jules. "She does, does she?"

"No, she doesn't," Jules replies as she tugs her brother from the door and shoos him away. "Get out of here."

I expect him to complain or whine at being dismissed, but instead he's filled with excitement as he races up the stairs, calling back to us, "I'll go get my Legos!"

"See what you did? I'll be playing Legos for the rest of the day." Jules laughs once we're alone at the door.

"Sorry?" I shrug, giving her another smile and not feeling bad at all. Star Wars and Legos rule. "Hi, by the way."

"Hi." She shifts nervously, a slight blush covering her skin. After all the kissing we did yesterday, I'm thrown off by this side of her. Her hand moves to her hair and her face falls.

"Your brother said you just got out of the shower." My eyes flick to her wet, tangled hair. I sense her self-consciousness, though she has no reason for it. "I should have called first. I can go."

Jules shakes her head immediately, stepping aside. "It's fine. Um, did you want to come in?"

I brush against her as I enter the foyer and explain my appearance on her porch. "I was driving by and thought maybe we could hang out."

"You were driving by? Where were you heading?" She calls my bluff. There's no logical reason for me to drive by Jules' house; she lives in a neighborhood full of dead ends.

"Truthfully?" Shrugging, I stuff my hands into my pockets again.

"The truth is always nice," Jules nods as I shake off my rambling thoughts.

I close the gap between us. She smells fresh and clean, like flowers and fruit. "You didn't call me back last night." Removing a hand from my pocket, I catch a bead of water that's dripping off her hair with my fingertip. "I wanted to see you. Thought maybe we could go for a ride; get away to a little cornfield I know."

She frowns. "I'm on duty today."

"On duty?"

"Yeah." She nods behind her. Jase appears on the staircase, talking ninety to nothing about . . . something . . . and I rock back on my heels, putting my hand back in my pocket. Jules slips back a step. "Kid brother duty."

"Oh. I really should have called first," I apologize for the fourth time.

"No, I'm glad you didn't. Er, I mean, I'm glad you're here. You can hang," she lowers her voice as Jase's socked feet hit the landing, "if you don't mind a shadow."

"I'm not a shadow." Jase ruins his protest by bumping into Jules and thrusting a spaceship into my face. The move gives me the urge to thank my brothers for putting up with me growing up. Jase reminds me of my younger self. Star Wars obsession and all.

Plastering a smile on my face, I check out the Lego ship he's holding up for me. I recognize it vaguely from the more recent movies. "Oh man, wow. I don't have that one."

"You don't? Want to see my other sets? Can I show him, Jules, please?" he begs hopefully.

"Of course, as long as West doesn't mind," she turns her smiling eyes on me.

"Do you want to see all my sets? I bet I have a lot you don't, since you're older and don't get them anymore."

"What do you mean I don't get them anymore?" I ask as Jase motions for me to follow him upstairs. Giving Jules one last look, I follow her brother as he reminds me how old I am.

"Obviously, you don't buy Legos because you're too old, so you can't have all the cooler sets like I do. The new sets are way better than the old ones."

Can't argue with him there since I can't recall the last time I was given Legos as a gift.

"I'm going to change really quickly, if you don't mind hanging with Jason for a minute," Jules calls after me.

Studying her, I shake my head. Her cropped leggings leave nothing to the imagination with the way they hug her curves, and while the simple, pink tee should clash with her fiery hair, it doesn't. Her face is void of make-up and I'm amazed at how perfect her porcelain skin is. She really does have the most amazing skin I've ever seen, so smooth and soft and—*damn!*

I need to think of Legos before I embarrass myself physically. "You look great. Don't change on my account." I shift a little.

Our eyes hold each other's, then the moment is broken by Jase shouting my name. "Excuse me. I have some Legos to inspect," I tell her with a wink.

Jase's room is like going back in time to mine or Austin's. Filled with sports posters, action figures, and a Lego-covered floor, I'm propelled back to memories of hours of rainy day fun.

Unable to ignore the temptation, I throw myself onto the floor and jump right into a battle scene that Jase has spread out among his bed, floor, and a child-sized desk.

"You can be the dark side," Jase informs me, grabbing up two Jedi-looking figures and making blaster sounds my way.

"So I'm evil, huh? Cool then," I chuckle, shooting back at his Jedi with the troopers I find. I scan the floor in search of the best characters and smile when I come across Darth Vader, who must have been in the middle of fighting with Luke before I arrived because Jase has them on a platform with Lego fire and trees around them.

Jase laughs as his men rush mine and his voice rises higher and higher with each fake explosion, gun sound, and war cry he makes.

"Argh," I utter a low, tortured grumble as I knock all of my storm troopers to the floor in defeat. Jase looks about to declare victory until I grab Darth and raise the little red lightsaber he's holding in his hand.

"You *will* join me," I order as I throw in two heavy breathing sounds, trying my best to mimic the movies.

Jase bursts into a fit of laughter, raising Luke's lightsaber in return. We engage in a well-choreographed battle that the movies wished they'd had. Apparently, Darth was skilled in gymnastics; if only the movie directors knew this way back when.

"Come play, Jules." I look up, surprised to see we're being spied on.

Part of me feels ridiculous and wants to drop the toys, as though I have to prove I'm cooler than this. Then Jase's laughter rings in my ears again and I simply ignore my embarrassment, smile at Jules, and pick up another man and set him next to a ship as if he's ready for battle and as though Jules isn't there.

"How about a snack instead? Why don't you go make some popcorn?" Jules asks. Her voice catches and emotions run across her face. She's trying hard not to cry. Jase notices it too and his face falls as he watches his sister, and I immediately step in to ease his worry.

"Yum! Using the force sure does make me hungry. I could really go for some popcorn," I agree with Jules a little over-enthusiastically. Jase gives me a questioning look. Nine-year-olds aren't easily fooled so I add some Star Wars for good measure. "Besides, you know we have to follow the Princess's orders, young Padawan." I raise a brow, daring him to disagree with me.

Jase laughs. "She's not a Princess," he scoffs, standing and dropping his Lego men.

Setting my men on the dresser next to me, I stand and look at Jules. She didn't change her clothes or put on make-up like I'd expected her to. The only change in her appearance from when she opened the door is her slicked-back ponytail.

"I see a Princess," I smile, because it's true. Looking at Jules Blacklin causes me a physical reaction, every time.

Jase, on the other hand, isn't as enamored. He groans and heads for the exit, mumbling. "Ewwww! I'll be downstairs."

Jules chuckles as she watches her brother leave the room. "We'll be right behind you, bud. You can turn on cartoons if you want, or pick a movie."

I listen as Jase hums the galactic theme song, hearing it as he moves down to the first floor where it fades out. I smile internally, as I'm reminded once more of my younger self, before returning my attention to Jules.

She's standing in the doorway, and the ever present gravitational pull constantly calling me to her goes into effect. I move behind her, a new scent tickling my nose and making me grin. She might not have gussied up herself with makeup and fancy clothing, but she absolutely made sure she smelled good. *As if she doesn't always smell incredible.*

"Thanks for that," she whispers once the sounds of Jase are gone.

"For what?" I ask from directly behind her. She flinches, evidently not expecting me to be so close. She spins around, wrapping her arms around me and tucking her head into my chest, but not before I spy the shimmer of tears on her cheeks.

"For playing with him. He's had a hard time getting over the tornado, and I haven't seen him truly laugh that way since it happened."

Rubbing the back of her neck with my thumb, I hug her closely. "Then I'm happy I came by, if only for him," I tell her, and it's true.

If I had to leave right now I wouldn't care because knowing I made her brother smile makes me content. She says he's had a hard time dealing with the storm and I can only imagine what it must be like for a kid his age to process these things. His sister was trapped, her best friend died, much of the city is a mess. Children are resilient, but it doesn't mean lasting impressions aren't being made.

"You're totally going to lose your bad boy reputation, Rutledge," Jules teases into my shirt.

"Do I have one?"

"You did, but I'm wondering if it was all part of some elaborate ruse."

"Reputations often are."

She tilts her head, looking up through wet lashes at me. "I'm sorry I didn't call last night. I fell asleep, if you can believe that."

"I thought maybe you changed your mind," I confess.

"Changed my mind? About what? You and I? Why in the world would you think that?" She stretches up, pressing a kiss to my chin. She's so tiny compared to me, her head fitting perfectly under my chin whenever I hug her.

"I keep thinking you're going to get your memory back from before the tornado."

"Huh?"

I'm stunned myself. It's as though my subconscious is coming through and saying things my brain hasn't considered, and I realize I really am worried about her changing her mind. "I know; I'm crazy, right? I don't know if I could handle it, Jules. You're not going to wake up and be all 'Dude, I love Stuart! What am I doing with *this* loser?'"

"Dude? What the hell? First, I have all of my memory from before the tornado and I'm not changing my mind. Second, don't call my boyfriend a loser, you loser," she growls, kicking the toe of my shoes with her bare foot.

My lips curl into a smug smile. "Your boyfriend, huh?"

"Yeah, my boyfriend. Didn't we just agree to this last night? Or are you already leaving me? Is that part of your bad boy charm—love 'em and leave 'em?"

Jules grimaces, looking away as though she's said something wrong, and I skim her cheek before tipping her jaw up.

"I told you, gorgeous, I'm not leaving. As for love, well I've never been there with another girl," I admit, liking the sound of the word on my tongue. *Love*.

Jules looks doubtful. "You haven't? Not even with Carley Raine?"

"Nope. Not even Carley. She was fun, but she wasn't love."

"And what about me? Am I just fun?"

Her question makes me inexplicable angry. Tightening my arm around her back, I answer her a little sharper than I intend. "You, Jules Blacklin, are not for fun. You are—" I swallow hard, biting the inside of my cheek.

"Never mind, I was playing," Jules rushes her apology, her hands resting on my chest.

In less than two weeks I've become so attuned to her facial expressions and tone that I know when she's lying. She might say she's playing, but somewhere inside she is obviously worried about the player West. I see it in the way her eyes shift nervously. I want her to know where she stands. No second guessing between us anymore. I might have trouble with insecurities and thinking she'll leave me any day to go back to Douche Canoe Stuart, but I don't want her to second guess my intentions.

I steal a kiss and explain. "No, you should know. You're not for fun. *You* might even be love." I step back, rubbing my hands over my face and into my hair. "I think, or at least I'm pretty sure, I could fall in love with you. Does that scare the crap out of you?"

Everything stops as I wait for her to process what I've said. Spilling your heart out isn't for the weak, but when Jules grabs my face and forces my eyes to meet hers, I know the years I may have taken off my life are worth it.

"The only thing that scares me right now is that I feel the same way," Jules admits, steering my face down to hers. "This is crazy," she murmurs against my lips.

"But real," I smile, as though I have to prove to myself that it is, in fact, real.

"Perfectly real," she agrees with another kiss.

My hand finds its way to her backside as our lips tease each other. Jules doesn't laugh this time as my fingers dig into her rear, pulling her closer to me. Her yoga pants are more like second skin, leaving nothing to the imagination and kicking up my libido. Five more minutes and her brother is bound to see something only appropriate in R-rated movies. I let go of her butt, as much as it pains me.

"Do I get to see your room?" I ask, not wanting to be an exhibitionist for a nine-year-old.

Twisting in my arms, Jules tugs at the end of my shirt and pulls me to the entrance of her bedroom. Her unmade bed beckons me with the fluffy comforter and mound of pillows, but I resist the urge to drag her there.

This relationship is real; we just established that. Real is more than the physical stuff. Working hard to forget the need in my pants and the bed, I look around her room and take in everything that makes up this girl standing before me.

Her bookshelves are filled with mementos of a charmed life, there are stuffed animals in the corner chair, large boards are covered in pictures of people I know from school; these things are Jules. With the exception of an overturned laundry basket sitting near the door, the room is spotless. I'm not surprised.

I move into the room to get a closer look at the pictures on her walls and spot a stack of snapshots piled on her desk. Curious, I pick up the one on top and smile when I see what it's of.

"I've never seen these." I tell her as I shuffle through the candid shots from a middle school football/cheerleader yearend pool party. Memories wash over me as I take in the faces of my past, including my own. "Man, we look so young."

"We *were* young."

"I would do so many things differently if I could go back to those days," I confess. "So many things."

The what ifs threaten to overwhelm me; regret sucks. A heavy pall hangs over the room as I flip through the shots. I'm mesmerized by a shot of my younger self—my thick wavy hair completely out of control back then—smiling broadly for the camera with my arms slung around the necks of friends. This was the end of sixth grade, shortly before my mom was diagnosed with cancer and the last summer I spent as a carefree boy.

"Jules! No boys in your room!" Jase's voice screams from downstairs.

Jules' light touch on my back releases me from the past and I drop the pictures to the desk and whirl around on her with a smile, grabbing her waist.

"Come on, cheerleader. No boys allowed in your room," I tease, casting away my heavy thoughts. West Rutledge, master of subject change.

○○○○○○○○

In honor of the 'no boys in your room' rule, we spend the day with Jase wedged between us, watching *Star Wars* movies and pigging out. Jase falls asleep between us near the end of movie four and my arm stretches over the back of the couch to touch Jules' head. I tease my fingers through her hair as I attempt to concentrate on the action.

I spend the remainder of the film watching Jules. My eyes ache from the covert staring, but it's worth it. She's beautiful. She sends me small smiles every once in a while, letting me know she's as aware of me as I am of her.

When the movie ends, I help carry Jase to his room and watch as she covers her little brother tenderly. We maneuver the Lego minefield that is his floor in the dim light as we leave his room.

"You're a good big sister," I tell her as the door clicks closed.

"I was an only child for so long. He was always like a baby doll to me growing up."

"Must be a girl thing, I was a punching bag to my brothers."

Jules chuckles and I take her hand, pulling her away from her brother's door. For a fleeting moment I consider pulling her into her room and testing out the softness of her bed, but I think better of it. That's not the impression I want to make on her parents should they arrive home unexpectedly.

Either she's a mind reader or she sees the indecision in my eyes because she sighs and directs us toward the staircase. "It's close to ten. You should probably go before my parents come home."

I nod and allow her to walk me to the front door.

"I'm not worried about meeting them as your boyfriend, you know. I don't want you to worry about me," I tell her with a smile. I'm not really a meet-the-parents type of guy, but I can be. For her, I will be.

"I know. It's just—I told my mom there was something between us, but—I don't know. I guess I feel like I should tell them we're seeing each other before they walk in on us," she explains. I can't stop feeling a bit suspicious of her explanation, as though she doesn't want to fess up to being with me. West Rutledge—the quitter and screw up.

"You're going to tell them though, right? I mean, they don't hate me or something, do they?"

"West! Of course not." She kisses me as if those lips are going to change the subject. "They think you're awesome. You saved me, remember?"

I barely hear her words because her dang lips *did* change the subject and now I'm wrapping my arms around her and kissing her back. My mouth works at hers until she gives in and deepens the kiss. Today was perfect.

We're two for two, Jules and I, and all I can think about is having another day like this with her tomorrow—perhaps without a Star Wars movie marathon and a little brother then it hits me.

"Shoot," I groan, backing away from our kiss. "I completely forgot to tell you I'll be gone for the weekend. My dad and I are getting up early and heading to the big game at A&M."

Jules' face crumbles. "I'm jealous," she rubs her cheek against my chest. "So I won't see you until Monday?"

Ugh! Three days. Why does that sound like torture? Normally Dad and I wouldn't head up until late Friday night or early Saturday, but with school out our plans changed. Dad needed an extra day at the school for some broadcast interviews he wanted to do. He'd mentioned it Tuesday night, and since Jules and I weren't speaking at the time, and he'd caught me after my full day of work labor, I didn't think to disagree with him.

"Yeah. My oldest brother, Carson, and his girlfriend, Mindy, live about thirty minutes from campus, so we always stay at their place after the games. Austin lives there too, kinda, and he usually gets to hang too. It's a lot of manly stuff. We probably won't head back until late Sunday. I'll see if I can guilt Dad into coming back earlier so I can stop by."

"No, don't do that. See your brothers and have a good time. I'll be sitting here withering away without you."

"Jules?" I use her name so she knows I'm absolutely, one hundred percent serious when I speak. "Every minute I'm not with you, I'm thinking about you and wanting to be with you."

"Me too," she confesses her lips kissing mine goodnight.

Twenty-Four

Me: Usually I look forward to A&M football weekends
Me: I think you've ruined it for me. I want to stay home with your lips
Me: and your hand
Me: and not in a dirty way!

I send the texts to Jules as my dad's truck veers onto the highway. I'm not surprised at the lack of a response since it's 8:00 A.M. I'd be asleep too if my dad hadn't forced me into the car this early so he could make a lunch meeting with his producers.

Me: of course, we could discuss the dirty things.
Me: I'm game ;)

"What's got you smiling this early," Dad asks from beside me.

"Eh, I amuse myself," I wave my phone in the air for him to see I'm texting.

"Jules?"

"Yeah. Well, kind of. She's not answering so I'm actually having a one-sided conversation." I pocket the phone and reach into the bag of donuts we picked up before leaving town.

Dad shakes his head. "It's good to see a smile on your face."

"It's good to have one."

Jules: I'm not sure where to begin with those texts.

Her reply arrives halfway into our three-hour drive.

Me: Well, good morning Sleeping Beauty.

Jules: its 9:30, its not like I slept all day. Plus, I needed it

Me: yeah, you did.

Jules: And I was having this great dream. I'm kinda sad I woke up

Me: really? About what??

Jules: wouldn't you like to know. You there yet?

Me: Hey! Don't change the subject.

Jules: hahaha. I'll tell you all about it next time we talk.

Me: damn. I'm calling as soon as I get to the house.

Jules: No you are not. You're spending time with your brothers.

Me: I spent time with them last weekend

Jules: West.

Me: Jules.

She doesn't reply. I relent.

Me: I'll spend time with them, but I'm calling you as soon as I'm alone. Deal?

Jules: Fine. Showering now.

She ends her text with one of those kissy faces. Normally I'm annoyed by the over usage of emojis, but from Jules I can deal. Not only do I deal, but I deign to send her back a winky face. Then I delete the evidence, just in case.

"You're smiling again," Dad points out.

"She makes me happy."

He clears his throat, but I can tell he's merely covering the pause in his thoughts. "So, you two worked things out then," he asks.

"Worked what out?" I haven't told him much about Jules and I. Austin knows the most and he wouldn't spill it.

"Should I give you your play by play for the last week?" I frown as he looks over at me. "First, I should mention how you were extra cranky after Tanya's funeral. Which is understandable, considering the circumstances, but then you ran out of the house all excited only to return an hour later pissed at the world. Next, you spent the weekend pretending you were happy, but Austin's whispers and worried glances proved otherwise, as did your imbibing at the Sig party."

"Dad—"

His hand goes up. "We have an agreement, West. You be responsible, you don't drive, you don't get into any trouble, and I won't come down hard on you. I'm not talking about drinking right now, though. I'm talking about your change in attitude. You sulked all weekend, you ran off as soon as we got home Monday to go to Jeff's. You started a conversation with me about Jules and your mother. Then you threw yourself into work Tuesday and Wednesday. After all of that you disappeared yesterday only to return home being downright cheerful. Exactly how you've been this morning. So, either you're on drugs or something has changed. And since I've witnessed the way your eyes light up when you see Jules Blacklin, I can only presume she's the reason for this smile."

Wow. I sound certifiable when he lays it all out that way. "I haven't kept you in the loop, huh?" It's more of a statement than a question. I scratch my knuckles across my jaw as I think of how to respond. "Sorry."

"Are things okay?"

I nod. "They're better now."

"How is she doing, still suffering from her concussion?"

"She's feeling okay actually. She doesn't remember everything yet, but she's had flashes. She doesn't seem to have any other side effects. Remember how sick I used to get after the concussion I had in middle school? I couldn't stand up too quickly for weeks without getting dizzy."

"I had my fair share back in the day, too. Each one was unique and came with different recovery periods. How is she dealing with Tanya's death?" His eyes stay on the road as he questions me.

"Honestly, we haven't talked about it."

I chew on the inside of my cheek. I spent the last two days with Jules and we didn't talk about the tornado or all that's transpired in the last two weeks. We've kind of acted as though none of that happened, as though we were two normal teens who fell for each other. *Ignorance is bliss, right?*

"And we're here."

I look up as we pull into the drive of our college pad. That's what my brothers and I call it. It was the bachelor pad until Mindy moved in with Carson a year ago. I smile thinking about living here every time we pull up to this house.

"One more year."

"You so ready to be rid of your old man?" I didn't realize I'd made the comment out loud. I laugh as I pull my duffle from the back of the truck and follow him to the front door.

"Not at all. I just can't believe this time next year I'll be at school here. I can't believe this is my last weekend before senior year." *Shit, I'm feeling crazy sentimental these days.*

My mind wanders to Jules and I wonder about her plans for school next year. I've assumed she would be going to A&M, I'm sure I heard her say it before, but I'm not so sure. There's so much we've yet to discuss about ourselves. We moved headfirst into this deep connection without sharing ourselves.

"Alright, I'm heading to campus for my meeting. Do you want to come track down Austin or are you going to stay here?"

I drop my bag by the front door and head for the kitchen. "Nah, Austin told me he'd come here after the team walk-thru."

"I'll see you in a couple hours then," he waves, locking the door as he leaves.

Grabbing a bottled soft drink, I grab my bag and carry it to my room. I throw myself on the bed thinking a nap would be perfect. After running on empty for two weeks, I'm exhausted from the turmoil, the physical labor, and the nightmares plaguing my sleep. I yawn, kicking off my shoes, then Jules enters my mind. Not Jules so much as the dream she said she would tell me about. Then I think about her plans for next year and the fact that I'm all alone, and I pull my phone from my pocket and dial.

"Hey," she answers on the third ring, drawing out the word into three long, singsong syllables.

"Where are you going to school next year," I ask, not bothering with pleasantries.

"Uh, A&M. Why?"

"A&M, really? You're for sure on that?"

Jules laughs. "Yes, I'm very sure. I had early acceptance this year. You sound a little crazy. What's up?"

I smack myself in the forehead, feeling like an idiot. "Sorry, my dad and I were talking about next year and it dawned on me that I had no idea what your plans were for college. Whenever I come here I get excited about the future. Today for the first time I paused when I saw the house because for a second I worried about how maybe your plans wouldn't be the same as mine."

"Awe," she sings into the line. "You really do like me, don't you?"

"You're okay."

"Just okay? Well I guess you don't really want to hear about my dream, do you?" she teases.

Well hell, checkmate.

"Remember how I told you I have a top ten list of why I'm happy you're in my life?" I ask. "Number ten is you make me smile."

"The feeling is mutual."

"Good, so tell me about this dream of yours," I order, stacking the pillows behind my head and adjusting myself on the bed.

Jules chuckles. I hear rustling through the phone and a door click before she replies. "Well, it involves our favorite corn field, very little clothing, and a whole lot of R-rated material."

"R-rated for violence and language?"

"Definitely not for violence and language."

Closing my eyes, I picture Jules' red hair spread across her pale skin, and my body is immediately awake. "Maybe, we should save this conversation for when I'm not three hours away from you," I groan.

Her musical laughter turns me on more and I pull a pillow over my head. "It seems to me this might be the perfect time to tell you."

'Why? So I can't attack you?"

"Precisely." She laughs lightly, but I don't.

She doesn't remember our conversation when we were trapped so she doesn't know I know she's a virgin. She doesn't know how amazed I am by this either. I'm no saint and I don't ever want her to feel like I would force her into anything.

"Jules?"

Her laughter fades at my use of her name. "Yeah?"

"I know I tease you with dirty jokes and comments, but I want you to know I would never pressure you into anything. If talking dirty bothers you at all just tell me to stop. Okay?"

"Boy, your parents raised you right," she sighs. I wait for her to continue, but she doesn't. A moment later I hear her mother's voice and her mumbled reply.

"So, I've committed myself to a day with my mother."

"Well you go have fun then and I'll talk to you later."

"M'kay."

I'm about to say goodbye when she stops me. "Hey, West? I trust you."

She hangs up and I smile at the ceiling. Fifteen minutes later I fall asleep and dream of her barely clothed in our corn field, and damn if it isn't a good dream.

○○○○○○○○

"Remember Amy from the Sig party?" Austin asks as we're sitting around the backyard fire pit after dinner.

"Uh, not really. If you recall, I had a lot to drink."

"Ha, right. Well, she does this thing where she rubs my—"

"Whoa, whoa," I shout, nearly falling backwards in my chair. "I do not want to hear what you have chicks rubbing."

"Who's rubbing what?" asks Carson as he steps onto the back patio with a beer in hand. I point at Austin who groans.

"Amy is rubbing my back, you dirty bastards." Carson and I share skeptical looks and Austin leans forward, throwing another log into the fire. "She's a physical therapy major. Geez, you two must be hard up," he growls.

"Suuuurrre, therapy major," Carson and I echo with laughter, exchanging a fist bump.

"Uh, engaged and living in sin. I think I'm good, bro," Carson points out as he pulls a chair around the other side of the fire. The metal legs make a horrible scraping sound against the brick pavers of the patio and I cringe. It's like nails on a chalkboard echoing into the otherwise quiet night.

"West?" Austin prods, as though I would admit to being hard up.

They're both looking at me with expectant faces. "Why the hell you looking at me? I'm not talking about my sex life with you two."

"So you admit there's a sex life?" asks Austin.

"Shut up." I wish I had something to throw at him.

"Dude, just don't tie yourself down before you get up here next year. Carson tapped out on me way to early. I need a wing man."

Apparently I suck at hiding things from my brothers. Austin sits forward, his eyes narrow and his lips twitch into a smile as he studies my face. "You made a move didn't you?"

"What? On Jules?" asks Carson as he looks from Austin to me. What does he know about Jules?

Damn it, siblings can be a pain.

"Mindy and her big mouth," I mutter. "Or was it you?" I ask Austin, wondering who filled Carson in on the situation with Jules and I.

Austin shakes his head. "My lips are sealed."

Carson chuckles. "You must think we're all deaf and blind. We were worried about you, West."

I'm not mad. I love my brothers and my dad. They're the three people I know I can count on for anything in my life. I don't know why I don't talk to them more about how I've been coping. Especially Carson and my dad, except that I recall how they were after my mom's death. Austin is more like me—carefree and screws around too much—but Carson is responsible. He became a second father figure when I was dealing with my mom's death. He's an adult now, with a college degree and a serious girlfriend. Sometimes I find it harder to confide in him. Sometimes I just want to be allowed to wallow and act stupid instead of hearing sound advice.

"Austin would have told you if there was something serious to worry about. I'm good," I tell Carson before looking at Austin's curious face. "And yes, I made a move."

"And?" he prods.

"And—I'm whipped." I shrug, stretching my legs out before me as though I could care less about my self-diagnosis as my brothers laugh.

Giving them the Spark Notes version, I tell them about Jules and Stuart, and fill them in on the connection we felt from the moment we saw each other the night of the storm. I tell them how I stupidly fought it and how I eventually gave in, thanks in part to Mindy telling me to not be scared to fall in love.

"I told you you aren't a screw up," Austin chuckles.

"I'm still totally a screw up and I'm worried she's going to rethink being with me one of these days, but I don't care. I'm all in." The flames flicker across their faces as I admit my feelings. "There's something about her, she makes me want things."

"That's your testosterone talking. Didn't Dad tell you about the bird and the bees?" Austin slaps his knee, cracking himself up.

Carson's long leg stretches out to kick at Austin's shin. "Ignore him, he's still got the mentality of a thirteen-year-old boy."

Cursing Carson and rubbing his shin, Austin checks his phone. Letting out a deep breath, he jumps to his feet. "I've got team curfew; I should head out."

"Kick ass tomorrow," Carson offers as they exchange a fist bump.

I stand and pull him in for a hug, telling him what I always tell him before his games. "Run like the wind, Bullseye."

"Always," he agrees with a nod.

And he does. He scores twice in Saturday's game as Carson, Mindy, and I cheer in the stands. Football Saturdays at A&M—the Rutledge family lives for these. I pull my phone out of my pocket when I have a moment during a timeout and send Jules a couple texts.

Me: Reason #9 - your smile. I close my eyes and I see it. It makes me happy.

Me: Reason #8 - the crease in your forehead when you're thinking. It's damn sexy.

Play resumes and I pocket my phone, getting back into the game. I don't check my phone again until much later.

Jules: You have this smile . . . I call it the signature West look. It melts me every time. And, you think my forehead crease is sexy? I suppose this bodes well for me if we end up old and gray together.

My smile hurts my face, it's so wide.

Me: #7 - you admit we might just make it together long enough to end up old and gray
Me: #6 - your brain. You're one of the smartest girls I know. See #7 for proof.

Her response comes in the way of a phone call and I have to excuse myself from the dinner table to answer it while we're out having a celebratory meal.

"I miss you."

She laughs into the line. "Do you think either of us will ever just answer the phone normally?" she asks.

"Eventually, when we're old and gray."

"I'm sorry for calling, I know I told you to spend time with your family and I hate interrupting it," she apologizes needlessly, "I just wanted to hear your voice."

There's something sad in her tone and I'm immediately on alert. "You okay?" She tells me she's fine. I don't believe her. "Jules?"

"I'm just feeling a little down today. I miss her. I came across a shirt of hers I'd borrowed and I grabbed my phone to call her, then it hit me," she whispers. *Tanya.*

"Awe, babe, I'm so sorry." I remember the days when I would walk into the house after going somewhere and there was this part of my brain that was always expecting to see my mom in the kitchen. It happened for months. The scent of fresh baked cookies still brings out the feeling of loss.

"Babe?"

"Uh oh, do you not like babe? It kind of came out on its own," I admit. I'm so used to calling her 'Buffy' or 'cheerleader'.

She's quiet for a moment. "No, it doesn't bother me. What can I call you? Pumpkin?"

I groan.

"Sweetie, baby, love bunny?" she teases, and I face the wall so my laughter doesn't fill the waiting area around me.

"I don't care what you call me as long as I'm yours," I whisper into the line. *So. Freaking. Whipped.*

"I think this is the start of a beautiful relationship, West Rutledge." The rich timbre of her voice sends shivers down my spine.

"Damn straight, gorgeous."

Twenty-Five

When I wake up Monday morning, it has finally arrived. Senior year. This is the last first day of high school I'll have. Two weeks ago I sat on a bench with Jeff after his last first football game of the year and we chuckled at how we couldn't believe we'd made it to this point. That conversation has a deeper meaning now.

As I shower I think of the eight students who died during the storm. I think of Mike Brown and Tanya, who would have been seniors with me today. I think of all the students, teachers, and administrators who, because of the storm, will not be at Hillsdale High this year. Instead, we've been redistributed between several other local schools while rebuilding takes place.

I wash my hair and I wonder if I'll ever get over the feelings I have when I think of the storm. Emotionally, I know I'm still searching for something I've lost. It's there on the outskirts of my mind teasing me, but I can't pinpoint it. And I have Jules now. Thinking of her grounds me, she makes me forget what I can't remember.

Pulling on my jeans, I think about Katie's plans for this morning. Jeff texted me last night to fill me in on her surprise for Jules and asked for my help. Of course I agreed. I would do anything for Jules, and if Katie think she'll love it then who am I to disagree? I just hope they can both handle it.

Once I'm ready I shoot Jules a message because I miss her. I haven't seen her since Thursday, and because of her orders to visit with my family, we barely spoke over the weekend.

Me: Hey gorgeous! Sure I can't pick you up?
Jules: You know I'm riding with Katie
Me: I know, but I can't wait to see your face. I want everyone at Rossview to know you're mine. Sit in the car & wait for me?

Jules: LOL. You're kidding, right?

Me: No

Jules: West!

Me: You don't know those guys. They're vultures when a hot girl is around. You're wearing a bag, right?

Jules: Of course! See you soon

Stuffing my phone into my pocket, I head for the garage and out the door where I find the motorbike. I warned Austin over the weekend that I wanted my Jeep back this week. For a while I didn't care, but now I want to drive Jules to school and I want to take her out on dates and show up at her house without helmet head. Plus, her parents have made it very clear that she is not allowed on the bike.

Ready to see my girl, I head to Memorial Gardens and Tanya's gravesite. Katie and Jules will be there, starting their first day of senior year together with Tanya. Three best friends who have been together on their first day of school since they were in Kindergarten.

Katie asked that Jeff and I be there, along with Tommy Wilson since Tanya was sort of seeing him before the storm. They were on and off, much like Katie and Jeff were, and from what I've learned since the tornado, he really liked her. Jeff told me Tommy's had a hard time dealing with her death.

He was with her, they ran together, and were apparently separated. Tommy ended up with a broken arm from debris, and Tanya ended up dead. I can't imagine the guilt he feels. I know it's not his fault, but I think of Jules and I know that if something had happened to her I would feel the same way.

I stop at a grocery store and buy one red rose on impulse—probably another side effect of all the romance movies I watched with my mom. Wrapping the flower carefully to avoid the thorns, I tuck it into my shirt to keep it safe from the wind. I ride past Jeff's car and Tommy's huge monster truck and park in front of them.

The girls aren't here yet. When the site comes into view I spot Tommy squatting at the side of Tanya's grave. Scanning the area, I find Jeff waiting by a tree, so I head his way.

"They were stopping to get coffee first. A before school tradition," Jeff tells me. The image of cheerleaders walking on campus each morning with their frothy iced coffees in hand before school flashes though my mind. Of course *my* cheerleader would be one of them. I shake my head.

"So," Jeff drawls a little tongue in cheek. "You and Jules Blacklin?"

"Looks that way," I shrug. "And you and Katie, one hundred percent on now, huh?"

"Looks that way," he shrugs back with a grin.

"I guess our senior year isn't turning out to be the way we planned it then, is it?" I ask as I think back to a time when we stole a case of beer from a party my parents were having in middle school.

We spent the night getting plastered while talking about how awesome we were going to be when we were seniors. The imagined debauchery is humorous now. We thought we were going to be the big men on campus. Parties, girls, football fame; we were the kings of our futures. Jeff laughs as though he's remembering too.

Katie's car comes into view down the winding road.

"You know what, man? I think, considering all that's happened since then, we've done pretty damn well," Jeff points out as I lean against the tree behind me, waiting for Jules to arrive.

"So, no big pimping at the parties?" *The ghetto phase was strong with us, once upon a time.*

Two heads appear around the trees and bushes, one light blonde and the other golden red, and my breath catches.

"Who needs pimping when we've got them?" asks Jeff with a low voice.

"We don't deserve them."

"Hell no we don't, but I'm keeping mine."

He turns, letting Tommy know the girls have arrived, and I straighten from the tree just in time to catch a crying Jules as she walks into my arms. She's carrying a drink from Starbucks in each hand, but her arms manage to loop around my waist as her shoulders shake. I wrap her up.

I'm keeping mine too. I press one hand to her back, careful not to knock her drinks, while my other hand goes to the base of her skull and toys with her hair. My chin rests on top of her head, and as I inhale her strawberry scent I still.

Reason #5 - This feeling right here. The peace she brings when she's in my arms.

"This isn't a bag you're wearing," I whisper into her hair, thinking of the fitted dress she's wearing and her shapely legs. She lets out a half-laugh, half-sob as I kiss her hair. "You look gorgeous, though."

She looks up and I press another kiss right on the crease in her forehead.

"I can't believe you're here," she sniffles.

Removing my hand from her hair, I brush the tears from her cheeks. "I care about you, why wouldn't I be here?"

"You were playing with me this morning?"

"Was I?" I tease. "My bad. Actually, had you told me you wanted me, I would have come."

I knew Katie's plan, but at any time had Jules said she wanted me to pick her up instead of Katie I would have found a way to be there for her. Everything within me wants to do whatever it takes to make her happy.

She stretches up and kisses me. "I did want you, but I knew Katie would need me today just as much as I needed her."

My arm tightens around her back. "I missed you this weekend. Next home game you're coming with us."

"Deal." She smiles at me once more before she faces Tanya's grave and leaves my arms.

The five of us look down at the mound of flowers marking the spot as Jules and Katie hold hands and step forward. Jules sets the extra drink she was holding down on the ground before stepping back.

"It's not going to be the same without you, Ya-ya," Jules whispers.

"You'd be proud, though. Juju's already picking up your bitchiness. What'd you do? Possess her?" Katie asks, sending a teary-eyed smile Jules' way. I wonder what the story is there.

"Help us all now," Tommy groans, and we all laugh lightly. I squeeze Jules' hand again, giving her my strength for as long as she needs it.

Katie holds up her frappe, "To senior year and to Tanya."

"To Tanya," we chime in as Jules taps her cup to Katie's.

As we break up, the girls each give Tommy a hug before Katie steps up to me. "Thanks for being here."

"Of course."

"And for being there for Jules."

"Again, of course," I tell her, almost insulted by her need to thank me.

Katie nods. "You know the two of you were funny to watch. Both of you pretending there was nothing between you, then going crazy when you made each other mad. I'm glad you found your way together."

"Hey, Jules, another reason on my list—" I call out, and she and Jeff turn to us as Tommy heads for his truck. "I like your friends." I wink as I hug Katie, who giggles.

"Not too much, I hope." She walks to my side and tells Katie she'll meet her at the car in a moment.

"So, cheerleader, you sure you don't want a ride to school on my bike?" I ask as we walk toward our vehicles.

"And mess up my first-day-at-a-new-school-hair? You don't know me at all, West Rutledge," Jules balks, sending me a sassy smile while she plunks her fists on her hips.

I set my hands over hers and tug her closer. "I think I'm getting to know you better and better each day."

"And what about the rest of your top ten?" she asks, coming up on her toes and kissing my chin when she can't reach my lips.

"I'm leaving those open." She raises one brow in question. "Every second I'm with you, I'm finding something new I like. I don't want to fill my list too quickly. I only have room for ten."

"Well see, that's funny because my list is already filled with fifty things I love about having you in my life."

Love. This does feels a hell of a lot like love.

My best reply is to remove the drink from her hand, set it on the grass at our feet, and kiss the hell out of her. My hands tangle in her long, silky hair, messing up the first day of school hair she seemed so worried about only moments ago. My lips mold and press against hers as my tongue sweeps into her mouth. She tastes like chocolate and caramel. Jules' fingers play lightly over my ribs, my back, and up into my hair. We lose ourselves in the kiss.

It's an epic, grand gesture type of kiss my mom would be proud of.

Sliding onto my bike, I follow behind my friends' cars as we head to our first day of our last year as high schoolers. I'm not worried about attending Rossview the way Jules seems to be. I know a lot of the kids there, and with the exception of being around some of the girls I've hooked up with over the past year or so, I like the idea of starting over. New school, new girl, new West.

New West? The thought makes me laugh behind my visor, but it's the truth. I'm not the same West I was two weeks ago, that's for damn sure.

For one, I'm opening up to the friends I used to have. I'm opening up to my dad and brothers and Mindy more than I have in years. Most importantly I'm in love with a girl. It's a crazy thought to be in love with Jules after only two weeks, and I'm not stupid enough to think it's this all-consuming permanent love yet. It could be, though. The way I feel about her transcends the way I've felt about anyone. Ever.

I was the guy hell bent on letting the tides of life toss me around whichever way they chose. I didn't care, I just went with it, but with one touch of her hand, my whole world changed.

Jules Blacklin is my anchor. She's my mainstay, the one thing holding me in place and making me want to change the way I think and the way I do things. In two weeks she's made me rethink what I lost when I went into hiding after my mom's death. And she's making me rethink what I want going forward.

People make decisions every day. Spur of the moment choices, long thought out and carefully planned choices, life changing choices, mundane choices.

Every day.

Go this way, go that way, do more, do less, say hello, walk away; every step, word, thought we make is a choice. I've made a lot of choices in my life and I've found one thing to be true. Each one is made using either my head or my heart.

I'm not sure which decision making tool has won out over the years, but I know they both saved me in the last few weeks.

On that Friday night, before the twister struck, I turned and saw a beautiful redhead sitting on the table next to me and it was my head that told me to speak to her. I thought it was my heart at first, but it wasn't. It was my brain telling me to take the chance to know this girl again. It was my head that knew there was something there, that there was always something there between us. It started when we were younger and I made the choice to stop it. I went into hiding.

This time, I made a better choice.

Yep, my life has changed because of a storm and a choice. Funny enough, it's for the better. The best part is the knowledge that this is merely the beginning. We've just begun to fall in love, to know each other, to heal.

There is so much more to come.

Please consider reading the Author Note about the *From The Wreckage* series on the following page.

Author's Note about the *From The Wreckage* series

Dear Reader,

Did you know that *West* is a part of a larger book series called *From The Wreckage*? I wrote *West* with the intent of providing readers with the opportunity to choose your own beginning for this series. *From The Wreckage* is the same story as *West*, only it is told from Jules' point of view (POV).

So now what? Well, you could go back and read *From The Wreckage* and get Jules' POV. The e-book is free on all sites. OR you can move forward with *Out of Ruins*, book 2 in the *From The Wreckage* series. *Out of Ruins* is told from Jules' POV and picks up right where *West* left off. Don't worry, you get to read more from West's POV in the final book, *All That Remains*.

I've included the first chapter of Out of Ruins below for you.

One note: Jules is telling the story of the tornado as she makes a Video LOG for her school's time capsule.

I hope you will continue their journey now whether you move on to *Out of Ruins* or you go back to *From The Wreckage*.

Thank you for allowing me to take the time to tell you a story. Happy Reading!

~Michele

Out of Ruins

From The Wreckage, *book two*

One

"Five minutes."

"For the longest time, my brain was set on this time. That's roughly how long we had from when we first heard the sirens, to when the twister hit the Ice Shack. Five minutes."

"What can you do in five minutes?"

"Can you change the entire landscape of your life?"

"As we drove from the cemetery to school that first day, I was once again reminded about how different my life was from only two weeks before. Typically, the first day of school for me has always been easy. I'm not a nervous person; I've always known who I am." Jules holds up her fingers as she checks off facts about herself. "Cheerleader, debate team, homecoming court, student council. I'm well aware that, technically, I am the girl most people would want to hate. Except, I'm nice." She shrugs with a little smile.

"I don't say that to sound stuck up or anything, it's just me. Like I said before, I've never played the snooty role to get what I want. So to me, walking into a new school that day seemed like it would be a piece of cake. I wasn't the cheerleader anymore and I wasn't with the golden boy any longer, but I was still me. I could be nice, make friends and get through the year." Jules pauses and raises an eyebrow at the camera.

"Right?"

* * *

They pull into the student parking lot with five minutes to spare after their stop by the cemetery; a processional of Hillsdale students all arriving in the nick of time for their first day of school. Katie's car passes by the throngs of students making their way to the building, following Jeff's car to the far reaches of the lot before finding a vacant spot. Jules adjusts her sunglasses to avoid eye contact with the curious glances they receive.

"I don't think we're in Kansas anymore," Katie teases as she turns the car off and looks at Jules.

At Hillsdale, the cheerleaders and jocks were used to the prime parking spots; popularity had its advantages. Tanya always parked directly outside of the gym, a few feet from the overhangs that protected students from severe weather. When it rains here at Rossview, they'll be soaked before they make it half way to the school.

"It's like starting all over again," Jules mutters as she climbs out of the vehicle slowly.

West missed the light turning into the campus, which affords Jules the amazing view of watching people stop and stare as his bike purrs its way to the space on the other side of Tommy's truck. She finds the attention he garners interesting, seeing as how most people ignored them as they drove in. She leans against the trunk of Katie's car and watches as West makes his way through the crowd of students.

"Ready?" Jeff calls, throwing one arm around each of their shoulders. The heavy weight of his body practically causes her knees to buckle, and Katie laughs as she throws her hip into his side.

"I figure if I have to be new man on campus I might as well show up with the two hottest girls in Texas," he says with a wink. It's on the tip of Jules' tongue to make a snide remark, but the moment she turns to speak, Jeff falls away from her.

With a playful growl, West grabs him from behind and they jostle for position; leaving Tommy looking on with an amused expression plastered on his face.

"Ugh," Katie groans as Jules joins her. "Boys." They sigh simultaneously and decide to leave them behind.

The parking lot is almost deserted and they rush to get to their classes before the tardy bell sounds. The guys catch up after a moment and West takes Jules' hand without missing a step. They pass a group of stragglers still huddled by a beat up car and Jules smiles politely at one of the girls, who merely glances up as she takes a long drag of a cigarette. The raven-haired girl simply turns away.

The warning bell sounds as they open the main doors, causing a frenzy of motion in the crowded halls. The five of them stand there for a moment, taking in the foreign building and breathing in this new life.

"Well, well, well, look who we have here," murmurs a low voice.

The sultry tone causes Jules to turn and search for the owner. She spots a tall brunette with her thick hair teased up into one of those messy ponytails that look like they take no effort, but in reality take thirty minutes or more to create.

"West Rutledge," she purrs as she walks up to West; placing her palm on his chest and leaving scant inches between them. "Hi, good looking. Nice to know *something* good is coming from this Mustang invasion," she teases; her lips curling into a smile.

"Bri," West acknowledges warily; his hand going to her wrist as he takes a step back.

She pouts when he pulls away, and looks over at the rest of the group. Her large eyes stop on Katie and Jules a tad longer than the guys, taking them in. "So, my little loner *does* have his own little friends?"

Jules bristles at her reference and steps forward as Katie coughs and West gives her a guilty look.

"Bri, this is Jeff, Tommy and Katie." He points around the circle and makes introductions before turning towards Jules, now glued to his side. Wrapping his arm around her waist, he adds meaningfully, "And this is Jules, my girlfriend."

Jules doesn't miss the emphasis he puts on the word 'girlfriend' and she smiles inside as Bri's eyes narrow.

"You have a girlfriend? Well, that's unfortunate."

"For you, maybe," Jules quips rudely. West pinches her side lightly, but she doesn't care. Who is this chick? She looks like she should be at some nightclub with her smoky eyes, bright red lips and skimpy little outfit.

"Most definitely for me," she admits, before leaning into Jules' face. "I know all too well what I'm missing."

Jules' jaw drops. Katie, who is close enough to overhear the comment, pushes her way in with an angry, "Back off."

"Bri," West warns angrily; stepping in front of Jules while grabbing Katie's arm. Bri laughs and shrugs off her indifference.

Through her red hot anger, Jules can see the curious glimpses they're getting standing there as everyone else tries to make their way to their first period classes.

A voice shouts "Parker!" and pulls all their attention temporarily, giving Bri a chance to step away.

"We'll catch up later," she promises; wiggling her fingers at West with her bright red nails flashing.

Jules looks up at West. "Who was that?" she asks as a group of guys from Hillsdale descends on them. She's not an overly jealous type, but with so many changes in her life lately and so much uncertainty, she finds her emotions are all over the place, especially when it comes to West.

"Hey man." Jeff smiles at the group, and fist bumps and man hugs ensue.

"Ladies, looking good. Tommy—what's up, man? West. Can you believe this place? It's like some other planet here," complains the new addition to their group. Jules thinks back to freshman year when Fred played special teams for the Mustangs. He had always been nice and was one of her pep buddies—each cheerleader was assigned several members of the team to make good luck signs for each game day. She used to bring him Fanta and Skittles every Friday as his favorite treat.

She can't help but feel guilty when Fred's eyes rake down her body and find West's arm around her waist. She holds her breath, expecting a comment from him, but instead he winks at her with a short nod and turns his attention back to Tommy and Jeff.

She looks around at the student body, seeing what Fred sees. Rossview is certainly a bit more 'country' than Hillsdale was. Many of the students here actually live on farms, whereas Hillsdale and north up to Robinson is more of a business suburb. While cowboy boots and mammoth belt buckles are commonplace everywhere in Texas, at Rossview they are a little more prevalent. *So is the camo and NASCAR gear*, she notes.

"Get to class, ladies and gentlemen. No lingering," a teacher calls out as he makes his way down the still crowded hall.

Ignoring the others, West pulls her to the side; his body barely touching hers but making her pulse race. He looks worried as he eyes her. "Hey, she's just a girl I've hung out with, okay?"

Caught in his brown gaze, it takes her a moment to catch on. Girl? Oh, the Bri chick. "Hung out with? You want to define *hung out?*"

"I do, but not right now and not right here." He speaks clearly, not hesitating for a moment. His hand runs down her arm and takes hold of hers. "I can't help what others do or say."

She gives him a huge smile as he lifts her fingers to his lips. "I'll see you in third, okay?"

Jules is happy they were lucky enough to get assigned the same history class and lunch break. She's looking forward to getting to see him during the day.

"Yeah."

"You okay, Buffy?" She nods and plasters on a happy face as he leans down to press a quick kiss to her lips. "My first class is upstairs, so I better run."

She nods again as he takes off, and then he turns and makes the hand signal for a telephone. She assumes it's his way of saying to text him if she needs to. When she looks away from his back, she discovers the hall is nearly empty. Jeff is whispering in Katie's ear, Tommy's gone and across the hall a small brunette, whom she knows is a cheerleader for Rossview, is giving her the dirtiest looks she possibly can.

"K, let's go," she urges; pulling her gaze from the hateful stare. They rush down the hall to find their fourth year Spanish class and begin their first day of senior year.

By the time Jules reaches third period she's endured enough dirty glances from Rossview students to make her feel like a leper. Thankfully, her first two classes are liberally peppered with Hillsdale students, and although she's happy to find friends to keep her company, the cold shoulder treatment still bugs her. Hillsdale and Rossview have always had a spirited rivalry, and she assumes that's the reason for the hostility, but come on. It's not as if she, or any other Hillsdale student for that matter, wanted to change schools.

"Hey gorgeous." West startles her; wrapping her in a monstrously tight bear hug as he comes up behind her.

"Hi."

His face buries into her hair as he asks, "How many days left until graduation?"

Jules groans with him as his arms drop, and he takes her hand and leads her into the class.

"Right? One hundred and what, seventy-something?"

"Too damn long, babe, that's how long." Pulling her behind him, he leads the way to some seats along the back of the room. She gives him a weary glance and he laughs. "Bad boy, remember? You didn't want to sit up front, did you?"

She doesn't answer, but he sees it in her face. "Oh, hell. You're such a good girl, it's cute," he teases with a wink as they take their seats.

"What? I'm not a good girl."

"Oh Buffy, I think you are." He leans to the side, his desk lifting up off the floor onto two legs as he tilts towards her. "Don't worry though, babe, I happen to find your good girl vibe sexy."

Two girls in obscenely short jean skirts walk past slowly, pausing to say 'hi' to West. He gives them a polite smile and nods hello before returning his attention to Jules almost immediately. Their eyes follow West's to her face and they both frown visibly, letting her see their annoyance at her presence, and she's amazed.

"I feel about as welcome here as a Kardashian at a legit Hollywood party," she mutters to West; rolling her eyes as the girls take the empty seats two rows up.

The taller blonde looks over her shoulder, letting Jules know she heard her, but says nothing. As West leans his desk closer, he skims her arm with the tip of his fingers.

"Did something happen in your other classes?"

Her reply is interrupted by the low vibration of her cell phone going off.

Katie: Bathroom! First floor near cafeteria

Throwing a glance at West, Jules reads the message a second time and checks the time. She has one minute until the bell rings and no teacher has shown up yet. If she leaves she'll be tardy getting back.

Stay. Go. Stay. Go. She muses when the phone goes off again.

Katie: PLEASE!!!

The over usage of exclamation marks and the caps make up her mind for her. Sliding from her chair she throws West an apologetic glance. He moves to follow her, his eyes full of concern, and she leans forward slightly to whisper an explanation.

"It's Katie. She's asking me to meet her in the bathroom. I'll see you at lunch if I don't make it back."

He nods and his fingers skim her arm as she hurries out the door before their teacher shows up. Her steps are light and quick as she ducks into the restroom halfway down the first floor hallway and nearly crashes into three girls as they come out.

"Sorry," she murmurs; pushing past them and taking in the vacant bathroom. The air is a vapor cloud of freshly sprayed perfume; the flowery scent tickling her nose as she looks around. All of the dark blue stall doors are cracked open slightly, with the exception of the last one.

"Katie?"

Sharp snaps sound on the vinyl floor and the door clicks open.

"Were you hiding in there?" Jules asks as Katie steps out of the stall. Her face is red and blotchy from fresh tears and Jules rushes forward immediately. "What happened?"

Katie holds out her phone without a word.

"What?"

"Just take it and look for yourself," she offers and her hand trembles as Jules takes the phone.

Casting an unsure glance at Katie, she looks at the screen. It's a calendar appointment – a reminder actually, upon further inspection – and it takes Jules a moment to understand what she is looking at.

"This is your monthly reminder to continue being awesome! - You ROCK! <3<3 Tanya"

Jules' sharp inhale of breath echoes off the tile walls as she is reminded of the monthly "appointments" Tanya made in Katie's phone late last school year after some stuff went down with Katie's mom and dad.

"It shocked the hell out of me." Katie looks at her reflection in the mirror. "For a moment, I started to text her. I forgot for the briefest of seconds, and then my heart plummeted to the floor and I ran from class like some lunatic."

"You're not a lunatic."

"No, I'm not. I'm angry. Aren't you angry, Jules?" Katie pleaded.

"K—"

"No, really. I mean come on, Mother-freaking-Nature!" Katie drops her bag and purse from her shoulder and throws her arms up. "A tornado in Tyler? What did *we* do to deserve it? Too many keggers on the farms? Our short skirts offending you? You couldn't have sought revenge on a town a little more perverse?" She laughs manically.

"Sweetie, I don't think Mother Nature takes revenge on depraved societies," Jules deadpans.

"Well, God, then. Do we blame him? Who do I blame for this piece of shit hand that we got dealt, huh?"

Taken aback at the venom in her best friend's voice, Jules tries to maintain her calm. She thinks about how she speaks with Jason, calm and cool, when all she really wants to do is knock him over the head.

"It just happened. We can't blame God. We lived, didn't we?" she points out. Jules is well aware of the desire to want to pin the blame on someone. She's gone over all the places to lay blame and comes up empty every time; with the exception of herself, of course.

"We lived," Katie repeats and then lowers her voice. "But she didn't."

Tears spring to her eyes. "No she didn't."

"I hate this school already."

"Yeah, I don't think they're known for their friendly student body."

Katie snorts. It's a half-cry, half-laugh type of sound that brings a chuckle from Jules' own lips. "Girl, they sure seem friendly. I've had to tell off two hoes already for hitting on Jeff. And that was just in the hallway!"

Jules knows the feeling well after seeing the covetous looks West received in the parking lot and halls this morning.

"Are we going to get through this, Jules? This year, I mean. All of the 'last times', and she isn't here with us," Katie bemoans. She closes her eyes as tears streak her face again. She's a mess and Jules' restraint finally breaks as she pulls her best friend into a tight hug.

"We have to make it for her. Okay? We take every second we have and we live. We make up for the time she didn't get."

"You know she would be so bored to walk a mile in our shoes, right?"

The wild child. That was Tanya, Jules thinks to herself.

"So we walk a mile in hers."

Katie pulls back from their hug with a sad smile on her face. "Deal."

* * *

"Seven words. 'So we walk a mile in hers'. Those seven words set off a series of events that completely changed my senior year. With that pact, my grieving heart took on a new mission. Find closure, retrace Tanya's steps and, understand the part of her I never knew. It had hurt the night of the tornado to learn from West that Tanya partied with him more often than I ever knew. It hurt earlier that summer when Tanya confessed to her secret relationship with Carter, and then again when Katie said Tanya was confiding things to her about her love life."

"Suddenly I was hungry for answers and understanding. It's a downfall of mine; always curious. Never leave things unresolved. Walk a mile in her shoes . . . I was ready to try."

Acknowledgements

Whenever I finish a book I come to this spot and I debate on what I'm going to say. I'm nothing without the people behind me. My readers, bloggers, Facebook and Twitter friends, my family, and my local fast food providers. I kid, kinda! All of you are the reason I survive day to day as stories consume my life and mind.

I want to give a special shout out to Mandy with I Read Indie for falling so deeply in love with Jules and West last year and for sharing them all over the net for the past six months. You, my dear, are a gem!

The professionals who back me up:

My editor, Samantha—This has been a *true* labor of love. Thank you.

My cover designer—Starla, you've made this series beautiful. Thank you.

My cover photographer—Regina, I adore you.

My PR agent, Rick Miles and the crew at Red Coat PR—You're the best pimps ever. Thank you for your advice and for making me look good.

My Literary Agent, Italia Gandolfo, and Gandolfo Helin Literary Management—Here's to the future and #NOLA

My biggest supporters:

J, Gray, Gabe and Belle—my family, my life, my first and best fairy tale. I love you like crazy.

My Fierce sisters—Starla Huchton and Christy Foster (aka Iron Man and Black Widow) sharing this writer life on a day to day basis is a pleasure with you ladies by my side. I heart you.

My Mindy Hayes—Captain America, critique partner, Fierce sister, best friend. Cheers to all of the road trips, white cheddar popcorn, bad movies, good movies, karaoke, dance parties and adventures shared. And to those yet to come. In this insane world of writing, I'm profoundly happy to have you by my side.

My Jessica Surgett—you weaseled your way into my life and I'm a better person for it. I love you.

My Megan Toffoli—I miss you Canada! I'm so happy you're so busy though ;)

My Chele's Belles and Mischief Makers—Aisha, Amanda, Cathy, Cheri, Courtney, Danielle, Destiny, Kayla, Laura, Mandy, Marla, Megan B., Nancy, Nicole, Rachelle, Tanya, Tess, and Veranda. Thank you for supporting me in whatever way you're able and always lending an ear when I need one.

Special thanks to Melody Wade who allowed me to use her name. I got her name and she got to be West's past hookup, not a bad deal.

About the author

Michele writes novels with fairy tale love for everyday life. Romance is always central to her plots where the genres range from Coming of Age Fantasy and Drama to New Adult Romantic Suspense.

Sign up for my monthly newsletter (http://bit.ly/MGMNews) to keep up with all the latest, exclusive first peeks and other perks.

Email: authormichelegmiller@gmail.com
Facebook: https://www.facebook.com/AuthorMicheleGMiller
Twitter: @chelemybelles
Instagram: Chelemybelles
Website: https://michelegmillerbooks.squarespace.com/

Printed in Germany
by Amazon Distribution
GmbH, Leipzig